7 $\frac{20}{}$

The Spy Next Door

The Spy Next Door

Cathy Liggett

Five Star • Waterville, Maine

First Edition, Second Printing

Published in 2005 in conjunction with Tekno Books and Ed Gorman.

Set in 11 pt. Plantin by Ramona Watson.

Printed in the United States on permanent paper.

Library of Congress Cataloging-in-Publication Data

Liggett, Cathy.
    The spy next door / Cathy Liggett.—1st ed.
      p. cm.
    ISBN 1-59414-327-7 (hc : alk. paper)
    1. Spy stories—Authorship—Fiction.   2. Women novelists—Fiction.   3. Divorced women—Fiction.
    4. Single mothers—Fiction.   I. Title.
    PS3612.I343S69 2005
    813'.6—dc22   2005002234

To the guy who took me to upstate New York . . . and so many other memorable places . . . over the last twenty-plus years. What a sweet, blessed journey it's been, sharing my life with you!

Acknowledgements

I don't think I could ever go through this process of writing if it weren't for the suggestions and encouragement of my critique partners and friends Shelley Sabga, Heather Webber, Hilda Lindner-Knepp and Julie Stone. And honestly . . . even if I could . . . it wouldn't be half as enjoyable. Thank you!

Also, a special thanks to my family—near and far—for their continued love and support . . . to my friends next-door whose antics always stimulate the imagination . . . and to my editor Gordon Aalborg for recommending this book and John Helfers for taking him up on it.

Chapter One

Everything had been just a bit too quiet lately. That's why Sela Theodore wasn't surprised at all, when the phone rang early in the morning and her superior's wheezy voice panted in her ear.

"Merrily, merrily we roll at one," he sputtered between labored inhales and exhales. To anyone else his message may have sounded cryptic, but to Sela it all made perfect sense. The only thing she wondered was why the man always seemed to be out of breath. Shouldn't the head of the country's most formidable counterintelligence agency be in better physical shape than that? At least for appearance's sake?

But that wasn't going to change anytime soon, Sela knew as she pictured her boss's rotund body squishing out of his expensive gray suits. Not that it had any bearing on her life anyway. For life, as she knew it, was a series of espionage missions—and, of course, with that came a tantalizing lover every now and again.

So, the Mary Lee Ferry at one o'clock, huh? That's where she'd receive instructions for her next assignment. Not exactly what she had planned for the day. But that was the life of a spy for you—totally unpredictable!

Luckily, Danielle had a flexible schedule, too, and could flip-flop lunch in town to brunch near the dock, thought Sela as she climbed into her shiny red Boxster to go meet her dearest girlfriend. She threw her black cash-

mere coat onto the passenger's seat; she had just enough time to drop it off at the one-hour express dry cleaners along the way. After all, who knew? She might be going out of town—or even out of the country—sooner than she thought.

"Time to wake up, sweetie."

Hope bent over Theo's bed and brushed his baby-soft cheek with a kiss. One day, all too soon, that smooth cheek would be covered with bristly, manly whiskers. But she didn't want to think about that right now.

No. Instead, she wanted to hang on to this feeling of contentment as she watched him savoring his last moments of sleep . . . his final remnants of some adventurous dream.

His nose twitched. One eye cocked half-open, then abruptly shut again. And his body lay very still, until finally his arms reached out to hug her around her neck.

"Good morning, my man among men," she whispered, smiling at their daily ritual.

Still not stirring, Theo murmured, "Fifth grade starts too early."

"Well, you know what they say," she chirped, "the early bird gets—"

"Worms!" he croaked, the thought awakening him suddenly, like he'd been doused with cold water.

"*The* worm," Hope corrected him.

"No. Worms." He shot up in bed, grinning widely, rubbing his sleep-filled eyes with his fists. "Really gross worms like Taylor's dog has. Have you ever seen a dog with worms, Mom? It's so disgusting when they go to the bathroom and out of their behind comes—"

"Theo, please!" Hope exclaimed, stopping him in midsentence. Or mid-repugnant-thought would be more like it.

She reached out and tousled his already-mussed mop of strawberry blonde hair, making a mental note to run him by Dani's salon for a haircut. "What were you dreaming about, mister? How can a sweet, sensitive, wonderful boy like you wake up with such nauseating, repulsive thoughts?"

"I dunno." He shrugged. But the beaming smile on his face let her know he was proud of the fact.

What a funny age, she thought, as she watched him push back the covers and straighten his pajama shirt, all twisted around his torso from the night's dreamy escapades. Figures of action heroes lined the shelves above his bed, and yet peeking out from under his pillow was a CD player and headphones. It seemed he had one foot in boyhood and one venturing toward a sea of teenagers, where he was sticking his toes in, testing the waters.

"Did you write that part in your new book, like I told you about? I left Post-its by your computer. About Spiderman helping Sela? Or maybe Triple X Threat? Or she could get that smoke emissions device on her sports car like James Bond has on his BMW." He rifled off a slew of ideas.

Hope shook her head. "Sorry. I didn't get very far this morning, bud."

In fact, she had only written a page and a half. Not a great start for her fourth romantic spy novel. Not a great start at all. But the editor had given her a generous deadline, and there was no need to panic—yet. "But I'm still taking it under consideration."

"Maybe you need some of Uncle Cary's magic java juice to make you write faster."

"You know, I'm thinking you're right. Maybe I'll run next door and grab a cup while you're getting dressed. Then I'll come back and make you—"

"Cocoa Puffs with chocolate syrup mixed in?"

"Speaking of gross." She made an exaggerated grimace. "Besides, they'll never give me the Mother of the Year Award, if I let you have that for breakfast."

"But I will." He bared his slightly uneven teeth in a pat smile, and she made another mental note to make an appointment with the orthodontist.

"You will, huh? Well, that might be a good reason to do it, then."

"Really?" His eyebrows arched.

She gave him a wry look, like he should know better. Evidently, he did.

"I didn't think so," he mumbled.

Hope laughed and shooed Theo out of bed. Then, tightening the belt of the plaid flannel bathrobe that covered her favorite tattered long-johns, she made her way down the back stairs to the mud room, smiling all the way.

Who needs a man to wake up to in the morning, when I have a bundle of joy like Theo? How easily and cheerfully that kid woke up! And how blessed she was to have him. He had a smile on his face from dawn till dusk. Nothing at all like his father, Robert, her ex.

Thank goodness for that. Hope lifted her eyes to the heavens.

It would be a sad day when those whiskers did come in, first fine and soft, and then all at once prickly. A pang only known to mothers flitted through her heart. Who would cover her computer with Post-it notes then? And try to gross her out? And watch James Bond movies with her? Who would she look in on at night? Who would fill her days . . . her thoughts . . . her heart?

Again, she pushed aside such thoughts and began pawing through the pile of rubber galoshes, mismatched gloves and stretched-out scarves spilled out on the mud room floor.

12

Finally, she unearthed a pair of hiking boots. Yanking them on without bothering to tie them, she almost knocked the glasses off her nose as she pulled a striped woolen stocking cap over her morning mess of uncontrollable curls.

Then, wrapping a pilled purple wool scarf around her neck, she donned one glove and one mitten, and grabbed some keys from a hook on the wall. She'd start up the school bus on her way to Uncle Cary's bed and breakfast next door . . . even if she did feel a twinge of guilt about wasting the school district's gas.

On a frigid morning such as this, she liked having the bus all warm and toasty for her load of elementary school kids. Besides, it made things especially cozy for the few minutes she and Theo had the bus to themselves before picking up their first passengers. That alone time was one of the perks of her morning route, one of the reasons she enjoyed driving the yellow box on wheels. Well, that and the fact that she needed the extra income.

Once the bus promised a steady chug, she headed across the icy patch of lawn that joined her home with Uncle Cary's property. From a distance, most of the inn's imperfections went unnoticed, hidden by a veil of turn-of-the-century charm.

A massive yet quaint home with a wrap-around porch, it was the only bed and breakfast in Bearsville, New York—a good thing, since Uncle Cary couldn't have stood any competition. After all, Bearsville was truly a town in hibernation. A quiet little place, as sleepy as the inn looked to her now, pitched against the midnight blue of the dawning sky with one porch light on, one burned out and clapboards randomly breaking loose from their places.

She made a promise to herself to help Uncle Cary patch everything up in the spring. Although who would ever really notice anyway? The place rarely had more than one boarder at a time these days. Its heyday had come swiftly—and was gone just as fast—with the historic Woodstock concert in 1969, when Bearsville, which abutted the famed town, and Uncle Cary's bed and breakfast got to play host to greats like Janis Joplin, Stephen Stills and Neil Young.

But that was thirty-some years ago. Another lifetime. Nowadays nothing much surprising ever happened in Bearsville. Well, not to her, anyway. And not since her divorce—which had been more of a shock than a surprise. But that was old news now. Eleven years old, to be exact.

Nope, life in Bearsville was pretty darn predictable these days. No surprises there.

What the—?

Chandler Adams rubbed a large circle on the frosty pane of the inn's dining-room window and peeked out curiously.

What a sight for sore eyes that is, clomping across the lawn!

And his eyes were truly sore . . . and blurry . . . and heavy-lidded. The transition from international to domestic spy missions was supposed to make his life easier. But instead, over the last couple of weeks, he'd had to circle the globe several times, tying up loose ends. Bangkok. Prague. And Sydney last week. And before that, Maui and Paris. Without a doubt, his sleeping habits were so totally screwed up, who knew when he'd get his hours straightened out again?

But even with all that, he could still see that the frumpy form outside the window was a real live-wire. *Only in Smallsville, U.S.A.,* he mused. You'd never see a sight like that in Monaco. Or Cannes. Or even South Beach, Florida. Oversized boots. Layer upon layer of loose, ragged material. And a floppy toboggan hat with a mane of mustang-wild

14

curls flowing out from under the rim.

What was it—uh, she? The Queen of Flea Markets? Bag Lady Extraordinaire? Blunder Woman? Whatever the case, she seemed to be headed this way.

Well, this should be entertaining. He shook his head with a chuckle. And prepared himself to be amused.

Hope opened the door of her home-away-from-home and tiptoed inside. Seeing her uncle's bedroom door still closed, she was thinking she'd have to make the magic java juice herself, when the pleasantly familiar aroma of coffee sent her olfactory senses leaping to life. Puzzled but pleased, she followed the scent into the dining room.

Curiously, there was already a fire blazing in the fireplace, taking the morning chill off the room. Hope paused at a serving table near the doorway and poured herself a cup of coffee. Waiting for it to cool, she surveyed the room where "diners could get carried away on Cary's cooking." Or so the brochure used to say.

Just like the exterior, the interior held a myriad of quaint, charming possibilities, but was in dire need of a makeover. The scuffed antique tables needed refinishing, the worn forest-green carpeting replaced. Or maybe Uncle Cary should opt for hardwood floors and strategically-placed area rugs? Hope was lost in a redecorating fog as she blew at the steamy cup and took a tentative sip.

"Yuck!" she sputtered, spewing out the vile liquid. "This stuff is rancid," she complained aloud.

"Sorry about that. Never too sure how many of those darned scoops to put in."

At the sound of the stranger's low voice, Hope nearly jumped out of her skin. Not that it wasn't perfectly normal for a stranger to be in Uncle Cary's place. But she felt like someone had snuck up on her, and gasped at the sight of the sneak as he emerged from the shadows.

Her glasses were still slightly steamy after making the transition from the cold outdoors to the warm, cozy room. But she could still see well enough to realize the guy appeared to be the epitome of calm as he casually ambled toward her.

Coffee cup in hand, he looked like an Eddie Bauer ad, wearing an olive brushed-cotton shirt halfway buttoned up over a white T-shirt which hugged his obviously taut chest. Faded jeans covered the remaining portion of a build that was definitely kind on the eyes. He had that carefree, hadn't-shaved-for-a-day-or-so look going, and the rugged darkness of it seemed to accentuate lips most women would die for in more ways than one.

A lock of hair, dark as a starless night, had fallen across his forehead. For an instant, Hope had a slight urge to reach out and put it back into place.

It's just the mom in me coming out, she assured herself. Certainly not the woman locked inside that yearned to do so. All she knew was that she was looking upon someone who could give her own personal heartthrob Keanu Reeves a run for his money.

"What are you doing here?"

It certainly wasn't one of the friendliest greetings she'd ever given anyone, but she truly did wonder. What *was* he doing here? Gorgeous creatures like him didn't drop into Bearsville every day of the week—or even once a year, for that matter.

In fact, the last time she could recall a bona fide specimen of male pulchritude passing by the area was when that blonde-haired Federal Express driver's truck broke down on his way upstate a few years ago. What a hunk on wheels he was! Every woman in town suddenly decided to stop by Ralph's Auto Repair with some inane mechanical question just to get a glimpse of heavenly Fred X, as he came to be known.

If confused by her question, the stranger still seemed happy enough to answer it.

"Well, this *is* a bed and breakfast, right?" he asked, a mere hint of a smile lining his lips.

Hope nodded, suddenly unable to tear her own eyes away from the penetration of his chestnut ones. It had been a long time since she'd looked into the eyes of a man—besides Uncle Cary, of course. And this one, well, he seemed to have a steady, practiced kind of gaze. Like maybe he thought if he stared long and longingly enough at a woman, he could turn even the most frigid heart torrid.

Well, Mr. Suave and Debonair, she stared right back, *I'm not falling for any of it.* Besides, the coffee was strong enough to give her heart a kick-start this morning. She certainly didn't need him to.

"Well, I bedded down here last night," he said slowly, smoothly. "So that's the bed part. And now I'm ready for breakfast, that's the breakfast part." He smiled easily—too easily. "Although no one mentioned just how informal the dining-room attire was," he added, casting an amused sideways glance at her getup.

Oh, and a bit of mild sarcasm mixed in. Ha, ha. What an amusing guy! Though she had to admit, his words did make her hideously aware of how pathetic she must look. Like a waif wandering around in the wee hours of the morning, a hapless spinster mooching coffee along her way. It was enough to make her cheeks burn.

The truth was, she hadn't really thought about her appearance in *so* long—not since Theo's dad had left them

17

when Theo was a newborn. She had been so busy taking care of her son, and escaping into Sela Theodore's world where she could dress her heroine any way she liked, without spit-up and creamed peas, that she'd just throw on overalls and sweatshirts—or whatever was handy. And who on earth—at least on the minuscule part of the earth she inhabited, Bearsville to be exact—cared? There certainly wasn't anyone around here she wanted to impress.

"Maybe if you add a little sugar to it, it'll help," he offered, trying the charm routine one more time. He set down his own cup and reached for the sugar bowl. Before she could even respond, he was stirring in the sweetness with one hand and steadying her cup with his other hand just slightly covering hers.

"Everyone can use a little sugar from time to time." His eyes smiled down into her own spectacled ones.

Okay. So he had the penetrating eyes going for him big-time. And he'd probably written the book on smooth one-liners. *But I write books, too, buddy. And I create slippery characters just like you!* He needed to know she wasn't that easy or that naïve—no matter how her physical self responded to him at the moment.

Sure, there was that tingling, flushed feeling that she'd almost forgotten existed creeping through her insides. And a warm sensation spreading its way throughout the universe of her being. But that was just hormones talking. And everyone knows hormones can talk some crazy mumbo-jumbo at times. The thing is—you just don't listen to them, that's all. Not even if it had been a long time since you'd felt much of anything. A really long time . . . like say, when did she have that fling with Tony Pascali? When Theo was five or so?

"So—so—so—" She was stuttering for God's sake, a grown woman stuttering. What was her problem? *Pull your-*

18

self together, Hathaway. "So you made the coffee? And started the fire?" Her sentences came out clipped. "Uncle Cary overslept?"

He nodded. "All affirmative, except for the Uncle Cary part. He, uh . . ." The stranger paused, seeming reluctant to say more.

But he didn't have to. Because at that moment Hope's ears picked up the sounds she realized he'd already heard. Utterances of lovemaking coming from down the hallway, making her face turn as fiery red as her hair.

"Oh, geez, Uncle Cary . . ." she groaned, closing her eyes and shaking her head.

But the stranger seemed intent on ignoring the titillating proceedings within earshot. "So does everyone in town call him that?" he prodded.

Hope shrugged. "Well, I do. He's my uncle." Although at the moment, she was loath to admit it.

Just then, a female voice cried out in pleasure, making the awkward moment even more uncomfortable. At least for Hope anyway. Shifting on her feet, she tried glancing everywhere, except at the stranger's face. Meanwhile he appeared unaffected. He sauntered over to the serving table and topped off his cup of coffee.

"Care for some more of this awful, 'rancid' stuff?" He pointed the coffeepot in her direction.

"No, thanks. Even though you do make it sound appealing." Her lip curled slightly. "Anyway, I really need to be going." But she stood frozen. If only she didn't have to walk past Uncle Cary's bedroom door . . .

"I didn't get to meet your aunt last night. Her name would be—?" He set down the pot of coffee and turned back to her, seemingly fixed on keeping their conversation nonchalant.

"Huh? Oh." Hope shook her head. "There isn't any aunt exactly. Well, there was Aunt Maggie, but she's been gone for a while now."

The stranger's eyes appeared instantly sympathetic. "Sorry to mention it."

"No, no, nothing to be sorry about," Hope assured him. "I didn't even know her really. I guess she and Uncle Cary were young marrieds, madly in love, and then—" Hope snapped her fingers. "One day, shortly after Woodstock, I'm told she ran off with some hippie passing through town. I don't know, I guess they were going to open a macramé shop in the Adirondacks. You know, make their fortune selling macramé plant holders and potholders." *Why am I telling him all of this?* Hope wondered. Well, at least her voice drowned out all the other sounds in the inn. And the stranger did appear amused, so she prattled on.

"Then in the eighties," she continued, chronicling Uncle Cary's love life, "after the incident with the wrecking ball and the retirement home—"

"The what?" The stranger interrupted with a deep, rich laugh. He set down his coffee cup and crossed his arms over his chest, as if settling in for a good, long tale.

"Oh, well, never mind, it's not really critical to the story. It's just a time reference we use around town. You know, the year the wrecking ball accidentally knocked the roof off the Bearsville Retirement Center, and everyone had to come and stay here for a week." Hope couldn't resist a reminiscent chuckle herself.

"Anyway, a French circus came through town. And one day Uncle Cary spied this young French girl, Fiona, cleaning the animal cages, laundering the performers' costumes and so on. He asked her if she wanted to earn some extra money and clean the inn, too. So over the course of the week she did, and they became quite smitten with each other. She never left."

Hope shrugged and then added, "Since then she does the cleaning. She does the windows. And, well, she does—"

Fiona's female wail echoed again, reminding them of her extensive range of skills. But the stranger was gracious enough not to make mention of it.

"—floors?" he helped her out.

"Uh, yeah. Floors." She nodded, with a slight smile. Okay, maybe the guy wasn't as bad as she'd first thought.

"So a French maid, huh? Your uncle must be the envy of every man in town." He winked at her.

"Oh, Fiona's a sweetheart, for sure." Hope nodded. "But wait till you see her." Hope stretched out her hands to give shape to an imaginary short, round person. "She has a sweet tooth, too, especially for French pastries. Oh, and she makes the most delicious crepes this side of the Atlantic. My favorites are the raspberry. You may get a chance to sample them for yourself, if you stay long enough." For some odd reason, Hope found herself wondering how long that might be.

"And what about you?" the stranger inquired. "Do you work here, too? Are you the cook?"

"Hardly!" she blurted out. "Though I have been known to make a mean frozen pizza from time to time. But no, I'm not the cook." It might be shallow of her, she knew, but she loved telling people what she did for a living. And every time she got the chance to say it, which wasn't too often since everyone in town already knew, she savored the moment and the proud feeling it gave her inside. "I'm a writer."

"Really?" The stranger drawled out the word, looking genuinely interested, and she had to admit that was one plus about him. He looked like a man hanging on to every syllable—which, wait a minute, wasn't that a contradiction in itself? "What do you write? Articles for glitzy women's magazines? Like fashion do's and don'ts?"

"Is that supposed to be funny?"

He shrugged. "Hey, this could be the latest fashion you're wearing. Do I look like a man who would know the difference?"

He was attempting to appear self-deprecating, but it hardly worked because, yes, he did look like a man who knew all about chic and style.

"Seriously." The stranger urged her with a nod of his head. "What do you write?"

"Spy novels. I write the Sela Theodore series of romantic spy thrillers. My name is Hope Hathaway, but I write under the pen name of Hope Starr. I wouldn't expect that you've heard of my books though. They're not best-sellers or anything. They help pay the bills is all."

"I'm sure they're great," he said, staring intently into her eyes in that unnerving way he did. "It's just that with my job I don't get out to bookstores much. But you know, I've been meaning to change that. So, wow, it's not every day that I get to meet an author." The stranger extended his hand. "I'm Chandler Adams by the way. Nice to meet you . . . uh, was that Mrs. Hope Hathaway?"

"Nope. Just Hope." She shook her head. Was that a flicker of relief she spied in his eyes? But why would it be?

"Nice to meet you, Hope Hathaway, a.k.a. Hope Starr."

Hope stared at his hand momentarily. It was a nice hand, soft-looking with long fingers. *A hand that would feel so good as it . . .* Whew, it was warm in here! Actually it was stifling really, what with the fire roaring, Uncle Cary in heat, and this stranger standing next to her, sizzling with

22

possibilities. Hope wiped her sweaty palm on her robe be-fore reaching out to grasp his hand.

Her new acquaintance held her hand for just a bit longer than necessary before letting it go, then took his own turn at swiping his palm on his jeans.

"So that's what gets you up so early—writing?"

"Writing, my fifth grader and—ohmigosh—"

Hope thrust her coffee cup toward him. It jostled on the saucer and coffee sloshed over the side. "The school bus is going to run out of gas before I even start my morning route. But, hey," she said, hurriedly backing out of the room, "thanks for the coffee. Next time, less is better, more is bitter, got it? Only one scoop per cup."

"Next time? As in tomorrow morning?" he asked.

But Hope didn't answer as she took giant, mother-may-I steps backward toward the door. She didn't answer because she couldn't, didn't know what to say. Wasn't even sure, after all, if she was truly awake or if she was dreaming this all up.

"Hey, you didn't say what you do, Chandler Adams."

"Me?" He raised her cup and saucer in the air in a blasé gesture. "Oh, I'm a spy. An international spy, actually. But I've been reassigned DOM-15, so the bulk of my assign-ments will be in the U.S. from now on."

Ha! Hope howled inwardly. Mr. Looker also had a sense of humor. How interesting was that? She wrote spy novels. So he said he was a spy. Funny. Very funny. Her smile broadened till she laughed aloud.

"Right!" She pointed a mock gun at him with her finger as she backed out the front door of the inn. "That's very hu-morous. Well, have a safe day out there, double-o-whomever you are!" she said gleefully.

"You, too, Ms. Starr."

★ ★ ★ ★ ★

Well, there you have it, he thought, staring after Hope as she made her exit. She wasn't buying the spy bit at all. Of course, he hadn't actually expected her to, had he? Hardly. Why else would he have blurted it out like that?

Though he knew if he had some phony-baloney British accent, she may have been more inclined to believe him. After all, he'd learned from past experience that the term "spy" was synonymous with James Bond the world around. The smooth talk. The *GQ* look. The gentlemanly ways. The elegant, cool daring. And, of course, the incomparable sex, too.

How could a mere man like himself live up to all that? No wonder it took a fictional character to pull it off.

Still, James Bond was just what people expected of someone in the espionage profession. That's why it was so easy to play the part of a CPA and make playful remarks about doing espionage work on the side. It amused him, and it was a rare person who ever took him seriously. Especially since he, Chandler Adams, didn't quite match up to the total spy image anyway.

Oh, if he tried hard enough, he could come across that way to some degree. Just like this morning. He'd tested a bit of the double-o-seven coolness on Hope Hathaway with that "everyone can use a little sugar from time to time" line. But he could tell right off she wasn't really into it, was put off by it. And rightfully so. It was just a mask anyway. Not something he could carry off easily—or completely—being the hybrid he was.

He wasn't really a Sean Connery or a Roger Moore. He was much earthier than that. Not as stodgy as, say, a detective character like Columbo. But something more like . . . Mel. Yeah, Mel Gibson was more his speed. Only a tidier version.

Satisfied with the self-comparison, he slipped his hands into his jeans pockets and sauntered back to the window. The wild-haired woman had made her way across the crunchy, ice-tipped grass and was retreating into her house. All cozy looking, with white wisps of smoke curling out of the chimney, her home looked small-town picture-perfect.

Though a world traveler by trade, it wasn't surprising the picturesque scene held some underlying appeal for him. At heart he was simply a small-town guy who enjoyed big-time adventures. But even that was starting to wear thin these days. You could only circle the globe so many times till the world began to seem as small as your own backyard, and the jet lag didn't seem worth the trips anymore.

That's why he was making the switch from international missions to domestic assignments. Well, one of the reasons. When his dad passed away a couple of years ago, his sister and her family had stayed in Nyack, New York, to be close to their widowed mom. But currently his sister's husband was actively searching for a new job that might take them out of state. And Chandler's brother and his family had already moved to Colorado a year ago. So, it was his self-appointed time to watch over his mom now, to be close by. He had enjoyed his escapades, bopping from one continent to another. Surely, his siblings deserved an equal chance to test their wings.

A young boy emerged from the snug-looking house, lugging a backpack behind him. Throwing the pack onto the bus, he then climbed up the steps and disappeared into the dimly-lit tomb.

Hmm. Hope had mentioned a fifth- or sixth-grader. But had Chandler heard right? She did say she wasn't married, didn't she? Though he guessed it didn't really matter. He'd only be holed up in Bearsville for a few weeks anyway, just until he completed the art fraud mission in Manhattan.

Suddenly his stomach growled, and he remembered why he'd wandered into the dining room in the first place. When was the last time he'd eaten? In Lancastershire? On the flight over from London?

Whatever. Breakfast at the bed *and breakfast* seemed a remote possibility at this point. From the sound of things, Uncle Cary still had his hands full and cooking was on the backburner.

Well, Chandler had to hand it to the old guy; he certainly had quite the stamina. Maybe Uncle Cary should try out for a double-o-seven role. Shaking his head with a bemused grin, Chandler grabbed his jacket and headed into town—hopefully, to find something to eat.

Chapter Two

As the details of her next assignment unraveled, Sela's heart lurched in her chest. She grabbed onto the ferry's railing to steady herself. Had she heard that right? Venice, Italy? Was life in the present actually taking her back to her past?

It wasn't the bodily harm that caused her apprehension. After all, she was a first-degree black belt under Master Chi Dong and exercised regularly with those Billy Blanks Tae-Bo videotapes. So physically, she was in great shape.

But what about her heart? Her last visit to Venice was also the last time she had seen Giorgio. She had fallen in love with him there long, long before her life as a spy was a concrete thought in her luxuriously curly, raven-tressed head.

At the time, Giorgio was an aspiring writer, his written words so magical and melodic that surely he must be a successful author by now. And yet, when it came to words, she and Giorgio hadn't needed them. For they spoke a language of love . . . communicating with a look, a touch, a caress—which was handy, since neither of them could put a sentence together in the other's language!

Ultimately, maybe it was the frustration of her unfinished romance with Giorgio that had led her to her dangerous, wanderlust profession. Whatever the reason, now that she *was going back, questions ran rampant through her mind. Would she have another chance with Giorgio? Could she deny her heart's yearnings for him once more? And should she check out some "Italian Made Easy" tapes from the library before she went?*

"Here, take this and don't lose it." Hope handed Theo a twenty-dollar bill as they stood outside Dani's Shear Magic hair salon. "And don't forget to give Dani a tip."

"Aw, why do I have to get a haircut?" Theo whined as he stuffed the bill in his pocket. "Why can't I grow my hair long?"

"Because you make a much better-looking boy than you do a girl."

He rolled his eyes at the response, having heard it umpteen times before. Hope pretended not to notice. Sometimes it was just easier that way. "I'm going to make a quick stop at Mitchell's. Then I'll be back at Dani's in just a few minutes. Okay?"

"All right," he grumbled.

Shuffling his feet slowly toward the door of the salon, he looked as inconsolable as he would have if Porky, his guinea pig, passed on to great mounds of shavings in the sky. But Hope knew that wouldn't last long. Dani would have him smiling in a millisecond. Her best friend simply had that effect on people.

In fact, as Hope began her short trek to Mitchell's department store, she caught herself smiling just thinking about Dani's open pixie face, bright blue eyes and mostly her contagious, enthusiastic ways. Hope wondered for a moment if her friend's short, cropped hair was still blonde this week. If so, that would mark three weeks in a row and would be apt to change soon.

Whatever her hair color, every man in town was crazy about Dani's perfect little build and pert personality. Some even had their hair trimmed a bit more than their wives and girlfriends really thought necessary. But Larry Lighter, the town's veterinarian, was the one who tugged at Dani's heartstrings. Little by little, he was lassoing in this free-spirited filly.

Good for you, Dani. Hope wistfully sent her friend telepathic best wishes.

Good for Dani that she could find her one true love in Bearsville. As for herself, Hope had pretty much extinguished the idea.

Strolling down the pavered sidewalk through the heart of town, she took in the full view. The town certainly had every nuts-and-bolts necessity of life lining one side of High Street or the other. There was the post office, combination dry cleaners/Laundromat, hardware store and drug store on one side; obviously, the more rudimentary services. And on the other side—whoa, you could really live it up at Mitchell's department store, with both floors newly renovated. Or you could drop by the fifties-styled movie theater, Gloria's Gift Shop, the ice cream parlor, the Village Pantry restaurant, and of course, Dani's hair salon.

Yes, Bearsville had every basic need for a very basic life. But for Hope—that's about all it had.

Admittedly, after Robert made his abrupt exit from her and Theo's lives, she had wanted to take flight and whisk them away from all this. Away to some new, uncharted habitat. Robert's out-of-the-blue departure had left her completely stunned. Devastated. Bruised.

Here she had thought they were the perfect married couple, trying to make a go of their own ad agency, with him as the ad exec and her as the creative expert. Sure, their sex life had slowed up a bit at the time. Why wouldn't it? They were tired after all, working hard side by side, putting in long days to make a life for themselves and whatever offspring they might be blessed with. But, ha! Apparently, that was solely *her* reality.

While she had her nose to the grindstone, his was sniffing up their office assistant's skirt. Then when she had news for him that she was pregnant, he had news of his own—he was leaving her for the skirt and what was underneath it!

Ultimately, losing Robert and gaining Theo was an incomparable trade, one she'd make a zillion times over again if she had to. Theo was a far greater joy than Hope could've ever imagined. For his sake, she dismissed her impulsive ideas about moving, running away from Bearsville. In her heart, she knew her hometown would be a safe, wholesome place for a single mom to raise a son. It was the times, though, when she'd see her ex in town with his new family that the sting of his leaving resurfaced a bit.

She paused outside of Mitchell's and glanced up and down the street again, trying to take it all in with a stranger's eye. How would it appear to a newcomer seeing it for the first time? Say, a six-foot male newcomer with hair the color of double fudge brownies and the slightest dimples when he smiled. Though she hated to admit it, she wondered what Chandler Adams thought of the out-of-the-way burg, her home.

Would he think Bearsville quaint and peaceful? Too provincial and quiet? A nice place to visit, but boring if you lived there? Not that it mattered, of course. *Why should it?* she thought, taking the escalator up to the second floor in pursuit of new, pristine white panties. Three pairs for thirteen dollars, Mitchell's newspaper ad had read.

More basics, she sighed, duplicating her son's earlier display of sulkiness.

But as the escalator ascended to Lingerie, a captivating cloud of pink caught her eye, lightening her mood. All thoughts of tightie whities poofed into thin air. In a dreamlike state, she floated over to the cloud, which in reality was a long, blush-colored silk robe.

Delicately, she ran her hand over the luxurious fabric. Slowly. Softly. *Heavenly!*

True, the robe was impractical. Impulsive. Plus impossibly expensive. But did she ever want it! And only one S/M size left. That had to be a sign from the gods for sure, didn't it?

Ohmigosh. Hope shook her head. What had come over her? The last time she'd bought something sexy and expensive like this was when Tony Pascali was in her life for that brief episode. *But there certainly isn't anyone in my life now,* she thought, push-push-pushing and finally shoving the tempting image of that Chandler Adams character out of her mind.

And she wouldn't let there be anyone. Mostly for Theo's sake. He really didn't need to get hurt by some man again. Some man who pretended to care for him. That is, until that man didn't care for her anymore. First it was Theo's own father, and then Tony—the phony. How could she consider letting that happen again?

So you can shoo, too, Adams. Shoo!

But his face . . . and those dark eyes of his . . . lingered in her mind. And all at once she wasn't just Hope Hathaway, single mom living in Bearsville. She was Hope Hathaway, off-duty single mom and on-call enchantress . . . tempting the new stranger in town, letting the pink silk slip off her shoulders and employing a few flirtatious techniques that always helped Sela Theodore get her man.

Still wrapped in the tantalizing haze of her daydream, Hope touched the silky softness again. What a lovely, out-of-the-question thing it was. *The robe—and Chandler Adams,* she thought to herself.

So why then was she carrying the flowing gown on its hanger up to the cash register? And peeling off three twenties and a five to buy the darn thing? And why, with the package under her arm, was she skulking out of Mitchell's as if she'd stolen the robe, when in fact, she practically had to take out a home equity loan for it?

Like Theo's sourpuss feelings, Hope's guilty ones at having made such a frivolous purchase dissipated the moment she stepped into Dani's salon. Void of customers, Dani rushed to the door to greet Hope, acting as excited as the day that Norm Hobbs won ten thousand dollars in the state lottery and left her a twenty-five-dollar tip.

"I'm so glad you're here," Dani bubbled over, pulling Hope into her salon, nearly knocking the Mitchell bag out of her hand. "Doesn't Theo look so grownup? And such a cutie, too."

Dani nodded toward a row of chairs surrounded by end tables overflowing with magazines. Theo was sitting there, sporting his new haircut and looking totally content, a *Sports Illustrated for Kids* spread out on his lap.

Hope smiled proudly at her son and nodded in agreement, while wondering what had brought on Dani's burst of enthusiasm this time. Surely it wasn't just her son's adorable face.

Plopping down at Dani's workstation with her overpriced package, Hope knew she was right when her friend, animated as ever, began pacing the floor. It was clear something else kindled Dani's mind, and Hope swiveled from left to right in the pumped-up salon chair, trying to keep up with the vivacious woman spilling her news.

"You wouldn't believe the guy who came walking in here a little while ago!" Dani exclaimed. "My horoscope said it was going to be a day full of surprises. And for once, it was right. First of all, I see this black Porsche pull up in front of the shop, right when I was finishing up Mrs. Marsh—who you know I hate to do." She wrinkled her nose. "The little old thing passes so much gas, I'm afraid to use the aerosol hairspray she likes so much. Why, her gas, combined with that spray, could blow a block of Bearsville to smithereens!"

At the mere mention of passing gas, Theo burst into giggles from his corner of the salon, reminding them he was privy to their every word. Evidently Dani didn't think that was such a good thing at the moment.

"Hey, handsome." Bearsville's primo stylist pulled some singles from the pocket of her much-too-tight black pants. "I could sure use a vanilla Coke. How about you? Want to run over to the ice cream shop and get us a couple?"

Without the slightest hesitation, Theo hopped up from his chair, grabbed the money with a shy "thanks" and bolted out the door.

"Anyway," Dani continued once he'd gone, "this Porsche pulls up and my mouth just falls open—"

At this point Dani gave a visual reenactment of her body facing the window where the famed Porsche parked, and her jaw going slack when she saw it. "I was so dumbstruck. But then my mouth dropped to the floor when this incredibly, and I do mean incredibly—" Dani looked up to the heavens as if the guy had descended directly from there, "—good-looking guy with this divine head of dark hair gets out and heads toward my shop. He's the best-looking guy—

well, minus Larry, of course—I've seen around town since that UPS driver had his truck break down here a few years ago."

"Fed Ex," Hope corrected her.

"What?" Dani stopped in her tracks momentarily.

"I said Fed Ex. It was a Fed Ex guy."

"Really? I thought it was UPS." Dani scrunched up her face.

"Nope." Hope shook her head assuredly, knowing she was right. "It was Fed Ex all right. Remember, you said he could absolutely, positively get you there, and it wouldn't take overnight." She arched an eyebrow at her friend and chuckled.

Visibly tickled by her own wit, Dani cocked her head and put her hand over her mouth, hiding an amused smile. "Oh, yeah, I do remember that." Then she straightened up and added boldly, "And I also remember praying that he'd be a good deliveryman and deliver me from my celibacy. But not all of our prayers get answered, I guess." She shrugged. "Anyway, this Chandler Adams guy is staying at your Uncle Cary's. I couldn't wait to tell you, so you could pay Uncle C an impromptu visit."

"Been there, done that," Hope said without much expression, completely denying the anxious feelings bubbling up inside of her. *So, he'd already made it into town, huh? Is he still around? Will I run into him?* Her stomach did a flip-flop.

"So you've seen him?" Dani's eyes were wide. "Well? What did you think? A ten on the Richter scale or what?"

"Well, I guess I was too sleepy to feel the earth moving," Hope fibbed. "But, yeah, he was okay."

Avoiding her friend's gaze, Hope pretended to be fixated on a new hair spritzer in a cobalt blue bottle at Dani's cutting station. She reached for it from where she was sitting and caught a glimpse of herself in the mirror as she did so. *How I must've looked to Chandler Adams this morning!* Though, come to think of it, she didn't look much better at the moment, decked out in her patched-up overalls, still wearing the same ski cap with wild curls escaping in every direction.

Deep down, she knew the morning's embarrassing scenario had left her rethinking her wardrobe. That had been her prime motivation for the impulse purchase at Mitchell's . . . that and the person who had made her rethink it, though she hated to admit it.

Maybe when she got home she'd try to dig out some regular jeans or some nice pants from her closet, too. Something like other moms wore. *Theo would like that,* she thought, recalling a couple of random conversations when he'd made mention of her crazy, haphazardly-thrown-together outfits.

Dani appeared confused that Hope hadn't gone mad for this guy, but didn't let it daunt her gushing. "Anyway, I directed him to my chair, the same chair that you're sitting in now, as a matter of fact. So if you start feeling tingly all over," Dani wriggled around in her own skin, "you'll know why," she cooed.

Tingly. Yes, Hope had felt exactly that way this morning. *Those wacky hormones—who could control the darn things?* And if she thought too hard and too long about her encounter with Chandler—oh, she even liked his name and would have to use it for one of Sela's lovers—she'd be feeling that way again now. *Sure don't need that.*

She glanced at the "Directions for Use" on the blue bottle, trying to block out Dani's detailed account in an effort to assuage her own feelings. Maybe if she sang "The Star Spangled Banner" in her head at the same time, it would help.

"Then I snipped away at him. But I have to tell you, I never took so long to do a little trim job in my life. He was so easy to talk to, so congenial, especially for a spy," Dani ranted on. "I mean he noticed the Laundromat across the street and mentioned how handy it was having it there. Said he'd probably come back later to get a tub or two done.

"I guess I don't exactly think about a spy doing laundry, you know?" Dani continued without pausing for a breath. "But then, I suppose spies need clean underwear, too, don't they? I would just expect them to be a little more aloof than that or something. But then again when you see James Bond, he's absolutely charming, so maybe not."

Spy? Had Dani actually said *spy?* Hope slammed the spritzer a little too hard back into its spot.

"He told you he was a spy?" she sputtered, aghast. *Who is this guy anyway? Isn't he carrying the spy bit a little too far? Has the local insane asylum misplaced a patient?*

"Well, honestly, it's not like he just blurted it out or any-thing," Dani said confidentially. "It did take me a while to drag it out of him. But you know," her eyes gleamed victori-ously, "psychiatrist . . . priest . . . hair stylist . . . it's all the same thing. When people are in this chair, they pour their hearts out." Dani patted the arm of her salon chair with fond affection.

"Dani, believe me, you don't understand. He's not *really* a spy. He's just saying that."

"Yeah? Why would he make that up? I mean a brain sur-geon or a criminal lawyer or something, but a spy? Who would even think of it?" Dani dismissed the notion with a wave of her hand.

"Dani, really, he's not a spy. It's just that this morning, well, I kind of ran into him first, you know." Hope couldn't believe herself. She had actually added the word "first," like she was staking a claim on this guy. Calling dibs on him or something. Like Dani had Larry's heart clinched, and Hope had first right of refusal on the new man about town. How childish was that?

Embarrassed, she softened her tone. "It's really simple, actually." She pushed her glasses higher on her nose and cleared her throat. "I said I wrote spy novels, and so he said he was a spy. It was a joke. Honest."

"Well, it's true. He hasn't *always* been a spy," Dani pointed out matter-of-factly, drawing out the word. "He actually majored in accounting and even worked as a CPA for a while. But then he decided that he really wanted to travel more, so—"

"So he became an international spy," Hope finished her sentence, shaking her head at her friend's gullibility.

"Right!" Dani nodded. "That's exactly right."

"Dani, Dani, Dani, do you hear what you're saying?" Hope pleaded for some sanity to enter into Dani's cute, and typically more acute, little head.

"What?" Shrugging her shoulders, Dani stared at Hope as if she were the crazy one.

"Oh, my gosh! A spy doesn't go around telling everyone they're a spy. Or just drive their dashing little bodies around in some flashy spectacle of a car, for God's sake." Hope threw up her arms in frustration.

"Oh, yeah? Well, yoo-hoo, have you forgotten?" Dani stood squarely with her hands on her hips. "Sela Theodore drives a cherry red Boxster, and James Bond drives just about every sports car there is!"

"But, Dani, that's just fiction, and yoo-hoo yourself, have you forgotten? This is real life! And Sela and James certainly don't go around blabbing to everyone that they're spies!"

Hope pressed her fingers to her temples. This was the most ridiculous conversation she had ever had with anyone in her life. Well actually, come to think of it, some with her ex had been pretty irrational, too. But this was her best friend. They usually felt everything the same way. They were of the same gender, same spirit, same heart, and same mind. Was Dani really putting credence in a guy who had plopped down in Bearsville from out of nowhere?

"Chandler isn't telling *everyone*." Dani's tone turned haughty. "He told you, true, probably because he thought you could relate, being a spy novelist and all." Dani rolled her eyes as if that had been a huge miscalculation on his part. "And he just told me because people tell their hair stylists everything. All their deepest, darkest secrets! He knew telling me would be like telling a man of the cloth. My lips are sealed." She pursed her lips and added so tersely that Hope could barely understand her, "I, for one, won't tell anyone."

"You just told me!" Hope blurted, completely exasperated.

"Well, that's different. I tell you everything because there's no one else in town you'd tell anything to, except for me. And I already know what you'd tell me, because I'm the one who told you. So, see, it just doesn't matter if I tell you."

Hope narrowed her eyes into a painful squint, trying to follow Dani's logic.

"And it's not like he gave me any details about his assignment, Hope."

"How very covert and spy-like of him," Hope replied sarcastically.

"He just said he was holing up in Bearsville because his work would be in Manhattan, and we're a close—yet safe—distance away."

"I hope you know how ridiculous this sounds." Hope was the one to roll her eyes this time.

"You know what, Hope? Looking into his eyes, yes, he could probably sell me on just about anything. But he seems honest, intelligent, easy to talk to, and he's obviously well off." Dani crossed her arms in front of her chest. "I don't know . . . you might want to clean off your glasses or put in your contacts, and take a look for yourself, girlfriend. I know Robert did a number on your heart. But he was a lying—"

Dani stopped in the midst of slamming Robert—something she'd gotten very proficient at over the years—distracted by the sound of someone loudly slurping the last remnants of a drink through a straw.

Hope heard the same thing at exactly the same time. Exchanging concerned looks with one another, the two women turned toward the door simultaneously, knowing their worst fear was about to be realized. Theo was standing there. The question was, for how long?

"Theo, you're the best." Dani instantly brightened, pretending she hadn't just been talking about an international spy or Theo's dad, who had also gone undercover, so to speak, many, many years ago.

She held out her hand and Theo advanced toward her with her vanilla Coke, his lips still locked on his straw, now apparently sucking air.

"That was quick," Hope piped up. "The ice cream parlor wasn't crowded, huh?"

Theo shrugged and looked around, clearly not wanting to make eye contact with her, making her wonder how much he'd overheard.

"I was just trying to guess what your mom has in this bag," Dani told Theo, making an abrupt subject change.

She pointed to the Mitchell parcel in Hope's lap. "So, you're not going to tell me, huh?" She turned to Hope.

"It's nothing. Really." Hope clutched the bag tightly against her. She knew Dani was doing all this to divert Theo's attention, but she really was slightly uncomfortable about revealing the bag's contents.

"Nothing? Is it a birthday present for Theo?" Dani prodded and turned to smile at Theo.

"Maybe."

Dani arched an eyebrow, delighted disbelief shining in her eyes. "You're fibbing," she sang out. "I can tell these things. It's something for you, isn't it?"

Hope glanced at Theo, who looked relieved not to be getting a birthday present from boring old Mitchell's department store, then back at Dani. She didn't give an answer, which meant a sure "yes."

"I think we should tickle it out of her." Dani gleamed at Theo, as if they were the truest of cohorts. "What do you think?"

Theo nodded back enthusiastically and together they dove onto Hope, tickling her wherever they could get their hands in. She howled with laughter, trying to defend herself with her arms. In the midst of all the grabbing and tickling, the bag dropped from her lap.

"I've got it, I've got it," Dani shrieked, picking up the paper bag. "And what do I have here but a brand-new, never-been-used—" She reached into the bag and pulled out the silk robe inside. "Oh, Hope!" she gasped, instantly reverent. "It's so pretty. You found this at Mitchell's? It looks like something out of a fancy catalog."

Dani was right, Hope realized. Maybe that's why she'd been so entranced by the robe. It looked like nothing generally seen in this chilly town, its hue as breathtaking as a summer-pink rose, its texture as soft as the flower's velvety petals.

"Yeah, I kind of liked it," Hope replied shyly, catching her breath.

Theo didn't seem much interested, now that the tickling was over and the mystery had been solved. He gave the robe an indifferent glance before sauntering back over to his magazine.

But Dani was clearly entranced and reached up to hold the robe against Hope's frame. Hope flushed when Dani complimented her in a soft, sincere voice. "Pretty in pink—actually beautiful in pink—that's you."

It was a warm moment between friends, but truly only a moment, because a knock on the salon's window startled both women and made them jump.

Standing there, between the "½ Price on Wednesdays" sticker and the flyer advertising Bearsville High School's production of *Bye, Bye Birdie*, was the man who had been the topic of their conversation that morning.

With a pillowcase presumably full of dirty clothes slung between his broad shoulders, he looked in on the scene with eyes that were both inquisitive and friendly. The women stood frozen, mesmerized by this undeniably handsome stranger who had abruptly come into their lives.

Dani still had the silky-soft robe displayed against Hope's full length, and now Hope's cheeks glowed with warmth under the gaze of Chandler's appraising look. Though she wasn't ready to admit it to her best friend—and barely to herself—the morning's events had awakened some long-lost kinds of feelings in her.

But, heck, who could blame her? It had been a long while since she'd let herself feel anything. Theo would be eleven years old next week, after all. Who knew if it was really the new man in town who was having this effect on her? Maybe it was just too much time spent alone, and the fact that she was getting tired of Sela, her alter ego, having all the fun!

Chandler Adams' gaze singled her out and traveled the length of her body, starting at her eyes and drifting down to the folds of silk puddled at her feet. Then he smiled up at her slowly . . . an appreciative sort of smile . . . his eyes never leaving her face. With his free hand, he gave her a "thumbs-up" sign. *In approval of the sumptuous cover-up?* Hope wondered. *Or also of me . . . the woman behind it?*

Instantly, that tingling feeling was there again, starting at the essence of her being, breaking into tendrils that sparked all the way up to her cheeks. Needing to keep such strange, new—and at the same time, familiar and old—feelings at bay, Hope broke away from his gaze. But when she turned, behind her she saw a younger pair of male eyes staring at her, too. Theo's. Wary and skeptical-looking, he seemed to be reminding her that they'd both been hurt before.

If I'm smart, she thought, *I'll follow my son's lead.*

Chapter Three

The plane rocked, jarring Sela out of her light sleep, though she was somewhat thankful for that. After all, every time she closed her eyes, the image of Giorgio came to mind, stirring up a gamut of feelings inside her.

She remembered him as if it were truly yesterday . . . his brown-black hair . . . deep, dark eyes so full of mystique . . . enigmatic, crooked smile . . . and such kissable lips—lips that had rocked her to her core. She had torn herself away from him once. But it had not been easy, especially when her young, maiden body had pulsed with desire.

However, she was a professional now, and couldn't afford to be distracted by such memories. Once the plane landed in Venice—city of romance or not—she'd have to get cracking on her designated mission. She'd have to forget the man she had once desired with all of her heart. She'd need to concentrate on the job she now put her heart and soul into.

Sela sighed heavily. Maybe a movie would help take her mind off things. She reached for the headphones and looked up at the screen toward the front of the plane. The film was just starting. Roman Holiday.

Well, then again, maybe not.

Chandler pushed back the curtains from Uncle Cary's dining-room window, allowing a morning splash of winter sun to filter through the lightly-frosted panes.

He stretched his arms into the air, one after another, deciding he felt pretty much at home in Cary's rundown, but oddly interesting place. His morning routine was getting more pat, for one thing. Once again, today he'd made a fire in the dining-room fireplace, and it was burning even better and brighter than yesterday's attempt. And the pot of coffee he'd brewed was far less bitter this morning, thanks to the advice of Uncle Cary's niece from next door. He felt rested, too, having finally gotten a decent night's sleep. Yes, all in all, life in Bearsville was comfortable at the moment.

Pulling out a dining-room chair near the well-lit window, he sat down at one of Uncle Cary's nicked-up tables and attempted to concentrate on the task at hand. The laser feature on his computerized multipurpose watch hadn't been working correctly lately. He'd been waiting for the right time and place to take the thing apart, hoping to determine the problem. However, minutes later, as he gazed at all the minute, puzzling pieces strewn out on the table before him, he was thinking that may have been a mistake.

They sure didn't make computerized lasers like they used to. When he first entered the spy business, used to be that the components were more simplified. You could even fix them yourself. *But not anymore,* he sighed, realizing he'd have to pack up the parts and ship them all back to headquarters.

But who was he fooling? It wasn't only the number of watch pieces that was perplexing him at the moment. It was the number that Uncle Cary's niece was doing on his head. Every time the wood creaked in this old house or a flickering ember crackled in the fireplace, he'd glance up, hoping it was the sound of her footsteps bringing her near to him.

He wasn't sure why she'd had such an effect on him, except that she was so different from the other women he was used to being with. Women from around the world. Famous women—incomparable beauties—and all well aware of it. All so full of pretenses, you could never be too sure just what their true motives were.

Not that he'd rate his experiences with those women as exactly agonizing by any means. But still, after a while, one came to realize that the glamorous life was like real life, only with a glossy enamel coating on it. And once that enamel began to chip off—well, there was no guarantee you were going to like what was underneath.

Take the supermodels, for instance. He'd met plenty of them from a slew of different countries. Plenty who were obviously great to look at, but talk about bony to the touch! At least they were for his tastes anyway. And what was most disturbing was that they never seemed to get a hankering for a greasy cheeseburger, fries and a chocolate shake. Or if they did, they'd rarely admit it. And if they did admit it, they still wouldn't eat it. Now where was the fun in dating someone like that?

And then there were the heiresses. Greek. Iranian. Texan. No matter where they came from, they were all on the same level. So concerned about spending as much of their daddy's money as they could get their hands on. It's practically all they thought about. How could a regular guy—even a regular spy—compete with that?

Ah, and the movie stars. Call them schizos, for all he cared. It was hard to tell what the real deal was with those people. Always looking for some hot spot to get noticed in—and then shying away or pretending to be angry when the paparazzi got close by.

They're certainly not the kind of women you settle down with, his mother's voice echoed in his head. And not for the first time.

She was right, of course. Though what guy wanted to admit that to his mom? And what did it matter anyway? Who said he was thinking about settling down? And even if he was searching for a special someone, someone a little more down-to-earth—a frump in a ski cap, hiking boots and thermal underwear was a bit far-fetched. Talk about going from one extreme to the other!

Only . . . Hope Hathaway wasn't a frump, and he knew it. Sure, maybe her taste in nightclothes and outerwear was uninspired—and that was being kind. But in her unique way, Hope was beguiling.

Her long, russet hair, peeking out from under that ridiculous hat, was the kind a man would love to get his hands on and run his fingers through for the pure, soft feel of it. And her eyes. Their rare blue-green color was truly hypnotic. Even though the way she looked at him was guarded and not particularly trusting. *Is that distrust only aimed at me,* he wondered, *or every male?* Whatever the case, it made winning a smile from her seem even more special, like he'd won first prize in a million-dollar sweepstakes.

Small-town girl or not, something about Hope let you know she didn't look to be a pushover either. In fact, as far as her looks were concerned . . . Chandler took another sip of coffee and, cradling the warm mug in his hands, leaned back in his chair. Momentarily he closed his eyes, letting his imagination do what his hands dared not to.

First, he'd take off those glasses of hers, so he could get the full, alluring effect of her enticing gemstone-colored eyes. And then that curly hair. It shouldn't be tucked under some floppy ski hat. Hair like that should be free to flow in wild abandon, cascading down her shoulders and pushed back from her face when a man bent to kiss her luscious lips which, by the way, could stand to be enhanced with a berry-colored gloss.

And the overalls he'd seen her in yesterday? They were fine once in a while. But legs like hers, which began at her chin and never stopped, well it was a crime not to show those off in some snug-fitting blue jeans. Or expose them in all their bare beauty, like from underneath that pinkish sort of robe he had seen her showing to Dani yesterday.

Yeah, he could just envision her in that now, standing before him, as seductive as ever. Slowly he would untie the robe's sash and push the silk back from her delicious shoulders. Down it would fall, skimming the small of her back. Slipping past the curve of her buttocks. Right before landing in a swish of softness at her feet. And then he would take a moment to just admire the exquisiteness of her nakedness before he began to . . .

Chandler settled deeper into his chair enjoying the places his mind was taking him. The computerized laser watch could wait. His daydreaming could not.

"Uncle Cary!" Hope's voice rang out in the silence of the bed and breakfast. "Uncle Cary?" she called again, making a path down the hallway and into the dining room.

At the sound of her voice, Chandler's eyes jolted open. His body jerked upright in the chair, slopping coffee onto his lap.

"Oh!" She startled at the sight of him. He was always taking her breath away by one means or another, wasn't he? Theo was probably right. They should be leery of the guy.

"I—uh—" she stammered. "Have you seen Uncle Cary?"

"Earlier." He nodded, a besotted grin glued on his face, like he'd just been dreaming his favorite dream or something. "Before he and Fiona took off."

"Took off?" That sounded odd. How often did the two of them "take off"? She glanced around the room warily, suspecting the stranger of some kind of foul play. But nothing looked amiss, as far as she could tell. "He didn't happen to mention when he'd be back, did he?"

"You know, he did say. Let me try to think." He rubbed his dark, whisker-stubbled chin thoughtfully.

Why did she get the impression he was toying with her? Maybe she was wrong, but he seemed so pleased with himself that he had all the information—and she had none. "Let's see . . ." He pondered, tapping his lip with his index finger. "We were on our second cup of coffee . . ."

"You and Uncle Cary? You had coffee with my uncle?" The idea annoyed the heck out of her, although it shouldn't have. After all, it wasn't unusual for Uncle Cary to share a cup of coffee with his guests.

"And Fiona too," Chandler added, saying the name as if he'd known the French woman all his life. "She was fresh out of raspberries this morning, but she did make an incredible breakfast crepe for me. We all ate together."

"You ate together," Hope repeated flatly, arching an eyebrow.

"Really nice people, your relatives." He nodded, his eyes twinkling with playfulness.

Surely, he knew he was getting under her skin. Of course, it was her own fault for letting him. Why did it bug her to picture the three of them together talking, laughing over breakfast? Imagining how Fiona would enjoy cooking for this attractive man, and how Uncle Cary would relish talking to him, rehashing Bearsville history?

Probably because she still wasn't sure what to make of the so-called spy. Her skepticism meter was at full tilt. Though no one else seemed bothered.

"So when will they be back?" Her hands went to her hips, to the belt loops of the ages-old blue jeans she'd wrenched herself into earlier that morning.

"I believe he said around ten tonight."

"Tonight?" So the two of them really *were* gone? For the entire day? Even more odd.

"We were talking about great hiking places upstate, and I told them about the Mohonk Mountain House. Isn't it great? They decided to go and make a day of it," Adams informed her, smiling a smile that was searching for one of hers in return. A smile from her, or some show that she accepted him the same easy way Fiona and Uncle Cary had. Thankfully, she managed to remain expressionless.

"Just like that? Out of the blue?"

He affirmed it with another nod. "Just like that. I guess I'm a fairly good salesman, huh?"

She cast her deadliest, narrowed-eye look on him. "So that's what you are, huh? Because I'm not as naïve as Dani, you know. You're a salesman then?" She was going to pin him down once and for all.

"That depends," he answered vaguely, taunting her. "Are you buying?"

Okay. She didn't curse much, but this guy was bugging the h-e-double-hockey-sticks out of her. And what was it with everyone in town? *Wow, have we all gone a little daffy?* Hope wondered.

Dani believed every word this guy said. Uncle Cary trusted him so much that he had no problem leaving him to run his bed and breakfast for the day. And now here she was alone with him, and not making any moves for a hasty retreat. Were they all so hard up in this town for some kind of diversion that they were ready to embrace any old Joe that came along?

"Is your writing going well this morning?" he asked—too politely.

Instantly she crossed her fingers behind her back. "Great. I'm on a real roll." *Oh, yeah, a full four paragraphs. I'll never meet my deadline at this rate.*

Every time she'd try to picture Sela's Giorgio, the mysterious Chandler Adams would pop up in her mind instead. Finally, instead of writing, she'd spent most of the morning getting her new look going. Well, actually it was her old look resurrected. First she had to dig around and find some jeans. Then she had to try them all on till she found a pair that looked stylish, intact, and would zip up over the womanly curves that motherhood had bestowed upon her.

She had thought about putting her contacts in, but her solution was all dried up and so was most of her make-up. She did manage to splash a little color on her lips though, and blew her hair dry. How had she forgotten what an ordeal it all was?

At first, she'd felt so frou-froued up and self-conscious, she'd almost dismissed the idea of coming over to the inn altogether. But now that she was here, she was glad she'd gone to all the trouble.

She felt good, confident even, standing before him, her lanky legs feeling even longer in her pair of tight, stonewashed blue jeans, and a baby blue sweater hugging her breasts. Like yesterday, she was still wearing her glasses, but her hair wasn't stuffed under a ski cap this time. It was tied back in a loose rubber band and a few tendrils fell freely around her face. Hopefully, for all her trouble, she was getting under his skin, too. *Though for a completely different reason, of course,* she smirked to herself.

"Did you stop by for some coffee then?" he asked,

nodding toward the pot on the serving table.

"No," Hope said honestly. "I'm actually stuck on a section of my book. Usually Uncle Cary helps me out with some of the martial arts scenes. We go over them, so it's easier for me to describe in my writing."

"Oh, yeah?" He set his mug on the tabletop and stood up to come toward her. "I know martial arts."

"Of course you do," she grumbled under her breath. "Don't all spies?"

"What?" He inclined an ear her way.

"I said, you do?"

He nodded. "Maybe I can help," he offered, looking sincere . . . and well, darn it all . . . hard to resist.

"Thanks. But it looks like you're busy," she said, nodding toward the watch parts on the table.

"That thing? Forget it." He waved his hand in disgust. "They don't make computerized laser watches like they used to."

Geez, there he goes with that spy business again. Sure, it got a big laugh out of me yesterday. But he doesn't need to run it into the ground. Why is it every time I meet a guy—like every half-dozen years or so—he has some little quirk? Oh, as if having delusions would be considered a minor "quirk"?

"So what's the scenario?" he asked her.

"Huh?" Her thoughts had drifted.

"Your character. What's her name? Sarah? Selma? Tell me the setup."

"Sela. Her name is Sela. And really I think I'll just wait until tomorrow, when Uncle Cary is back."

"Don't you have a deadline?" he persisted.

Did he have to mention the "d" word?

"I'll be gentle," he promised, a slow smile building on his lips. "No broken bones. Trust me."

51

Hope Hathaway Life Lesson #1: Never trust a man who says, "Trust me."

But still . . . for days she'd been trying to figure out an alluring way to introduce Sela and Giorgio to each other again. Something totally novel, exciting, sensuous. And now that had she thought of it, a martial arts scene where they'd become entwined in one another's arms, she was anxious to get it down on paper. In the name of research, she found herself going on heedlessly.

"Well, the deal is this," she jabbered excitedly about the scene, talking with her hands. "Sela is going to break into a villa where she thinks some incriminating papers might be hidden. But she doesn't know the villa is actually the property of her former Italian lover, Giorgio. He hears something and is near the door when she picks her way in. Obviously he comes up from behind her and—"

"Like this?"

Before she could finish her sentence, with one swift move Chandler had spun her around, slipped his arms underneath hers, and locked his hands across the back of her head.

"Now," he explained authoritatively, his body spooned against hers, making it a challenge to concentrate, "Sela could do two things to break out of this position. Either she could bend over and flip Giorgio over her head, or she could put her right leg behind his, to lock him up while she makes her move. Which do you prefer?"

Obviously, the overhead flipping wasn't exactly a romantic way for her characters to get reacquainted. But the thought of acquainting herself with Adams with the leg-locking move made her body tense up. She didn't need to be this close to him. Didn't need to be in such a precarious position with such an unpredictable stranger.

Because he could do me bodily harm? she questioned herself. *Or possibly bodily good?*

"Option two," she answered him tersely, bracing herself.

"Okay. Try it then," he urged. "Loop your leg around mine."

The last thing she wanted to do was to wrap her leg around his. After all, she knew his leg would be muscle-hard . . . from his thigh to his calf. His chest taut and solid-feeling as she leaned up against him. But, again, it was all in the name of research, so . . .

Just go for it. Get it over with, she moaned inwardly, swinging her leg around his, trying to push all thoughts from her head, trying to ignore all the heated places their bodies touched.

"Okay, good," he said softly as they stood intertwined.

His breath tickled her ear. And with her back snug into his chest, she had to admit "good" was an understatement. They seemed a perfect fit. Strangely natural together. And there was nothing *good* about that.

"Now, uh . . ." He cleared his throat. "What's-her-name—"

Is he feeling something, too? she wondered when he couldn't recall her heroine's name.

"Sela," she answered him.

"Right. Sela can use the leverage with her leg to twist herself around against Giorgio. And the force of that will break apart his clasped hands behind her head."

Hope had turned her head to listen, and flushed at the feel of his breath on her cheek as he spoke to her. "Go ahead," her mentor urged. "See if you can do it."

"Twist around?" She hesitated.

"I'm ready for you."

With all her might, she swung her body around toward

his and felt his hands give way as she broke his grip. She was shocked that she could complete the move with such agility. Even more, she was shocked at the position she found herself in.

Suddenly, the two of them stood there alone, facing each other. Toe to toe. Pelvis to pelvis. Heart to heart. Not a fiber between them touching. Yet they were so close, it took little imagination to realize how each would feel to one another.

"And that way," Chandler's explanation was almost a whisper, "it would be a situation where the two characters could meet again by Sela coming face-to-face with—"

" '—the man whose kissable lips had rocked her to her core,' " Hope quoted her manuscript in a faint, breathy voice.

Their eyes continued to hold one another. His eyes looked sincere, just a glimmer of playfulness left in them now. And so dark and deep . . . in a warm way that caressed her. She realized he seemed able to do things with his eyes that most men could only do with their hands. Which left her with another unsettling thought—*imagine what he could do with his hands!*

No! Don't think about it! her mind shouted. But it was too late.

His closeness became so intoxicating that Hope's knee buckled from under her. Instantly he caught her and, cupping both of her elbows, he drew her more closely to him. She felt her chest brush against his, and his eyes once again searched hers. Looking for some kind of consent? Some kind of answer? Her mind full of questions, the only thing she knew for sure was that someone had to make the next move.

So she did.

"Yeeeeyaaah!" she yelped with a warrior's cry that even Bruce Lee would've been proud of.

She threw her arms up in the air, breaking loose from Adams' grasp. But what goes up must come down. And as her arms flipped upward, they came crashing down, sweeping wildly across the table, sending watch parts flying everywhere.

Shocked at her own outburst, she covered her mouth and stepped back from the scene. It was then that they both heard something metal squish underneath her left boot.

Looking up at Chandler, she felt all at once foolish, sheepish. "Oops! I—uh—crap! I hope that wasn't a family heirloom or anything."

He shook his head. "No. Just a lousy computerized laser watch, like I told you. I was going to send it back to head-quarters anyway."

"You mean the manufacturer?" she asked.

"No. Headquarters." He shook his head nonchalantly.

Oh, right, the spy stuff again! When is he going to give it up? She winced.

"It's okay. Really," he assured her, responding to the pained expression on her face. "I'm sure your dinner to-night will more than make up for it."

"My what?" Her eyes went wide in disbelief. Had she heard that right?

"Dinner. Cary said you'd be happy to provide dinner for me tonight, since he and Fiona are gone. At your place. I can make it any time," he added congenially. "Whatever's convenient for you."

Hope couldn't have been more stunned if she'd been poked with a cattle prod. And that would be extremely stunning in this part of the country. "Well, um, see here's the thing about that. It's really *not* convenient for me," she told him. "And besides, this is a B&B, not a B&D, you know?"

"Oh, yeah? Do you have other plans?" he asked nosily, looking all interested.

"Dinner plans?" She chuckled, unable to contain herself. "Ha, that's a laugh. No, not exactly. But I do have a son." *A son who's already spotted you and bestowed the hairy eyeball on you. A son who doesn't need some strange man lurking around, thank you very much.*

"I saw him going out to the bus yesterday morning. What is he? Fifth, sixth grade, did you say?"

"Fifth."

"Same age as my nephew Cory. One of my brother's kids." He nodded. Then his lips twisted downward, forming a slight frown. "But they moved to Colorado last year. Gosh, I miss those kids," he confided, sounding all at once wistful. "Luckily, my sister's family isn't too far away. But still, with work and all . . ." He shook his head. "I don't see them as often as I'd like. They grow up so darn fast, don't they?"

Oh, puhhlease! She wanted to scream out loud. *Please, don't do this. Don't be nice. Don't seem to be normal, when we all know deep down that you're probably some loony, or at the very least a renowned heartbreaker.*

But—his puppy dog eyes were imploring her, tugging at her heart. Damn those orbs of his!

"Six-thirty," she found herself saying.

"Perfect." He grinned openly.

Not really, she wanted to tell him. At least, Theo wasn't going to think so.

"Cary said his beautiful niece wouldn't let him down," he told her in a low voice. And there went those eyes of his again, fixed on her . . . brightening at the complimentary word, emphasizing it as if it were his thought instead of her uncle's.

"Yep, that's me," she said lightly, breaking herself away from his shiver-inducing gaze. *Ever the sop,* she mentally flogged herself, flipping a good-bye wave at him.

But as she backed out of the dining room for the second day in a row, her eyes couldn't help but be drawn from Adams' face to the wet spot on the crotch of his pants. *What the heck?*

"Coffee," he assured her, clueing in to what was going on in her mind.

Whew! she thought, flying out the front door.

Chapter Four

Sela picked open the lock of the elegantly-carved villa door, her heart pounding in her ears. Supposedly the occupants would be at the opera this evening, leaving her full rein to search for the incriminating documents. But plans always did have a way of changing. She'd have to be on guard.

Stealing through the foyer and down the hallway into a study lit by a full moon seeping in the window, she sensed someone behind her. Before she could make a move, the attacker made his—pinning her arms behind her with his own. With one fluid motion, Sela wrapped her leg around her assailant's. Then she turned toward him with all her might, breaking free from his grasp. That's when she came full face—and full front—with her aggressor.

"Giorgio?" Sela gasped in surprise.

"Sela?" Shock registered on the ruggedly handsome face of her former love.

"Giorgio?" Sela repeated.

"Sela?" he said once again.

Darn. Why hadn't she made it to the library for those "Speak Instant Italian" tapes?

Immediately, Giorgio's shock gave way to pleasure. It was there in his eyes. A look that told Sela that all this time it was still her—and only her—he desired. Except for—

"Che ella, Giorgio, che ella?" A woman's thickly-accented voice exploded from the doorway. She was a blonde-

haired, olive-skinned beauty in a chartreuse dressing gown, with dark eyes that glared at Sela.

Sela wasn't sure what the woman had said exactly. But she could guess from her acidic delivery, it was something like "three's a crowd." And Sela had definitely arrived third . . .

"What did you think about the Giants this year?" Chandler scooped up a bite of lasagna from his plate, and turned to Theo for an answer. "Almost snagged the Super Bowl, huh?"

"I'm not into football," Hope's son blandly informed the incredible-looking man sitting at her dinner table.

"Baseball then? The great American pastime?" Chandler tried again. "Got a favorite team?"

Theo stopped poking at his food just long enough to give Chandler a wary once-over, sizing up their guest not for the first time that evening.

To Hope, Chandler looked as casual as the meal truly was, an impromptu affair mostly prearranged by Uncle Cary. Dressed down in jeans—faded jeans hanging low on his slim hips—and a vee-neck sweater—a sweater the same golden brown as the flecks in his inquisitive eyes—Mr. Adams was no threat. No threat at all. *Well, okay,* she conceded to herself, *maybe to a female like me, who has been man-less for—*Oh, did she have to keep enumerating the years? But, he certainly shouldn't appear threatening to Theo.

But obviously her son wasn't seeing it that way. He was digging in his heels, not giving their visitor an inch, or a word either. Theo simply shrugged in reply.

When no answer came, Chandler stopped in the middle of his chewing. Eyebrows cinched, he looked across the table to Hope for help.

Maybe a few hours ago, she wouldn't have minded letting Chandler Adams squirm. But after watching him with Theo throughout the meal, seeing him struggle to engage her suddenly-turned-stubborn son in conversation, well, it made her feel kind of bad for the guy.

If his story was true and he really was an uncle, she'd guess from the effort he'd put out this evening that he was a pretty good one. Unfortunately, if he was looking for a surrogate nephew, he sure wasn't going to find one in the Hathaway household.

Theo had been incorrigible throughout the entire meal, passive and indifferent to their guest. Hope couldn't believe this atypical behavior, and had thought about reprimanding him right then and there. But she bit her tongue instead, containing herself, hard as it was. If Theo thought there was a contest going on between him and their visitor, scolding him in front of Chandler would definitely only make matters worse.

"Theo plays basketball." She turned to Chandler, trying to assume an everything's-hunky-dory posture, even though she was feeling terribly uncomfortable for all of them. "He's the center on his school team."

"Oh, yeah?" Chandler looked relieved to receive this bit of information, something he could run with. "I used to play some b-ball myself. How's your team doing?"

But while Chandler was ready to run with the conversation, Theo tripped him up with another taciturn shrug and blank stare.

"Probably too early in the season to tell," Chandler offered, answering his own question in a kind and patient way, endearing him to Hope even more.

He gave her a weak smile and ruffled his fingers through his hair. A lock escaped, falling onto his forehead just as it had the other day. *Yes,* she thought, feasting her eyes on him. He truly was one incredible-looking man, all right . . . sitting at her dinner table.

"The Knicks are on Channel 11 in about five minutes." Hope attempted to smooth over the awkward moment and quell the rush she'd gotten just glancing at him. Rising from the table, she dutifully began stacking dishes in her arms. "They're our favorites, aren't they, Theo?"

Again, without even as much as a glance at her, Theo shrugged indifferently, making her face burn. Her teeth clench. Her patience falter.

His behavior tonight was abominable—so unlike his usual, cheery self. She knew, of course, when she'd told Chandler that he could join them, that Theo would probably be less than pleased about it. But even if Theo didn't like the idea of some man being there, there was no reason for him to be downright rude to both of them. He'd certainly be hearing about this from her later.

Though as she made her way to the kitchen, Hope's ire defused a bit. How much had Theo overheard Dani saying? Had he heard something that upset him? Caught the slurs Dani had made against his father? Or Dani's suggestions about Hope getting back on the prowl for a man? Or even the silly spy stuff about Chandler?

She glanced over her shoulder at the man she'd met only yesterday and marveled. What a good job he was doing, overlooking her son's boldness and coolness, taking it all in stride.

Thankfully, one of the males present is behaving admirably, she thought. Though regrettably it wasn't the one she'd given birth to.

Chandler stood and, picking up his plate and wineglass, he took a final sip as he followed behind her. "I thought you said you couldn't cook. That was some of the best lasagna I've ever had," he raved, placing his dishes on the kitchen counter.

"Hah!" Theo finally let out a sound, a snicker that erupted as he towed behind them with his dirty plate and milk glass.

"Yeah, it did turn out pretty good, didn't it?" She deftly skirted the issue, taking a moment to sneakily shove the Stouffer's frozen lasagna box deeper into the garbage pail. Then, taking Theo's plate from him, she gave her son her own version of a hairy eyeball. If he told her secret or mentioned that the famed Sara Lee was in the wings with a carrot cake for dessert, it was no allowance for him for a week!

Turning on the faucet, she began methodically scraping the dishes into the sink.

"Need any help?" Chandler asked over her shoulder. A bit too closely over her shoulder, she realized, as an involuntary shiver worked its way down her spine.

"Thanks, but I was just going to give these a quick rinse and finish them up later. It's not a big deal."

At least it wasn't until she flipped on the garbage disposal. She jumped back when it growled at her with a gnarly, metal-gnashing sound.

Apparently the noise had gotten the guys' attention as well. She could feel them standing frozen behind her, as she hurriedly flicked off the disposal's switch.

"Here, let me." Chandler stepped forward. Nudging her hip gently out of the way with his, he took over her position at the sink. But before launching into the job, he removed a bulbous silver ring from his finger and placed it near the philodendron plant on the windowsill over the basin.

She'd noticed the ring at dinner, and had caught Theo

staring at it, too. It was certainly different looking, void of any gems, and now that she could appraise it more closely, it appeared to have miniature doors that flipped open.

"Don't tell me," she said teasingly. "Your spy decoder ring, right?"

He didn't answer, just arched his eyebrow and smiled at her like she was one smart cookie.

Oh, great! More spy fantasy stuff. Well, if he was going to keep it up, she was going to start ripping on it.

"Oh, yeah? So, did you get it with Wheaties box tops?" she scoffed. "Or is it the Cracker Jacks model?"

"Something like that," he replied easily, sticking his hand down the disposal, routing around for the problem.

"Ah ha." He brought up his hand a minute or so later. "Who's the barbecued wings aficionado around here?" He held up a portion of bone.

She turned to look at the number one wing-eater in her family, but Theo's eyes weren't looking her way. Instead, they seemed fixed on the windowsill, his expression puzzled.

What a surprising evening!

Theo had acted worse than she could've ever imagined. And she'd actually enjoyed Chandler's company much more than she'd ever have thought. Not that it was worth all the strife that it'd apparently caused her son. But for one night . . . well, honestly, it had been nice to have some adult male company. Different. Entertaining, she smiled to herself as she went to turn out the lights and call it a night.

"Oh, shoot!" She spied Chandler's money clip, lying on the dining room chair. Oh, well, no big deal. She could just return it to him in the morning.

Picking it up, she ran her hand over the Chinese-looking

dragon etched on the silver clip. Then she examined the slim fold of money it held. Three singles and two twenties. Admittedly, she felt almost relieved. If it'd been a roll of fifties or hundreds, a wad to match the ostentatious look of his Porsche, she might've been more put off. But it appeared he really was a fairly normal guy after all.

Okay. The spy thing was a tad different. But not everyone shared exactly the same sense of humor, did they? And humor aside, he'd certainly done a remarkable job of handling her impolite son all evening. No laughing matter there.

Why, Chandler Adams had even taken over in the kitchen, clearing chicken wing bones from her complaining disposal. He'd simply stepped forward and given her a gentle nudge with his hip. So small a gesture, yet she could still conjure up the heated undercurrents she felt as they stood side by side at the sink, his hips and leg brushing against hers. How she had struggled to stay locked to her spot, though his slight musky scent invited her to lean closer to him . . .

Oh! Her heart skipped a beat, her hand rubbed over the silver clip. *Maybe tonight would be better than the morning.*

It wasn't very late really, and she still had to take out the trash cans anyway. For sure, it would be better to return his money immediately. Once things found their way into her house, they rarely resurfaced again. The Hathaway Triangle, she often called it.

Yes, she should certainly drop it off now and make sure he got it back. Well, that is, drop it off after she brushed her teeth. Sprayed on a smidgen of perfume. And freshened up her lip gloss.

Funny, she thought as she headed to the bathroom, *maintaining my new look doesn't actually require as much effort as I thought it would. Maybe I just needed the right kind of incentive,* she mused, conjuring up the image of Bearsville's most recent visitor once again.

However . . .

If he says anything about staying, the answer is unequivocally, undeniably "no," Hope told herself as she exited her house and started out across the lawn. Not even for a minute. She didn't want to leave Theo asleep alone in the house for long, even if all the doors were locked. Who knew? He could have a bad dream. The aliens could show up to take him away. There could be a blast of spontaneous combustion. Mothers knew about these things. Whatever, the answer was "no."

Her mind was resolute as she glanced up at Chandler's window at the side of the weatherworn inn. Resolute . . . until she got an eyeful of his compelling backside through the window.

Woo-hoo! The sight of him stopped her dead.

So is this what a voyeur feels like? she wondered, unabashedly staring into the window, prickles of heat rising up her neck. Her shame should've far outweighed her pleasure, but it didn't as she watched him pull his sweater over his head and drop it carelessly to the floor. He stretched then, his arms up in the air, and the flex of the sinewy muscles across his back gave extraordinary shape to the ordinary white T-shirt he still wore.

Well, I am only right next door . . . Hope reconsidered, a warmth spreading through her. *Maybe I could stay a minute or two. Five, tops. Yes, five minutes—that's it. Would that be so bad?*

Hope tried to avert her eyes from the bedroom window as she scurried toward the house.

But seeing Chandler still posed there, it was proving to be too tempting.

He had a rather nice rear. Kind of like that tight end on

the Giants' football team, she giggled to herself. Leading up to his fit-looking torso . . . hmm, did he use some elliptical machine, jog, or was it just Adams *au naturale?* She'd love to get a look at his abs, too. But for right now, his backside would do just fine with a strong, slim waist where some woman's hands were reaching around to—

Whoa, replay that again! Hope shook her head, adjusted her glasses and squinted into the lit room again.

For cripes sake! Yes, that was definitely Chandler's waist. And yes, there was definitely some woman's hands wrapped around it. Hands with brightly painted red nails and plenty of flashy, sparkling rings. Hands that were tugging at Chandler's T-shirt to release it from the confines of his jeans. Hands that Hope couldn't identify because the woman's face behind those hands was obstructed from view by Chandler's upper body.

Still, she could see enough to make out the straight blonde hair that grew just past the woman's shoulders. And for sure she could see the way the woman moved in more closely to Chandler . . . how her arms hugged him as she freed his T-shirt, pulling it over his head to reveal his toned back underneath.

Geez, what a hunk! What a low-lying, two-timing hunk! Hope wanted to scream.

The woman threw the cotton T-shirt onto the bed. Then something else must have occurred to her, because she walked determinedly toward the window. Suddenly, she seemed to be looking right at Hope. Could she really see her out there in the blackness of the night? Instantly, Hope made a break for it, dashing for cover in the shrubs directly under the bedroom window.

"Ye-ouch!" She muffled what under normal circumstances would've certainly been a healthy yelp. Grabbing at the banged-up toes of her right foot, she cursed at her beloved uncle. Would he ever learn to put things away? The paint can she'd tripped over had probably been there for decades. Hopping up and down on one foot, she tried to soak up the pain and keep her moans to herself.

After the pain subsided a bit, Hope stepped up on the paint can to peek in on the bedroom scene. But, she was out of luck. The blonde woman had already reached the window and closed the blinds.

Still, with her ears perched just below the window, Hope could hear their voices. Though what language they were speaking in, she couldn't be too sure. It was something truly foreign, not a Latin language by any means. Maybe Dutch? Or German? All she knew is that the woman laughed frequently while she and Chandler exchanged words. *Words, and whatever else they are probably exchanging,* Hope thought disgustedly.

Well, she'd seen and heard enough for one evening. Of all the places in the world this creep could have landed, just her luck he had to settle in right next door to her. She clenched her fist around the dragon-laden money clip and had a mind to throw it out into the dark oblivion.

Thank goodness she hadn't fallen prey to his "everybody needs a little sugar from time to time" line yesterday and given him some sweet part of herself tonight. Had she really thought she could trust him? *He is a man after all,* she thought, disgruntled by her own naiveté.

When will I ever learn? She asked herself as she stomped back home on her good foot, her right foot throbbing and her heart not feeling so hot either.

Men!
What distractions they were!

Not that she'd had many men in Bearsville distracting her for the past six years. But that just further proved the point, didn't it? One finally shows up, and suddenly her life goes all out of whack again. Buying expensive lingerie for no apparent reason, for goodness' sake! Spending way too much time on her appearance . . . though Theo had been kind of nagging her about that anyway. And now, sitting at the computer with a deadline looming, and she couldn't even write anymore. Couldn't even begin to concentrate.

And how could she? How could Sela and Giorgio's lovey-dovey words flow from her brain when steam was hissing out her ears? How could she concentrate on keeping Sela alive and out of harm's way, when she was having murderous thoughts about the guy next door?

Seeing the creep's money clip perched on top of her thesaurus sure didn't help. And recalling how the silver edges had nearly cut into her clenched hand as she looked in on the scene last night was even more disturbing.

Ho, boy! I'd sure like to clip off his . . . you-know-what, Hope grumbled to herself.

Wonder what Roget would have to say about the newcomer?

She flicked the money clip off the bulky book. Feeling a momentary comfort just holding the thesaurus in her hands, she flipped through the pages. *78.4. Newcomer: new arrival, immigrant, intruder, gate-crasher, disconcerting, frustrating, no-good scoundrel, not-to-be-trusted man.* Well, she had added the last parts, but if the synonyms fit . . .

The best thing to do was to just get rid of the damned clip. Exorcise the louse from her house. Drop it off to Uncle Cary, so she could get on with Sela's fictional life and close this short chapter on her own reality. Let Uncle Cary deal with the new weirdo in town.

★ ★ ★ ★ ★

Uncle Cary was standing down the hallway outside his and Fiona's bedroom when Hope grudgingly made the trek over to the bed and breakfast.

"How's my favorite niece?" Uncle Cary gave her his customary greeting. He was as tall, lean and average-looking as Fiona was petite, pleasingly plump and exotic. Together, they reminded her of that Jack Sprat nursery rhyme. Yet they were so noticeably compatible and in love that their physical differences seemed to be of no consequence.

"Fine," Hope shot back curtly, and then caught herself. "I'm fine, Uncle Cary. Thanks." She tried to soften her voice, but somehow the silver clip clutched in her hand wouldn't let her. "Just wanted to drop this off. I believe it belongs to your boarder."

"You mean Chan, my man?" her uncle replied, sounding happy to have made a new buddy.

Despite having passed the middle-age mark, Uncle Cary had a youthful, bright-eyed aura about him. And while Fiona thought Uncle Cary's graying ponytail was artsy and European, Hope wondered if it was just a hold on an era and an attitude that he didn't want to totally let go of. "Did he leave it at your house last night?"

"Yes, as a matter of fact. Thanks so much for warning me ahead of time about that, by the way."

"Ah. It wasn't so bad, was it?" His eyes twinkled. "Ed Gusweiler said Chan stayed pretty late. Saw him saying good-night on your porch at about ten-thirty or so."

Instantly her cheeks inflamed like a blowtorch. "Ed Gossipweiler knows?"

"Honey, you know you can't make a move, or make a plate of food for someone around here, without the whole town knowing."

"Oh, great." She sighed. She wondered if the whole town also knew that right after Chandler Adams left her place, he had moved right on to his second female of the evening. Another female, who didn't even have to go through the trouble of heating up a frozen entrée for him.

"Too bad you didn't bring his money back last night though. You could've met Chan's sister," Uncle Cary continued.

"His sister?" She couldn't believe her ears. "You really believe that woman was his sister?" From what she had seen, Chandler and Blondie looked to be involved in hot-blooded relations—a far cry from your everyday blood relations.

"You mean you did meet her?" Uncle Cary looked confused.

"Uh, no," Hope stammered. "No, I just saw her in the window, kind of when I, uh . . . when I took the garbage out," she fibbed.

Uncle Cary bought it and nodded. "Yeah, seems like a very unique family. Hearing them through the walls, I'm thinking one of their parents must be from the Baltics or somewhere. That's probably how they ended up being bilingual." He seemed satisfied with his convoluted conjecture.

"Whatever works," she said passively, tiring of everyone giving Chandler Adams the benefit of the doubt. "Well, will you just give this to him?" She held out the clip and money.

"Can't right now." He shook his head. "Fiona needs me in the bedroom."

The bedroom! The mere mention of the word instantly made her seethe. What on earth was this place coming to? Fiona and Uncle Cary in one bedroom carrying on. Adams and Blondie in the other. Was it a bed and breakfast or a bordello?

"Can't you guys go a minute without, well, you know," Hope blurted out huffily, exasperated by all the hormonal activity.

"A minute? It's been at least a month." His eyebrows furrowed in bewilderment.

A month? She had just heard Uncle Cary and Fiona in the throes of passion two mornings before. Was he now going to join the ranks of every other deceitful male and start lying to her, too? "Are you sure that's accurate, Uncle Cary?"

"Well, sure. Once a month, I help Fiona flip our mattress over when she changes the sheets. It really saves on the wear and tear of a good mattress, you know." He paused and eyed her warily; a look of concern shadowed his face. "Hope, honey, are you okay? You seem kind of pent up. Is there anything I can help you with?"

"No, I'm just . . ." She shook her head and didn't even bother to finish her sentence. What was the point?

He patted her back consolingly, even though she knew he had no idea what she was upset about. "Just go put the money in Chan's room. And then do something nice for yourself today. You seem like you could use it."

"But, I don't want to barge in on him . . . them . . ."

Uncle Cary waved his hand and shook his head. "They're not there. I'm not sure what time of night his sister left. But Chan got out of here early this morning."

"He did?"

Suddenly it hit her that one day Chandler Adams was going to leave Bearsville for good—and it would probably be one day very soon. The thought was sobering, yet for the life of her she couldn't figure out why. And, surprisingly, the tight, knotted ball of anger that had been lodged in the pit of her stomach since last evening began breaking away involuntarily, turning into something else. Something that felt more like an ooze and left behind a lonely, empty kind of feeling. Melancholia. That was the feeling. She suddenly felt melancholy at the thought that he'd be leaving. And why? Why should she care?

She fumed inwardly, trying to regain control of her body's physical reactions toward him. After all, Chandler was a newcomer; a newcomer turned rotten intruder on her heart. Ask Roget, he knew.

Fiona's voice called out to Uncle Cary, bringing him to attention. "Fiona hasn't cleaned Chan's room yet." He waved to Hope as he started off to join Fiona in their bedroom. "But that's okay. You can put his money clip in there anyway. The door's unlocked."

Hope stood alone for a moment, feelings of dread making her legs turn leaden. No way did she want to walk into Chandler Adams' room and see the remnants of his and Blondie's lovemaking. Mussed up sheets on the bed . . . pillows strewn everywhere . . . a pair of thong panties left behind in haste . . . the lingering scent of their combined colognes. Life may have been boring before Chandler, but at least it hadn't been this torturous.

With trepidation, Hope walked down the hall and held her breath as she cautiously poked open Chandler's bedroom door and peeked into the room. *You'd think Freddy Krueger was lurking inside instead of a pair of black, lacy undies,* she thought wryly.

Amazingly, the room was immaculate, even without Fiona's cleaning. Not a thing was out of place. Adams' slippers were even tucked Ozzie-and-Harriet style side-by-side underneath the bed. A compulsive neat-nik! *Ew, bet that makes for an exciting lover,* she snorted facetiously.

The fastidious scene turned her from timid to brave. She

entered the room and walked over to the dresser. It was un-cluttered, with just a silk floral arrangement on top and a couple of papers neatly pushed to one side. He'll see the clip here for sure, she thought, depositing it there.

She was just about to turn and go, when something caught her eye. It was Uncle Cary's name on one of the papers, an income tax form. She picked it up just to make sure. Had Uncle Cary actually entrusted Chandler with his taxes? So, did he buy into the notion that Chandler was a CPA, while Dani still believed that he was a spy?

And next week, in the next town, would Chandler Adams have everyone believing he was an astronaut and a dune buggy wholesaler? A race car driver and a pantyhose sales rep? A cardiologist and a blackjack dealer? The possibilities were endless!

Well, that did it. She'd had enough of this guy. She'd track him down like a hound and expose him for what he really was—whatever that might be. After all, *she* was a cre-ator of all kinds of undercover characters, wasn't she? She could get out there and probe with the best of them. Now if she only had a clue to get started . . .

At that precise moment, just as it happened so often in her novels, a calendar page bearing the day's date fell out from behind her uncle's tax papers. Like a gift from heaven, it fluttered its way to her feet. She bent down to pick it up, scanning the handwriting she saw there. *MOMA—1:00.*

If she hadn't been a New Yorker, she might've thought Chandler was a poor speller who was getting together with his dear old mom that day. Instead, she knew without thinking that MOMA was the acronym for the world-famous Museum of Modern Art in midtown Manhattan.

With information in hand, and snooping instincts at full throttle, Hope walked briskly up the hall. She rapped loudly on her uncle's bedroom door. From inside, she heard Fiona squealing giddily like a young girl.

Geez, could they actually be at it again?

"Uncle Cary? Fiona?"

"Bonjour, cheri. We be out in a minute." Fiona's sweet trill of an accent answered her.

"No. No problem," Hope spoke to the aged oak door. "I just wanted to let you know that Theo's going to his dad's after school for the weekend. So I've decided I *am* going to do something nice for myself today. I'm going into Manhattan to do some shopping."

"Well, you deserve a break, honey," her uncle answered her from the other side of the door. "Hope you get lucky and find something."

You mean somebody, she corrected him in her mind. And as for the "lucky" part, well, she wasn't about to dwell on that right now.

Chapter Five

Mom, how many yellow sticky notes do you think I've written? A zillion?

I saw this Ripley's Believe It Or Not *book at Taylor's house. Maybe we can be in it for the most sticky-note notes. I don't have ideas for Sela today. I know you're thinking what's wrong with my son? Is he sick or something? I just wanted to ask why Sela and James Bond have so many boyfriends and girlfriends. Can't spies be monotone or whatever they call it? Don't you think that's bad? I do.*

Please make something good for dinner when I get home Sunday. Emily's cooking sucks, and I'll have to eat it all weekend. I know you're saying THEO!!!! Don't say that about your stepmother's cooking. But it does. Suck, I mean. You don't want me to lie, do you?

Love,

Theo, Your Awesome Son

P.S. I think I have written 1,234,567 sticky notes.

Though the ride into the city had been fairly uneventful, once Hope hit the infamous borough of Manhattan, all of that changed in an instant. She clutched the steering wheel of her Honda, while all around her the city noises blared, tempers flared, the smell of exhaust hung heavy in the air and traffic was in its perpetually congested state.

It was already 1:25, and she couldn't stand to sit in

traffic one moment longer. If she had driven all this way and had missed out on whatever Chandler Adams was up to, she really would have to do a whole lot of shopping to make herself feel better. Impatient, she ducked into the alley behind the museum.

She didn't know if she could find parking on the road adjoining the other side of the alley, but at least she was in motion and not stuck behind a cab or a truck blowing smoke at her. Yep, she was moving right along, right toward a beat-up, decades-old maroon Cadillac.

Two disreputable-looking guys were standing behind the mammoth car, and there was another guy who didn't seem to fit into the picture at all. In fact, Hope thought he looked liked someone out of an Eddie Bauer ad . . . hmm, hadn't she thought that about someone else recently? *Oh, yeah, Chandler.*

Geez, was the guy Chandler? This guy did have the same calm way about him, the same build. She squinted through her glasses.

He must have heard her car because he glanced in her direction. And she knew from the mixture of feelings she got just looking at him, there was no doubt about it. It was Adams.

At first she felt utterly gleeful at discovering him. But getting nearer, detecting the tension among the men, her heart pounded with dread. She hadn't intended to risk her life to save Adams' sorry excuse for one. But call her curious—didn't every writer need to be? And unrelenting—didn't every mom need to be? She was more than a little anxious to know what this was all about, especially since at the top of her list was a pledge to get to the bottom of Chandler Adams.

But now what? She had to think. *What would Sela do?* she wondered.

Sela? Forget Sela. I AM Sela, for goodness' sakes! And what would her alter ego do? Probably use her feminine wiles to wriggle in and out of the situation, that's what.

Peering into the rearview mirror, she studied her reflection and sighed. Did she even have feminine wiles anymore? Not that this was the best time to ponder the topic, was it? Beyond the windshield, she could make out Chandler's form, and she could see one of the gangsters shoving him against the car. Clearly, he could use some help.

Well, okay, she'd try it.

In one nearly continual swoop, she shucked her glasses, stripped off her white turtleneck from underneath her cranberry vee-neck sweater, hoisted up her bra straps, and removed the rubber band from her hair. She shook her hair till it fell free across her face and down her shoulders.

Ready for seduction.

Next, she rolled up the top of her black knee-length skirt till it was mid-thigh length, and grabbed Dani's "I'm available" high-heeled boots from where her friend had left them in the back seat after bowling the other night. They'd be too small and would surely hurt, but she could manage. She didn't plan on being in them for long anyway.

Scrambling out of the car, she smoothed down her skirt, and took a deep breath. Then she strutted her most salacious strut toward the monolith automobile with one hand on her hip and the other holding onto her leather jacket, which was slung casually over her shoulder. She tripped clumsily over a bump in the concrete that she'd overlooked without her glasses. That sent a hot flash up her back, and she cursed silently at the stupid, wicked boots she was wearing. Then she righted herself and tried to look cool and collected before continuing on in full sashay mode.

From her blurry line of vision, she quickly assessed the

two gangsters to be Italian. One was surely the boss man and looked to be controlling the situation. He was hard to describe, since he was all covered up with a full-length, black leather coat and sported round Lennon-type sunglasses though the sky was mostly overcast.

Probably the most notable thing about the boss man was that his right hand was tucked inside his coat pocket. And his coat pocket came to a definite point and was aimed right at Chandler's torso. The implication was frightening. It made her want to come unglued, and go screaming madly down the street. But instead, she carried on like a streetwise babe even though she could barely walk . . . what with her legs shaking and Dani's impossible boots pinching her toes.

The other thug was shorter, heavier and wearing the blazer version of the boss man's leather coat. He had his shirt opened halfway down his chest—a real mystery, since it was a blubbery chest no female in her right mind would ever want to see. He was also wearing enough gold chains around his neck to tow her school bus out of quicksand.

"Excuse me, gentlemen," she said throatily. Intentionally, she took a moment to eye each one of the men individually and present each with a lewd smile. The boss man eyed her suspiciously. His cohort eyed her lasciviously. And the shocked look on Chandler's face said he couldn't believe his eyes at all.

"Uh, lady, you're real attractive and all," the gangster boss did all of the talking, "but as you can see we're kind of in the middle of something here. Business. Not funny business, ya know?"

"Funny business? Do you think I'm some kind of hooker or something?" she gasped.

"Well, is there any other reason you'd be showing your

stuff in an alley in the middle of the afternoon in midtown Manhattan?" The boss shook his head and let out a guffaw that meant he'd been around. She couldn't fool him.

"Well, I—!" It took her a moment to remember this wasn't the time to be concerned about retaining the good-girl reputation she'd earned in Bearsville. Sap that she was, this was about saving Adams. And now that she was in the midst of it, also herself.

"Well, actually I was just admiring your big, bad machine there." She pointed in the direction of the car, but then lowered her lashes, allowing for a not-so-subtle glance to the boss's groin.

As the innuendo registered on the boss, he shifted on his feet uneasily, obviously trying to maintain his cool. Most likely *his* boss wouldn't like him getting caught up in some vampy broad's hot come-ons. "Huh? What? Oh, yeah. Admiring this old heap?" The boss nodded his head toward the old car. "Is that a joke or something? You some kind of cop?" He looked at her skeptically.

"Well, it looks like a classic to me."

"Yeah, right. A classic old heap," he retorted.

Hope bent over the car, slinging her buttocks high in the air, trying to muster up as much sexual prowess as she could. She felt ludicrous though, like a fish out of water. And not exactly a mermaid either—more like a cod. She hadn't tried to really turn a man on for years. What if these men started laughing at her attempts to be a temptress?

But when she stuck out her tongue and began to lick her index finger provocatively as if it were a melting Popsicle on a stick, she realized it was easier than she thought. She had their full, undivided, quivering attention all right. They couldn't tear their eyes away from her. Chandler included.

With renewed confidence and a moistened finger, she

rubbed delicately at a spot of dirt on the left rear bumper. "Oh, this baby's in fine shape." She swung out her hip. "Just a little dust on it here and there."

One look and she knew that gangster number two was having trouble concentrating on his task at hand. She hoped she was wearing the gangster boss down as well. If she could distract them long enough, maybe Chandler could make a break for it. However, when she looked at Chandler, she noticed he looked a mite distracted himself. She didn't know what to do besides continue with her sultry performance. She ran her hand over the bumper slowly, stroking it back and forth, back and forth, hypnotizing the trio.

"Are these radial tires?" This time she was standing and pointing at the tires, but she leaned forward slightly so that her chest dipped and the swell of her cleavage spilled out of her sweater. She didn't even know what she was talking about, but it didn't matter. She had to keep talking. She was too nervous not to.

"Hey, lady, another time, okay?" The boss man rubbed at his forehead fiercely, as if working to get his head back on straight. He let out a loud breath. "Seriously, this ain't a good time, awright?"

Hope felt the panic rise inside her. She couldn't let the encounter come to a close yet. What would happen to Chandler? Even if she didn't care about him, she couldn't abandon him. Her maternal instincts wouldn't let her. He needed her. And her imagination! She was the one who knew how to get out of sticky situations.

She added quickly, "And the trunk. It's probably huge. I'll bet it has loads of trunk space. I can barely fit a case of wine in mine." She pointed back at her own car. *Her dependable Honda . . . with a picture of Theo in his soccer uniform on the visor . . . her favorite go-cup in the tray . . . her*

80

half-listened-to Faith Hill CD . . . why in the world had she ever gotten out of it?

"Ya wanna see?" Now the boss man had an ornery grin on his face. And while he turned his head slightly in her direction and snickered, behind his back Chandler was shaking his head "no." But Hope didn't notice until after she had giggled and said in a low, seductive voice, "Sure, mister. You show me yours, and I'll show you mine."

All the while, she was wondering why Chandler didn't try to clobber the guy and make a break for it. But then, looking more closely, she noticed it was a situation where his hands were tied—literally—with a thin, fine wire.

The boss nodded for the gopher gangster to open the Caddy's spacious trunk.

When the trunk lay open before them all, the boss glared at Hope. "So get in and look around," he ordered.

She tried to force out a carefree chuckle. "Excuse me?"

"No joke, lady. Get in," he restated harshly. He nodded for the gopher gangster to do his dirty work for him once again and push her into the trunk.

That did it. Finally, Chandler spoke up. "Hey, I don't know why you're messing around with this tramp. Your deal is with me," he pleaded with the number one thug. "My partner will be here in a minute with the item you want. She's probably caught in traffic."

"Traffic *is* really heavy right now," Hope affirmed from inside the trunk, and the boss eyed her wearily.

"I'm tired of waiting for your person," the boss grunted at Chandler. "Next time ya want to deal, make sure she, he, whoever's on time. Now get in." The boss pushed Chandler into the trunk, nudging at him with the alleged gunpoint protruding from his pocket. "You two will be real cozy in there."

Hope had only meant to get Chandler out of a mess, not to get him more into one. She had seen enough movies and written enough books to know what could happen when mobsters locked their victims into the trunks of big, old Caddies. The thought filled her with panic, and she searched her brain for a solution. *Maybe the guilt approach?*

"Is this your mother's car?" she demanded to know.

"What?" The boss gangster had turned to walk away, having assigned his cohort the nasty business of closing the trunk on the two captives in it. Now he turned back, looking astonished that she wasn't a little more petrified of him. Even more, he seemed annoyed that she wouldn't shut up.

Yes, it appeared her small-town, sweet-talking self was driving this big-city, tough guy crazy. Meanwhile, she noticed that Chandler was working hard to suppress a smile.

"Do you know how angry your mother would be, if she knew you were using her car for this purpose?" she ranted.

The thug glowered into the trunk at her. "Hey, leave my mom outta this, okay? She's got enough problems with my brother Tony."

"Oh, I see," she countered. "And I guess you're her dream kid, huh? Lucky woman," she scoffed.

"Hey, lady, are we related?" the boss screamed, out of control. "No! Negative! So stay outta my family business, ya got it?" He nodded for the other gangster to close the trunk lid.

But Hope wouldn't be silenced. "You know, I just had my leather jacket dry-cleaned, and it cost me a bundle. Now it's going to smell like—"

The boss man shut her off. "Sorry I gotta do this to ya," he said to Chandler, referring to Hope's ongoing babble. "Good luck, man," he added, as he slammed down the trunk lid himself and the blackness consumed them.

"So much for the shocks on this heap." Hope's voice bumped over the words as the rusty, old Cadillac bumped over the New York City streets.

Cramped into fetal positions, their bodies were turned toward one another in the dingy trunk, bouncing in unison whenever their mystery driver hit a pothole in the road. Though her eyes hadn't adjusted to the blackness just yet, the feel of Chandler's warm breath on her face let her know they were only inches apart.

"Damn tire iron keeps jabbing me," he grumbled.

"So how do you plan on getting us out of this mess?" she asked, her words drenched in attitude.

Sure, she felt kind of bad for speaking to him like that, but she was scared to death. Her attitude was her last defense. If she weakened this very moment, she'd wet her pants. Besides . . . fair or not, Chandler Adams was the so-called professional in this situation. Shouldn't he be the one responsible for their well-being?

"*Me* get us out?" he snorted. "You make it sound like this was *my* doing. I wouldn't be in the smelly trunk of this dilapidated crate, if you hadn't been snooping where you shouldn't, you know," he scolded her.

"Of course," he paused momentarily, his voice suddenly turning mild, "you did put on one helluva show." He gave a low chuckle in that male way, letting her know that he had indeed more than enjoyed her brazen performance.

Face flushed, her words came out flustered. "Well, I wouldn't have been snooping, if—"

If what?

If she hadn't been so jealous of that woman in his room last night?

If she hadn't wished just a little bit that it had been her with him instead?

If she hadn't been so mad that she wanted to expose him for whoever he really might be?

She wasn't really sure how to finish the sentence, so it hung in the air.

"Forget it. I'm sure, given your profession, you just can't help yourself," he said easily, all agitation dissipated. "But don't forget, curiosity killed the cat."

"That's a comforting thought about now."

"Hey, do you have anything to cut this with?"

He raised his bound hands, and she could just barely make out their silhouette with the help of the slivers of daylight coming in through the cracks of the trunk. She felt around the trunk floor for something to cut with, and when she came up empty-handed, she searched her jacket pockets.

"I forgot." She pulled a rather humongous key chain out of her pocket. "I have a nail clipper on here. Oh, and a pen flashlight too." She turned on the light that dangled from the chain.

He whistled at the chunk of keys and odd items that mushroomed from her key chain. "That thing looks like it weighs more than you do."

"Elementary school bus drivers are always prepared," she said, as she quickly cut the wires that circled his hands. She laid the keys down between them.

"Ah, much better, thanks," he announced, rubbing his hands together.

Just then the Caddy hit a sizeable dip in the road. Hope's lighter body flew upward, her head thunking painfully against the trunk lid.

"Ouch!"

Instinctively, he reached out and cradled her head with his hands. "You okay? Sounds like that smarted. Here, let me hold you down. You're too light."

Without even waiting for a response, he slipped one arm under her head like a pillow and laid the other one lightly across her chest. Then he positioned his left leg over both of hers, his body weight protecting her from becoming an identified flying object again.

It should've felt unsettling, having a virtual stranger wrap his body around hers. But instead, there was something oddly familiar and comfortable about Chandler Adams. Too familiar. Too comfortable. Just like there'd been yesterday morning during their martial arts embrace. And annoyingly so, since she was still sore at him for double-dipping on desserts the previous evening.

However, given the present set of circumstances, if she had to be crammed into a trunk with someone, Chandler wasn't a bad candidate.

Not bad at all actually.

He was just the right size for a Caddy trunk mate. Just the right feel. And just the right scent with that ever-so-slight, luring hint of musk he wore. It had been growing on her for the last couple of days.

"Too bad my laser watch is broken," he mumbled. "And my decoder ring . . . have you seen it?"

"It's wherever you took it off last, I'm sure." She gave her standard mother reply.

"Which means it's on your windowsill."

"Which isn't possible, because I watered plants this morning, and it wasn't anywhere in sight."

Is he still insisting that glob of silver is a spy decoder ring? she wondered. Of course, with all that had just transpired, was she still insisting it wasn't? Whatever. She couldn't accept the idea of him being a spy quite as easily as Dani had. Maybe he was actually a gangster . . . and the gangsters were spies. *Now there's a twist for you.* Her mind automatically started to weave a story.

"You think Theo took it?"

His question snapped her to attention. "Took the ring? Theo would never steal anything," she exclaimed indignantly, hoping with all her might that Theo hadn't taken it. He had been acting strangely this past week. Could she be a hundred percent sure of anything these days?

"I didn't say steal. Maybe he wanted to get a closer look at it."

She tensed up in his arms, and tried to back away from him, but there was no place to go. "You know, I'm getting pretty tired of all this spy decoder stuff. Just because I write spy novels . . . I mean you can stop it with all this espionage bravado."

"Hey, calm down. It's not a big deal. You're getting all huffy over nothing," he said patronizingly, reminiscent of the way Uncle Cary had spoken to her hours earlier.

Well, she wouldn't have to get all huffy with everyone if it weren't for him—Adams. And was that his hand massaging the back of her neck, attempting to soothe her? Or was it the bumps in the road causing his hand to move against her?

"And you don't have to get defensive about Theo, Hope. There's nothing wrong about a kid not wanting to share his mom," he said. She could sense his slight grin in the dimmed light. "Hell, I wouldn't want to share you—I mean if you were, you know, my mom. I just asked about the ring because guys like to tinker with gadgets. That's all."

It *wasn't* the bumps in the road, she realized. It *was* his hand caressing the back of her head. Part of her wanted to sink into the tranquil feel of it. The other part wanted to ask which of Blondie's gadgets he'd tinkered with the night before.

But why? What was the use in that? They had no ties to each other. Right now, like it or not, they were bound together in a treacherous situation, stuffed in a trunk, cruising toward unknown danger. They might have hours—maybe even minutes—to live. And before she died, she just had to know . . .

"So, I saw you're doing some tax work for Uncle Cary. You're not a spy after all, are you? You're an accountant, right?" She braved the question.

"Or maybe that's just a cover."

"Could be. Or maybe you're in trouble for some illegal accounting screw-up you made with the mob or someone. And you're pretending to be a spy as, you know, another cover-up."

When he didn't answer, she got soft and pleading. "Chandler, I have to know, because we could die here and—"

"Shhh." He put a finger up to her lips just as the boat-sized vehicle swerved and came to an abrupt halt. The motor turned off, and for a moment there was dead silence. Then the trunk echoed with the sound of two car doors opening and slamming shut, one right after the other.

She clutched onto him, and they lay as still as they could, Hope fearful of what would come next. Once the creeps unlocked the trunk, would they be dumped into the river? Beaten and left for dead? Could she and Chandler overcome them? Would she ever see her precious son again?

Obviously, he could sense her nervousness, since her heart was practically leaping out of her chest onto his. Tightening his hold around her, he pulled her even more closely to him. Enveloped in the safety of his well-defined arms, she had to admit he didn't seem like some namby-pamby, pencil-pushing CPA guy.

"It's okay," he whispered. "I won't let anything happen to Theo's mom," he assured her.

The fact that he could read her mind was another plus for his *"If you had to be crammed in a trunk with someone, who would it be?"* column.

Lying there in a silent embrace, Hope held her breath, anticipating the gangsters' next moves. After a patient wait, Chandler finally spoke.

"They're gone."

"What?" Her body jerked in reply. "Gone?"

"I'm sure of it. I haven't heard a thing for a while. They probably ditched this car and got picked up by another one."

"So they're leaving us here in this smelly old trunk to suffocate?" She started to freak, and clutched more feverishly at the fabric of his jacket. He didn't seem to mind.

"We're not going to suffocate," he said evenly. "We'll get rescued."

"Oh, yeah?" she cried. "By who? Your contact at the IRS?"

"Not exactly."

His calm voice, calm demeanor . . . it was all so unnerving she wanted to scream. "Well, who then?" she spat out.

"You ask a lot of questions, you know that?" He brushed aside some tendrils of hair from her face, and suddenly she felt his index finger vibrating against her cheek.

"Uh, would that be your finger vibrating on my cheek?" Her jaw tightened.

"You weren't supposed to notice."

"And you aren't supposed to vibrate."

"It's an implanted homing device. See, I told you not to worry," he cocked his head. "Someone from headquarters will be here soon."

"Oh, my God. So you really are—" But she still couldn't say the "s" word.

"No more talking." His hand brushed her cheek again. Although this time she hadn't felt any loose strands of hair there. "We need to conserve whatever oxygen we have left in here."

She knew it was just an excuse to shut her up about the spy thing. Though he needn't have bothered. She was in too much shock to speak anyway.

He snuggled her body closer to his, and she eyed him suspiciously. "Might as well conserve body heat, too." He smiled impishly.

Only minutes ago she would've given anything to be home safe and sound, watching "Wheel of Fortune," throwing in a tub of laundry, popping some microwave popcorn. But now that help was on its way, she not only felt relieved but also excited about her state of affairs.

Imagine! Here she was in the trunk of a Caddy, curled up with a delicious-looking spy—yes, an honest-to-goodness spy—sporting an implanted homing device, for goodness' sakes. What a thrill for a thriller romance writer! It made her downright giddy.

"You know," she found herself saying, "I've been in the back seat of a car with a guy before, but I'm sure this is my first time in the trunk." She giggled, forgetting his caution about conserving oxygen.

"Really? I used to do this all the time with my girl-friends." He grinned back. "Well, except for the claustro-phobic ones," he teased. "So what do you think?"

"Mmm . . . not quite as romantic as the back seat. You can't turn on the radio for some mood music. And you can't look out at the stars."

He reached down at where her clump of keys lay between them. He fixed the gleam of the penlight so it shone on the cracked, gray underside of the trunk lid. The tiny ray spread out into a wide circle overhead, forming a soft light that showered down on them.

She grinned. "Very impressive, Mr. Adams. Do you always try so hard with girls you're shoved into trunks with?"

"Wait. There's more." He cleared his throat and began singing, his voice smooth and rich and melodious in the cavern of the trunk. The lyrics were somewhat familiar. They were something to do with needing and wanting—and a whole lot to do with holding and touching.

Hope laughed as if it were all in fun. In the meantime, her laughter couldn't mask the shivers that ran up her spine . . . couldn't dispel the yearning she had to yield her body into his. But, excuse me. It had been some time, after all, since she'd even been this close to a man. Try like six years—or 2,190 days to be exact! She had a river of dammed-up hormones that could possibly overflow at any moment.

And the two of them were so very close now, weren't they? Physically and emotionally. Their escaped danger had bonded them, holding them in an isolated world all their own. A union that made the rest of humanity seem far, far away.

Girl, you'd better stop feeling and keep talking, she warned herself.

"How, uh, how does your mother feel about the spy business?"

"My mother? Are you trying to ruin the mood I'm cre-

90

ating here?" He expelled a heavy sigh before answering. "My mother feels just the way you'd expect her to feel. She'd like for me to give it all up, settle down and present her with grandkids."

"But . . ." she prodded.

"I don't know. I've met a lot of dream girls, or what other guys would consider to be dream girls . . ." His voice trailed off.

"But . . ." she said again.

"But I haven't met the girl of *my* dreams. Yet."

His arms were still around her, making her feel comfortable, brave . . .

"And how will you know when you do?" Was it the giddiness making her voice sound that way, so overtly flirty?

"I don't know." Chandler paused. "Maybe by her kiss?"

She knew by his inflection that it was an invitation. The question was . . . should she r.s.v.p.? Did she want to be one of spy man's many girls, as Theo had mentioned in his Post-it note?

"I'm open for auditions, if you're interested." Chandler taunted her. Even in the dim trunk, she could sense his easy smile, feel its seductive force beckoning her.

Wow! There was no way that she'd ever be able to explain it to an almost eleven-year-old. But having lived through it now, she understood completely why spies had a tough time remaining monogamous, or monotone as Theo called it. It was simple, really.

First, there was the fear: the totally consuming, heart-stopping fear. And accompanying that was the gut-wrenching, soul-searching realization that your life was about to end. And then when that didn't happen—the relief came in mammoth waves. There was a depthless swelling inside of you. By contrast, it made you want to abandon all thought. Made you want to live in the moment. After all the graveness and fright, who wouldn't want to fling all caution aside?

Plus, here they were in the trunk of a car, of all things. Not as roomy as the back seat, of course, but still it did have a kind of déjà vu quality about it . . . High school. Saturday night make-out sessions with blue-eyed Tommy Miller. His full, hot lips, and his unsure hand cupped around the outside of her white padded bra.

Her entire body quivered in anticipation. Sweet anticipation.

"Are you interested?" he asked again, though he didn't need to.

His lips were drawing at hers like a magnet. One she didn't have the power to resist. Closing her eyes tightly, she moved ever so slowly toward him, tremors already coursing through her, imagining the arousing pleasure of his kiss. Closer she came, till she could feel his heated breath on her face.

"Moan . . ." Chandler uttered before their lips had even pressed together in a heated exchange.

Wow—had he actually let out a moan? What a titillating effect she was having on this self-proclaimed international spy, and she hadn't even touched him yet!

"Moan . . ." Chandler repeated.

She cocked open her eyelids to get a peek at him, wondering what he was getting so turned on about. But the consuming darkness her eyes had grown accustomed to was gone. Instead, she got a blast of blinding daylight that drew her eyes to a narrow squint. Because suddenly the trunk was open, and a blonde woman was looking down on them.

"Mona!" Chandler called out to the attractive female overhead. Breaking free from the circle of his and Hope's embrace, he sat upright instantly, not appearing to be peeved by the interruption in the least.

"At it again, eh, darling?" From her accent, Hope recognized the blonde as Chandler's so-called sister from the night before. She also noticed that the woman's words were no reprimand. In fact, she seemed delighted about his behavior, triumphant for him even.

And did she mean "at it again," as involved in a dilemma again? Or "at it again," meaning another day, another make-out session with another spy-whipped groupie? More than mildly chagrined, Hope sat up, too, patting at her hair and trying to distance herself from him. It wasn't too easy in the confines of the trunk.

"Mona, this is Hope." He introduced the two women. "Hope, Mona."

Before Hope could speak up, Mona spoke down into the cavern of the trunk. "Hope," she said coyly. "That's a new name, isn't it now? I'm so used to Britney. Or Elle. Or Christina." She winked in Chandler's direction. "Hope. I like it," she said decidedly. "How do you do, Hope?" Her smile was gratuitous.

"Fine, thanks, I—" Hope looked past the woman and saw her Honda parked on the shoulder of the road right behind the Cadillac. At least without her glasses the blurry image appeared to be her Honda. "Is that my car? But how did it—? I have the keys right here." She fumbled for her key chain.

"I hot-wired it and followed you most of the way," Mona explained, speaking directly at Chandler and excluding Hope. "And I put a call in to headquarters. Your Porsche is already on its way back to the Uncle Cary inn."

Oh, great! Not only is she blonde and beautiful, but she's resourceful, too. Hope groaned inwardly. *A woman any spy could love!*

She sighed and a wave of discomfort sloshed across her stomach. But, for sure, it wasn't jealousy. No, she just wanted to get out of this stupid trunk. Get some fresh air and a bite to eat. Yes, she needed a bite to eat . . . and a minute or so to digest the incredible qualities of Mona Hari here.

Chapter Six

"This is 555-8920. My mom and me aren't here right now because if we were, we'd be answering the phone. So leave a message, ok? Bye."

BEEP.

"Hi, Hope. This is Susan Clark, Beth Morgan's editorial assistant. Is that your son on the message machine? He sounds too cute. Anyway . . . Beth asked me to call to see how the manuscript is coming along. (Pause) Well, you're probably at your computer writing this very minute, and don't want to be disturbed. So, give us a call at your earliest convenience."

"Sorry about that," Chandler apologized after they had dropped off Mona in Greenwich Village.

"Oh, no problem. Elementary school kids. International spies. I'll pretty much chauffeur anyone around," Hope replied offhandedly.

She kept her eyes glued to the road, trying to quell her irritation with the espionage duo. All the way back to Manhattan and down into the village, Chandler and Mona had been engaged in a conversation. And they had conversed in a foreign language—so eavesdropping was definitely out. Not once had they spoken to her, except to direct her to Mona's trendy brownstone.

"No, really, I appreciate your driving. And I apologize for excluding you from the conversation. I hope it didn't seem too rude. It's just that whenever we talk shop, we discuss it in another language."

Apparently, he sensed her true feelings, and acknowledged their rudeness. Her fuming began to subside.

"What language was that anyway?" she asked curiously.

"Mostly Dutch," Chandler told her.

"Oh. Where is Mona from?"

"Sweden."

The idea of it registered. "Sweden? A real, live Swedish blonde? The kind of woman hair colors are named after?"

She wasn't sure if it was her astonished words or wide-eyed, astounded look that made him laugh.

"Well, I don't know about that. But she's a reliable partner. We hook up whenever we can." He smiled.

Hook up? She glanced over at him to see if there appeared to be any double meaning or underlying message in his words. But he was looking away from her, staring out the window.

"The day we met . . ." she started. "Why did you tell me that you were a spy?"

"Well," he turned to look at her, cocking his head thoughtfully, "I figured you'd never believe me."

"Really?" She didn't know whether to feel pleased or not. "Why is that?"

"Because you write fiction, and it was all too much like fiction," he explained. "Strange man comes into town, driving an expensive sports car, telling you he's a spy after you tell him you write espionage romances. It's all a little hard to believe, isn't it?"

"Well, yeah!" she agreed, her cheeks reddening slightly at the truth of his words. Hadn't she said as much to Dani?

"And why Dani? Why did you tell her?"

"Dani?" His eyes went wide. "The woman is like a

lamprey eel. She gets you in that chair of hers and sucks information out of you before you know what hit you. I know some Nazi interrogators who could use her tactics."

Hope laughed out loud. Yes, that was Dani for you. "But still, you told her."

"Again, I never thought anyone would buy it." He shrugged. "I'm not exactly the James Bond type."

Hope glanced over at him, at the fallen hair on his forehead . . . and the day's shadow beginning to darken his face. His masculinity more than filled her compact Honda. "Believe me, by Bearsville standards, you could easily be cast for the double-o-seven role."

They both seemed a bit embarrassed by her compliment, and it was a minute before she asked, "So, which agency do you and Mona work for?"

"Spies R Us," he answered, most seriously.

She rolled her eyes at him. "Very funny."

"Look," he told her, "right now we're working on some art fraud operation. It's not that big a deal, and we should have it wrapped up in the next week or so. But the fewer details you know, the better off you are. I'm just being honest with you."

Hope Hathaway Life Lesson #2: Honesty is for Boy Scouts—and how many thirty-somethings of those are running around?

He placed his hand on her arm in a sincere gesture. "You're okay with that, right, Hope?"

"Well, yeah, sure," she replied uneasily, aware that his touch was beginning to feel all too familiar.

Her stomach growled, changing the subject.

"Hungry?" he asked.

She nodded eagerly. "I'm starving. Would you mind if we stopped in Nyack for some dinner? It's just over the bridge." She pointed in the direction of the Tappan Zee Bridge, which they were fast approaching.

"Really? You want to stop there? They probably don't have any good restaurants."

"But it looks so inviting," she appealed, giving him a curious glance.

The town of Nyack appeared to be just slightly larger than Bearsville, though much more picturesque. Settled alongside the banks of the Hudson River, the village was afforded a dramatic skyline that embellished the town with an artsy feel. And with the bridge all lit up against the evening sky, a feeling of expectation and possibilities—romantic or otherwise—seemed to envelop the town.

"Do you mind terribly?" She hated to be a nudge, but it had been a long day and she was one hungry gal.

"It's fine." He nodded agreeably, though his tone sounded reluctant.

Exiting the expressway, Hope drove slowly up Main Street, impressed by the friendly appeal of the town. It was a burg that seemed to be both quaint and hip all at the same time.

Chandler didn't seem to want to participate in the restaurant hunt. So she looked for signs herself, while trying to avoid hitting the pedestrians walking about on the chilly evening.

"There's a Flannigan's Bar and Grill." She pointed to the left side of the street. "Mind if we try it?"

He shrugged, which she took as a "yes." After parallel-parking the car, they joined the other Nyackians on foot, and made their way to Flannigan's, settled among the other taverns, restaurants and small shops of the town.

Opening the door of the establishment, a blast of noise from the crowd and band almost knocked them over. A young woman sitting on a barstool near the entrance waved at them.

"Do you know her?" Hope asked.

"Hmm." Chandler seemed to be ignoring her question. "Too crowded in here, don't you think? Let's try another place," he responded absently.

They wandered a few doors down into the Coven Café. Hope thought another female summoned Chandler, calling out his name, although he appeared—or pretended—to be oblivious.

He shook his head at the crowd there too. "We'll never get served in here." He was already heading toward the door. "Let's get back in the car and drive up the street."

Once they were cruising up Main Street again, Chandler sighed heavily.

"Oh, forget it," he said finally.

"Forget what?" She hoped he didn't mean forget food. That's all that was on her mind at the moment.

"Let's just go to Mom's."

"Mom's? That's a cute name for a restaurant." She chuckled. "Where do you see that sign?"

"No," he said quietly. "My mom's. Let's just go to my mom's house. She'll have something to eat there."

Luckily there was a red light, because Hope brought the car to an immediate stop.

"*Your* mom's?" she specified, incredulous. "Are you serious? Mr. International Spy grew up in Nyack? This small town?" She began to laugh. "I can't believe this. This is great." She shook her head in disbelief. "I can't wait to tell Dani."

"I don't know why you're making such a big deal about it," he replied, clearly defensive. "At least Nyack is in the triple-A travelogs. Bearsville isn't even mentioned. The agency had a helluva time trying to find a place for me to stay in *your* hometown."

"I'm sorry," Hope replied, though she was still giggling, and he was still glaring. "I just pictured Mr. International Spy growing up somewhere—I don't know. Someplace fabulous."

"Nyack is fabulous," he retorted. "It was a great place to grow up. Go to school. Play football . . . baseball."

"So why did you leave, then?" She had loathed her hometown for a while now and had wanted to flee its smothering borders. But she hadn't for Theo's sake. Evidently, Chandler had loved his town, but had made up his mind to escape it. Every story had its share of conflict, didn't it?

Chandler shrugged. "Guess I watched one too many episodes of 'Mission: Impossible' as a kid." The gruffness had left his voice, and he gave her a half-smile. "I wanted to see more of the world."

Ah. Internal conflict.

"Does the rest of your family still live here?" she ventured.

"My dad passed away a couple of years ago," he explained quietly. "So Mom's living by herself now. Like I told you, my brother's family is out in Colorado. But my older sister, Julie, and her family live in town. For now at least. That helps Mom a lot. And it makes me feel better about being away on, well, you know, business," he added vaguely.

"Then why didn't you stay in Nyack during this assignment? Why stay in Bearsville?" *Why come and make my life all topsy-turvy?* she wanted to know.

"You sure aren't afraid to ask questions, are you?" He shook his head at her before shrugging. "Too many distractions here, I guess."

So then she really hadn't imagined women hailing him in the bars minutes before. Yes, guess that certainly could get distracting. "The town's big football hero, huh?" she pried.

"Something like that," he said modestly, avoiding her gaze.

"Will your mom be surprised to see you?" Hope thought for a second. "Will she mind that I'm with you?"

Chandler looked over at her, and she knew he was appraising her appearance. True, she looked slightly rumpled from the ride in trunk, who wouldn't? But nothing a visit to the powder room couldn't fix. Still, even in her post-trunk condition, his eyes seemed to tell her that he approved of her . . . quite a lot . . . and that his mom would, too.

"Mind? She'll probably have us married off by the time we finish eating."

He chuckled, but she didn't feel amused one bit. In fact, at the mention of marriage, she felt like she could gag on her own tongue.

"Hope. Relax. That's just an expression."

"What?" She faltered, her voice shaky. "Oh, I know. I'm fine, really. Let's go see Mom."

"Chandler!"

Mrs. Adams was visibly thrilled to see her son at her front door. She reached up to hug his formidable frame, but didn't let her excitement get the best of her good manners. Instantly, she turned toward Hope, her dark eyes lighting up with surprise and her silvery-white bob shining under the porch light.

"Come in, you two." She put an ushering, welcoming hand on Hope's shoulder.

Chandler took a moment to introduce the two ladies. Alicia Adams' hand seemed as warm as her presence. And

---

her motherly, all-knowing sense where her son was concerned made Hope smile.

"Don't tell me. You're hungry," she declared, looking into her son's eyes.

At that, she led them both into the kitchen, directing Hope toward a cushioned stool at the breakfast bar. From there, Hope watched as Chandler's mother scurried around the kitchen, talking all the while, seemingly quite pleased to be preparing a meal for them.

"What luck," his mother explained as she bent over to extract a pot from a cabinet. She set it on the stove. "I should've been at Bingo tonight, and would've missed this visit from the two of you. But they were having trouble with the furnace at the church rectory, so it was cancelled."

She moved on to the refrigerator and opened the door. "At first, I was disappointed. It's my big night out," she explained, turning to Hope and rolling her eyes. "But it couldn't have worked out better."

"I hope you're not going to a lot of trouble for us," Hope said.

"Yeah, Mom," Chandler chimed in. He was leaning over his mother's smaller frame and peering into the refrigerator over her head. "We can just grab something in here."

His mom chased him out of the refrigerator with a wave of her hand and motioned toward the stool next to Hope's.

"Actually, I babysat your sister's kids today. They have a three-year-old and a five-year-old," she informed Hope. "I made a big pot of beef stew, a huge salad and baked a loaf of sourdough bread. Of course, the kids barely made a dent in it. So, I hope that's okay." She began to pour the stew into the pot to heat it up, and then stopped. "Oh, I forgot to ask. Are you a vegetarian?" She turned to Hope.

"No, beef stew sounds wonderful," she replied, and Mrs. Adams beamed.

Minutes later, Chandler's mom served them her steaming, hearty meal. While Hope and Chandler ate, the talk was easy and the mood light among the three of them.

"Have you had any tough clients lately?" Mrs. Adams finally asked her son, watching him devour the last bits of food on his plate.

"You can be upfront, Mom." He nodded toward Hope. "She knows the truth."

"She does?" Mrs. Adams' eyes went wide with surprise. "You do?"

Hope nodded. Chandler's mom looked at her in a way that let her know it was quite unusual for her son to confide in someone. Quite out of the ordinary; and she seemed pleased about it.

"Care for some chocolate chip cookies for dessert, dear?" She pushed the plate of cookies toward Hope. "Have as many as you like."

Hope accepted Alicia Adams' offer, knowing the woman's gesture simulated her stamp of approval on Hope. She knew Chandler realized it, too, by his grin.

"She's in the same line of work, Mom. Only she's a stay-at-home spy."

Mrs. Adams gave them both a puzzled look. "A stay-at-home spy?"

"I write spy romance novels," Hope explained shyly.

"Wait a minute—Hope . . . Hope Hathaway. Where have I heard—? Oh!" His mother's face brightened. "Hope Starr? Are you one and the same?"

Hope nodded and smiled. "Gosh, I don't think I've ever been recognized before."

"Those are darling books, honey," Mrs. Adams commended her effusively. "I just love the way Sela always manages to find her way out of the most impossible situations. Oh, and the romantic parts." She blushed and shook her head. "What can I say? You should be proud of yourself, Hope."

"You mean you've really read them?" Chandler feigned astonishment, winking at Hope.

"You mean *you* haven't?" his mom answered derisively. "You might just learn something from Hope's books, son."

He shook his head. "Naw. You can't teach an old spy new tricks."

"Well, here's an old trick for an old spy then," his mom said, tossing a dishcloth in his direction. "You can wash while we girls talk."

Mom we need milk and Oreos.
This is probably my sticky note number 1,234,571.

Hope propped up the pillows on her bed, luxuriating in the quiet solitude of the Saturday morning. She reread Theo's stack of Post-it notes from the day before, and though his innocence tugged at her heart, his love for her made her smile.

Sons and mothers—what a sweet bond it was! And it was amazing, too, how early a young boy's protective nature sets in where his mother was concerned.

Her thoughts drifted back to the previous evening with Chandler and his own mother. Seeing the way they interacted with one another had been like watching a skit unravel before her eyes. She had been a captive audience, enjoying their rapport. The sweet hugs, the tender touches. The fondness that shone in their eyes. Their teasing and bantering. It was obvious they shared a close relationship and cared very much for one another.

Witnessing their endearing exchanges, Hope found herself scrutinizing Chandler Adams even more closely, and projecting scads of wonderful qualities on the guy. Warmhearted. Family-oriented. Loving. Upright. Good-natured. Supportive. Caring. A female sees the way a man behaves with his mother, and all of a sudden she thinks she's seeing him for real. However, that was a ridiculous notion, she reminded herself.

After all, the thing between a mother and son was a one-of-a-kind relationship, wasn't it? And sons had a hold on their mothers' hearts by default anyway. In fact, that's probably where men learned to take advantage of women in the first place. They learned very young that when a woman loves them, it takes a lot to shake that love up. And they learn much too quickly how disarming their charm can be to a woman who thinks they're adorable.

Her own son could sure take the fire out of her ire many times. During a scolding—at least for a minor infraction—he knew that he could get her to cave in with his "aw, you're not *really* mad at me, are you?" kind of smile. Suddenly Hope would find herself grinning, too, and the issue that had upset her just wouldn't seem so important anymore.

So no matter how great of a son Chandler seemed to be with his mother, it didn't necessarily mean he'd be equally great with another female. Actually it didn't mean a thing, did it?

And what did it matter anyway? She already had a man in her life—a young one who needed all of her attention and love. And obviously, after his ill-mannered display of behavior the other night, one who wasn't too keen about another male disrupting their lives.

Besides, Chandler had already said he and Mona would be concluding their mission in the next week or so anyway. So, it wouldn't be long until he was gone . . . out of her life . . . with no chance of him ever being in her heart.

His room at Uncle Cary's inn was still dim when Chandler rolled over on his back to greet the new day. His eyes were at half-mast; however, he readily noticed that another part of his anatomy was at full attention.

Normally, waking up to his boxers making a "pup tent" of sorts over his aroused state would have been a welcome, gratifying feeling. But this morning it was more disconcerting than it was delectable. It was because of the dream, of course. The dream had—in a manner of speaking, of course—awakened every part of him.

The problem was it hadn't been a particularly sexually-charged, provocative dream. In fact, it was actually kind of quaint, with a domestic backdrop. Basically, in the dream Hope was sitting at the computer working . . . which, if she'd been half-naked or something, would have explained his early morning excitement. But, no, there she was with all of her clothes on, in particular, a gray turtleneck and some lambskin slippers, Chandler recalled.

Meanwhile, outside the window Theo was kicking around a soccer ball with a friend. Chandler had been watching a sports program—a football game or something—and put the remote down long enough to go over to where Hope was typing. With soothing hands, he tenderly massaged the back of her neck, and gently kneaded her tense shoulders. Then he leaned over the back of her chair, and lightly kissed her right cheek.

That was it. That was all. That's what was so frightening!

"Aw, hell," he muttered, feeling like a doomed man, and he attempted to will his arousal away. This was all because of the homey evening he'd spent with Hope the night before, he was sure. Milk and chocolate chip cookies with her in his mom's kitchen. That could certainly bring on a dream like that, right?

Plus, what even made it cozier was the fact that his mom was already campaigning for Hope. He could see it in her eyes. Clearly, his mother admired Hope for working hard for her son, and respected her difficult position as a single mom.

Yes, Mom had liked her instantly. And what wasn't there to like? Hope Hathaway appeared to be much different from anyone he'd ever met. Everything good and strong and right . . . and somehow that made her everything desirous, too.

He smiled in remembrance of her performance the day before. He'd almost laughed out loud and blown his whole cover. She was something all right . . . and something to look at in those high boots and that black skirt skimming her smooth upper thighs.

It was apparent she wasn't about to give up or turn into a simpering mess in front of those gangsters. She might be all soft and luscious on the outside—*aw, damn, there goes that pup tent again*—but on the inside, the woman dipped from a deep well of strength.

Okay, so he was hooked. But the sad reality was he'd just have to unhook himself. Simple as that. He had a schedule, after all, a master plan. His life was neat, tidy and in order. Just the way he liked it. Sure, he wanted to settle down and have a family someday. But, according to his projections, that wasn't scheduled for another three and a half years or so.

He'd typed out his five-year plan on the computer and

could see it plainly in his head. Getting seriously involved with anyone right now was not on the list. It didn't add in to his current plans, and he *was* a man of numbers after all. Cutting back on his international travels to make himself more available for his widowed mom was one thing. He couldn't take on more family-type obligations right now.

And speaking of work, thank goodness there was Mona. What a lifesaver she was! They'd known each other for so long that there was none of that awkward sexual tension between them. It was so easy to work with her. They really were more like sister and brother, both of them appreciative of their truly platonic relationship. He needed Mona's help now to protect his five-year plan, to finish their art fraud mission and then get the hell out of Dodge a.s.a.p. In the meantime, he'd try to avoid seeing Hope as much as possible.

Convinced that he had a viable solution, Chandler hopped up and went into the bathroom to brush his teeth. His cell phone rang, but with his mouth full of foamy toothpaste, he let his audible voice messaging system pick up the call.

. . . *Chandler, darling, I'm so sick . . . like a dog, as you say. <Aaachoo!> Sorry. <Blow> You'll have to call that Hope rent-a-spy girl to go with you to the MOMA affair at the Plaza tonight. It's no big deal. It's just a black-tie dinner dance. <Cough> Nothing should come down tonight anyway. It'll all probably happen before the auction tomorrow. She simply has to <sniff> pose as your wife. Actually, I can picture the two of you <Aaachoo!> right now. How <blow> sweet! I'll call you when I'm <cough> feeling better . . .*

Ah, hell! Mona was sick? He had to spend more time alone with Hope? He cursed vehemently in every language he knew, nearly choking on his frothy fluoride.

He'd managed to survive lethal weapons. Life-threatening gunmen. And a variety of torture techniques. But now, damn it all, he was in real danger.

Hope threw her threadbare robe over her long-johns, and handily wrapped her wild head of curls into a self-contained knot as she headed toward her front door. She couldn't imagine who would be knocking this early on a Saturday morning. It couldn't be the teen-aged paperboy collecting subscription money. For sure, he'd still be asleep at this hour.

"Sorry it's so early," Chandler said meekly from where he stood on her front stoop. "Guess I caught you in your pj's."

Chandler looked good, as usual. Cooler than cool in his suede jacket, faded jeans and a slight shadow of a beard. On the other hand she, as usual, looked a sight. Silently, she damned herself that the silk robe from Mitchell's was still wadded up in a bag and lying on her bedroom floor somewhere.

"I had something to ask you, and I didn't have your phone number." He appeared apologetic. "So I thought I'd stop over."

Usually Chandler Adams had no problem making eye contact with her. In fact, many times his eyes penetrated hers in such a way that it created a burning sensation that would start at the back of her neck and tendril just about everywhere. But this morning, he averted his gaze from hers. He seemed nervous about something, and his nervousness only added to her ease.

"Go ahead, shoot!" she said gregariously. Then realizing what she'd said, she giggled. "Or come to think of it, that's probably not a good thing to say to a spy who could be toting a gun, huh?"

Chandler smiled, but just barely. His unease seemed to dissipate, but just by a bit.

"Not really." He nodded, fairly serious. "Actually, I, uh . . ." He stalled again.

"Yes?" Hope started to shiver from the cold. "Do you want to come in? It's freezing out there."

"No, no. Can't come in, no."

He shook his head so emphatically, she had to wonder what had changed since dinner the other night when he had slipped into her home and seemed to fit so comfortably there. Or even since last night. When they returned from Nyack, he had seemed so reluctant to let their time together end.

"I was just wondering," he tried to brave the question again, "would you, uh . . . what I mean to say is . . . Well, would you . . . be my wife?"

She had written about a character's eyes bulging out of their head before, but she'd never experienced it firsthand. Not until now at least. Here, she had just been lying in bed musing over what kind of guy Chandler Adams really was. And now she knew—just her luck—an incredibly weird one!

"Excuse me?" She clutched the lapels of her robe together, a gesture to shut both weirdo and weather out.

Chandler, meanwhile, was waving his hands wildly. "No, I didn't mean it like that. You'd just be my wife for a day. Today actually. Maybe even tomorrow. Not that we'd have to consummate anything . . ."

She blinked at him in disbelief. *Consummate anything?*

"What I mean to say is . . . Mona's sick. And, well, I

110

need someone to pose as my wife and accompany me to a black-tie affair sponsored by the Museum of Modern Art. It's part of the operation I mentioned to you."

"Oh . . ." She sighed with relief, and okay, maybe just the eensiest twinge of disappointment. "Well, as you can tell, I'm slightly clothes poor at the moment. Black tie isn't in my closet. And honestly," her teeth were chattering now, "after yesterday, I'm thinking I'd probably just get you killed—or myself kidnapped or something. And I do have a son to raise. So I think I'll just stick to fiction, even though they're right. Truth is stranger than fiction. But thanks just the same." She started to shut the door.

"Wait." Chandler's foot stopped the door from closing. "Do you really think I'd be asking *you*, if I didn't need for you to go?"

Was she missing something? On one hand, he was stressing the word "you," referring to her as if she had some sort of plague and was the last person on earth he'd ever ask. On the other hand, he was standing there in the freezing cold, pleading with her to go, wasn't he?

"I'm c-c-confused. D-d-do you want me to g-g-go or what?" Now her teeth were chattering so fiercely that her jaw had begun to ache.

"Well, no—I mean yeah. I just don't want to put you out or anything. It's nothing perilous, just a dinner dance. Although I guess dancing can be dangerous sometimes," he tittered, his skittishness still apparent.

What is up with him? Hope had to wonder.

"And the best part," Chandler clapped his hands, "you don't have to worry about a dress! I'll call in your size, and the agency will have a selection waiting for you at the Plaza Hotel when we arrive."

Of course! A hotel! Now she was beginning to see the

111

light—and feel the heat. For a moment, just the thought of being tucked away in a posh hotel room with a man singed her with an onslaught of desire. She didn't know what Chandler's true intentions were, but she really didn't know what her own reaction would be either. Maybe something regrettable? And if she couldn't even trust herself, how could she trust him?

"You know, I really don't think so . . ." she finally replied.

She started to close the door again, but he halted it with his hand this time.

"The dinner is being held at the Plaza. That's why we have reservations there."

She eyed him warily.

"Honest," he swore to her. *There he went with that word again!* "We have two rooms. Suites actually. Mona and I always reserve two adjoining rooms, even though it's necessary to check in as a married couple for our cover. And," he tried to make his voice sound as enticing as a game show host's, "you get to keep the shoes and gown. All compliments of the agency," he pitched to her.

"Well, that's r-r-really nice." The chattering started again. "But, as you may have g-g-guessed," she replied, glancing down at her worn jammies, "I'm not much of a clothes horse."

"But—"

"And it's S-S-Saturday. You wouldn't believe the ch-ch-chores I have to do."

Chandler exhaled heavily, and shrugged. "Okay. Well, sorry to have bothered you."

Hunched over and looking fairly forlorn, he turned and started down the steps of her stoop. But before he hit the bottom, he turned and gave it one more attempt. "A lot of colorful characters are involved," he worked to entice her. "You might glean some interesting ideas for an upcoming novel from the experience."

Suddenly the shivering stopped. The chattering ceased, and the thinking began. *The Museum of Modern Art. Midtown Manhattan. Cantankerous old curators. Docents. Artists' agents. Fraudulent paintings. Art enthusiasts.*

"Well, I . . ." Theo *would* be gone until tomorrow at six, and she'd have her cell phone with her if Uncle Cary needed her. Plus, he promised two separate hotel rooms. Was there really any reason she couldn't go?

"I have to be back long before six tomorrow," she said firmly. No way she'd want Theo to know where she'd gone and with whom.

"No problem." He clapped his hands, and rubbed them together. To keep them warm? Or because she'd succumbed to his plan?

Whatever, it couldn't daunt her excitement at the moment. "What time should I be ready?"

Chapter Seven

Sela was suddenly awakened by the voice of a gondolier singing outside her window. His notes weren't exactly hitting the right spots. But, she guessed his heart was at least in the right place as he repeated the chorus of "O Solo Mio" over and over . . . and, for cripes sake, over again.

Little by little, his off-key lyrics came closer and kept getting louder. What she had initially thought of as a sweet sound soon became a jangled, discordant noise that grated on her every last nerve. Like a needle stuck on a vinyl LP . . . nails screeching on a blackboard . . . or her Aunt Tildy's nasally whines.

ARRGH! She couldn't stand it any longer. She had to get up and see who this idiot was.

Drawing back the floral curtains on the terrace doors, she peered out onto the canal and the pleasantly sunny day. She focused her sleep-filled eyes on the glistening water and caught sight of the tone-deaf gondola driver.

"Giorgio!" she exclaimed, stepping out on the terrace, totally surprised to see him.

"Sela!" His expression was full of longing.

"Giorgio?"

"Sela!"

Oh, for crap's sake! This lack of communication thing was getting ridiculous. And she had so much to tell him— though, for sure, she wouldn't mention that he couldn't carry a tune worth a darn. She needed to warn him about Cirella Carducci, the lady he was sharing the villa with. Carducci was evil; she was dangerous. But how could Sela let him know? What words, hand signs, or mime expressions could she use to tell him?

"I'm sorry, sir, but there's only one suite reserved under the name of Mr. and Mrs. Adam Chandler. However, I can double-check that, if you wish."

The words of the meticulously groomed man behind the Plaza Hotel's reservation desk were courteous and compliant. But his movements, both crisp and precise, suggested the self-assuredness of someone who would never make a mistake. Still, he dutifully stepped away to go search the computer files for any errors.

"Aarr!" Hope hissed disgustedly as the desk clerk moved out of hearing range. "I can't believe you, Chandler Adams!"

"Shhh! It's Adam Chandler. Remember, my sweet bride?"

"How low can you get? Lying to me like that!"

His retort was strained but adamant. "I didn't lie to you about anything!"

"Pretending to have two suites when you knew all along . . ." She shook her head at him. "Is that how you get all your women? By lying? You should be ashamed."

"I swear," he hissed back, "I didn't know."

The desk clerk paused in his search, glancing over the computer in their direction. Chandler grabbed Hope's hand and rubbed it consolingly. Good thing for him he did, since she was about to belt him with it.

He seemed to be trying hard to look the part of the perfect husband; together, the perfect couple.

"Honey, now relax. Everything's going to be fine."

How could he do this? she wondered. Their ride into the city had been easygoing and relaxing, and for her part, enjoyable. In fact, compared to their time together in the trunk the day before, it had been relatively free of tension—sexual or otherwise.

Hope tried to recall the last time she'd spent even an hour with a man whose company she enjoyed so much. Someone who was easy to talk to. Someone she had so much in common with . . . including small towns, professions and her Uncle Cary's taxes. She tried to remember, but drew a blank.

And then this? Just when she was beginning to think he wasn't like every other male, he proved he was by counting on the fact that she was like every other female. Just when she was starting to form feelings of familiarity and trust, he left her with the impression she'd been duped. The disappointment must have shown in her eyes.

"I'm telling you," he whispered softly, his pursed lips brushing against her hair, "I didn't know."

The look on his face appeared agonizingly sincere. Still, could she believe him . . . even if she wanted to? Before she could decide, the desk clerk came back to face them.

"I'm sorry this has been inconvenient for you. I can see it's causing Mrs. Chandler some distress. Did you have guests joining you in the extra suite? Is that the concern?"

"Naw. She'll be fine. Won't you, honey?" Chandler nodded emphatically, trying to get Hope to nod along with him. She did, but not too convincingly. Finally, he leaned over the desk, and tilted his head toward the clerk, who moved in closer to hear what he had to say.

"What's your name?" Chandler asked politely.

"Griggs, sir."

"Well, Griggs, don't worry. She's just disappointed because she likes to have extra room to romp around in, if you know what I mean," he said quietly, with a confidential wink.

Raising an eyebrow, the clerk nodded back all-knowingly. Then he cleared his throat and spoke out loud, "Yes, well, our records indicate that a Mona Jergensen actually cancelled the suite. I assume our other desk clerk thought that would be fine, since Ms. Jergensen also requested a bottle of champagne be sent to your room, along with the message: 'Congratulations on your newly-formed union.' "

Blondie. Of course! Hope rolled her eyes skyward.

"Ah, newlyweds, eh?" Griggs clapped his hands together delightedly. "That's so wonderful. And, Mr. and Mrs. Chandler, since this is obviously a special night for you both, we'd like to make it up to you by offering you our honeymoon suite. At no extra cost, of course. It's very sizeable." He returned a wink at Chandler. "And if you need the suite for more than one night, it's available until next Thursday."

"The honeymoon suite?" Hope jumped in. "Till next Thursday? Thank you, really, but—"

Griggs held up his hand. "Mrs. Chandler, I'm sure your husband wants the best for his new bride, and frankly at the Plaza, we do too. Please accept our apologies for the mix-up," he replied with a smile, making it a done deal.

"Isn't that wonderful, sweetie?" Chandler raised her hand to his lips and left a delicate kiss there.

"Great," she said faintly, her face turning crimson, making her look every bit the blushing bride.

"Did you have to kiss me that way in the elevator?" Hope slammed the door of the suite—correction, the honeymoon suite—behind the bellboy before verbally slamming into Chandler.

"I just wanted to set the record straight. We want them to think we're newlyweds, don't we?"

It was a lie, of course. He hadn't meant to kiss her that way at all. When she had gotten onto the elevator, she looked so uneasy about the way things had turned out with the suites. But despite all that, it was obvious she was also trying to be a good sport and espionage partner. He felt bad and had the urge to smooth things over, to make things right. He had only meant to turn to her, lift her chin and give her a peck of reassurance. But then . . . who knows what happened? Maybe it was a residual effect of being locked in a trunk with her . . . linked in a dream with her . . . and lumped into a suite with her. He just couldn't stop himself.

"Set the record straight? Or set a new world record? That was the longest-lasting public display of affection in history," she ranted.

He couldn't say that he blamed her. Even if they really were married, it still would've proved an embarrassing kiss, in public and all. He had definitely taken advantage of their guise as newlyweds.

"And while we're setting things straight," she continued, wagging a stern finger at him, "I'll make you a deal. I promise to act my part so as not to blow your cover. But, you need to do me a favor, too. Don't try to treat me like one of your typical floozy, spy-groupie girls. Because in case you haven't noticed, I'm not."

Oh, he had noticed all right. She was anything but typical. Had she been typical, he would've already had her out of his system by now—or into his bed. The intense heat of the kiss would've followed them right into the door of the suite and would've carried over into a sweet round of passion. And right now, instead of being all balled up inside, he'd be curled up like a satiated tomcat in a contented, after-the-loving nap.

"I think we get along fairly well," she was saying, interrupting his thoughts. She paused, and he knew it was his cue.

"Sure." He nodded. "Me too."

"And I like you fine," she stated.

"Ditto." He nodded again.

"But lust isn't part of the deal."

"Definitely not." He shook his head, hoping his words would convince both of them.

"We're just here to get our jobs done. Right?"

"Right." He reached out to give her a brotherly high-five. "Want to toast to that?" He slid the champagne bottle from its gleaming crystal bucket.

"Champagne? It's a little early in the day, isn't it?"

"Probably." But, he uncorked the bubbly anyway. She might not need a drink, but he could sure use one, for God's sake.

As sick as Mona sounded, he couldn't believe she had the energy to toy with his life. Maybe she thought she was doing something nice for him by canceling the additional suite. But he'd only been in the hotel with Hope for ten minutes, and his nerves were already frayed.

Thankfully, Mona had ordered up the champagne. He needed something to help him settle down. He poured a lone glass for himself and took a gulp, knowing what was coming next. Knowing full well it was only going to get worse.

Damn! He sighed inwardly, already feeling defeated.

Sure . . . Hope was meandering through the suite right

this minute, checking out the accommodations . . . the luxurious bathroom, the fluffy robes, the view of Central Park. But any second now, she'd discover the long evening dresses in the closet right alongside his tuxedo. And then she'd want to try on each one, give each a twirl right in front of him, asking him to help choose which one looked the best on her glorious body.

Speaking of her body, then it would be time for a bath in preparation for the evening ahead. She'd soak in a hot, languorous bath laden with the scent of some mystical, exotic flower, or some other tantalizing fragrance which would seep out from under the bathroom door, teasing at him. All the while he'd have to sit on the bed and pretend that, no, there wasn't any lust involved. It was a job and only a job. Yeah, right . . .

Hope came running back into the main room, breathless with excitement. "You won't believe it. There are so many dresses to choose from. If we don't have any espionage work to do right this minute, I think I'll try on dresses before taking a nice, relaxing bubble bath."

Did she know she was torturing him? Was she doing it on purpose? Just to get back at him? True, he shouldn't have kissed her that way in the elevator. Absolutely not. Mostly because it only left him wanting more. For a moment, though, it seemed like . . . well, had he imagined it or hoped it? It seemed as if she had started kissing him back, had started to yield to him. Is that why he hadn't stopped . . . ?

"I swear, I feel like Cinderella," she bubbled. "I could really get used to this spy business. Do you mind if I try on the dresses for you, and you can help me decide which one is most suitable for tonight?"

"Not at all," he replied, feigning a nonchalance he didn't

feel. He took another sizeable gulp of the champagne. But realizing the fashion show would require more than a mere drink, he grabbed the bottle from the bucket, and set it on the nightstand. Plopping down onto the bed, he stretched out and crossed his legs at his ankles, trying desperately to relax. It was going to be a long night, to be sure.

He turned on the television, attempting to divert his thoughts. But that didn't work. A football game splashed across the screen, reminding him of the dream. Then the dream reminded him of his excitement that morning, and . . . he flicked through the stations. Why did hotel TVs have so many infomercials and adult channels? Quickly, he clicked off the tube and threw down the remote as if it were a hot iron burning in his hand.

"Okay." Hope breezed into the room, transformed into a goddess clad all in gold. "This is dress number one. What do you think?"

Chandler slugged down another belt of champagne, attempting to steel himself. The golden slip of a dress draped over her bare skin. It dipped in front. It dipped in back. And he'd be dipped if he were going to be around her all night, trying to keep his hands off her.

"I don't think it's the best color for you," he offered lamely.

"Really?" She looked puzzled. "I always thought this was a good color with my hair." She sighed. "But . . . well, okay. No big deal, there are two others I like. On to dress number two." She perked up.

The second dress was also a hot number. A black halter with a deep, wide décolletage that plummeted well past her breasts and landed at about mid-midriff. Embroidered scarlet and russet flowers vined up the left side of the dress.

"How about this one?" She twirled around slowly, and

Chandler caught sight of her back, bared all the way down to the top of her hips. He imagined dancing with her. Everywhere he touched, her naked skin would surely sear his fingertips. He winced at the thought.

"It looks a bit Spanish. Don't you think?" Another inane comment. "It's okay, I guess." He shrugged his shoulders indifferently.

Hope scrunched up her nose at him. "Oh, yeah? Spanish, huh? Just okay?" She looked in the mirror again, apparently trying to see the dress the way he claimed he was seeing it. "Well, gosh, there's one more gown that I like. Be right back." She scurried back into the smaller dressing room of the suite.

Chandler sat staring blankly, wondering at his fate. Dress number one was a knockout. Dress two was a killer. And number three? He'd probably wind up a dead man, for sure.

Hope emerged again, her good nature undaunted. "Actually, this may be the best of the three anyway. Even though the back is scooped out, the neckline is higher. I think it looks a bit more 'wifey,' don't you?"

Wifey? Was she kidding? How many guys had a wife that looked as incredibly voluptuous as she did? A really lucky handful maybe? He was pretty much convinced she hadn't a clue as to how attractive she was. Otherwise, he couldn't imagine her doing this; she certainly didn't seem to be the teasing type.

She stood on her tiptoes and looked into the Cheval full-length mirror that stood by the dresser. The luminescent quality of the dress reflected in her aquamarine eyes. And dress number three . . . yeah, he was a dead man all right.

The pale, silvery blue sequins covered her like a second skin, hugging every curve of her body. His eyes felt like they were on a roller coaster . . . and it was one helluva ride. They followed every intoxicating peak . . . passed around every thrilling curve . . . rode low and soared high. It was only a minute before one of his other senses, his sense of touch, awakened too, and wanted to partake in the joy ride.

"I think I'll wear this one," Hope finally said. "Do you agree?"

She looked so pleased with her reflection in the mirror; he couldn't deny her the satisfaction of a complimentary answer any longer.

"You look . . ." He paused. There were so many adjectives he could've chosen, but most seemed inappropriate or all too intimate. ". . . great."

"Oh, good." She expelled a long breath. "Now that that's taken care of, I guess I'll go take a bubble bath. But don't worry," she added sweetly, retreating from the room, "I won't use all of the hot water. I promise."

"No, really, use all you want," he replied generously, calling after her. He'd only be blasting himself with cold water anyway.

Once again, he tried to find something, besides Hope, to distract him. He turned on the television and cranked up the audio, trying to drown out Hope's combination of humming and splashing in the tub. Not that she was off-pitch. He simply didn't need to be reminded in any way that she was in the next room, cloaked only in wispy, clouds of bubbles, soaping every inch of her body.

He started to pour another flute of champagne, then gave up and took a slug from the bottle instead. He clicked swiftly through the channels again. Ah, a winner. The good old Ronco Vegematic infomercial. That looked like a safe bet.

★ ★ ★ ★ ★

"Damn!" Chandler cursed, clearly frustrated.

He was standing in the middle of the suite fumbling with a knotted cluster of plastic cords, when Hope exited the smaller sitting room.

Hot damn is more like it! she thought with a gasp—an audible gasp that she hoped he hadn't heard.

"I, um . . . I thought you'd be dressed," she stammered, attempting to get a grip on herself. She'd been camped out in the dressing room for so long, getting herself made up for the evening, that she hadn't given a lot of thought to Chandler's transformation.

But the sight of him now caught her totally off-guard. Clean-shaven. Chocolatey hair gelled into place. Black tuxedo pants hanging from his above-average frame. And his shirt . . . well, there was none. So came the gasp. She was only glad she wasn't close enough to catch a whiff of his aftershave, too. She didn't need anything else dizzying up her senses at the moment.

Chandler glanced down at his tux pants. "I'm decent though, right?" he asked, clearly not wanting to offend her.

Decent? Ha, what an understatement! She nodded numbly.

"I'm having trouble wiring myself." He held up the tangled mess of plastic cords which had microphones and suction devices attached to them. "Mona usually takes care of hooking me up in these ridiculous things. We tried it at your Uncle Cary's the other night. I really hate to ask you, but I'm all thumbs when it comes to this stuff. Do you mind?" He held up the device.

"Oh, sure. No problem." She ambled toward him, her walk slowed by the tight, sequined dress. Thankfully, it had a giving slit on the right side.

She hadn't wanted to get close to his bare, breathtaking

chest. *But I can handle this,* she told herself. In the name of espionage, she could do this.

She took the wires from him, and began to untangle them.

"Sorry about this," he apologized again. "But I don't want us to be late for dinner. One mike goes in front, the other in the back."

"Okay, I've got them all sorted out. Now what?" She stepped forward, holding the wires up to his chest.

But then . . . he unhooked the band of his black, formal pants.

And then . . . he unzipped the fly a couple of inches or so.

He never seemed to stop talking all the while he did so. "It's good equipment . . ."

Talk about another understatement, she thought, her eyes drawn to the hard, flat surface below his belly button. Imagining what that flat trail led to was more than she wanted to think about.

". . . but I don't know why they had to change the design. I'm sure the research people think it's progressive," he was saying, as he stood at attention ready for her.

"Wha—what are you doing?" she stuttered. She shook her head, incredulous.

"The wire goes right below my waist. I guess they figure that's not an area where another guy really wants to be feeling around for a wire."

Even in the evening glow of the lamp-lit room, she knew he could see her face was flushed. "If you're not comfortable doing this, I totally understand." His chuckle sounded as uneasy as she felt. "I can always try it by myself again."

"Don't be silly." She mustered up her resolve. "No big deal. It's all part of the job, right?" And if Mona could get the job done, surely she could manage to, too.

She just needed to disassociate herself, that's all. She needed to step back in the same way she had to with Theo sometimes. When kids came running in the door with hideously huge goose eggs on their heads, or were dripping with blood, a mom immediately took control. Beared up. Put them at ease. Got the job done. And then later, that's when your legs turned to Jell-O, and your nerves would quake and shake in the aftermath.

And that's just what she'd do right now. She'd step back and size up the situation—well, figuratively speaking, of course. And then she'd start in the back and work her way around to the front. She'd save the "worst" till last. Though as she recalled from her peek in Chandler's bedroom window the other night, his backside wasn't too shabby either.

Bending over carefully in her evening gown, not wanting to wrinkle it in any way, she worked to hook the wires at the small of his back. Chandler, meanwhile, held the other ends of the cords in the front. Smoothing out the wires against his backside, she tried to get the suction to stick, but wasn't having too much luck. She even moistened her fingertips and applied a little saliva to his skin, hoping that would help the suction stay in place.

"What was that?" He jumped, and the suction device started to dangle again.

"Nothing. Just a little saliva," she answered. "Do you have any tape to hold this in place a little better?"

Obviously, the suctions hadn't worked so well before, because he was ready with a supply of Band-Aids. She deftly unwrapped them and put them into place.

And then it was time—time to move around to his front side. Calmly, she took the wires from his hands and straightened them out. She tried to keep talking nonchalantly, maintaining a vision of her gynecologist in her mind. Dr. Friedman seemed to be an expert at removing himself from the situation. His mouth and hands were always moving at the same time, and not always on the same subject. It was nothing for him to be examining her plumbing while discussing how his sump pump hadn't kicked in during an overnight thunderstorm.

"So do you have to wear this wire whenever you're on assignment?" she chatted away.

"In many cases," he answered, looking dead ahead.

"Just in case something pops up?"

He glanced down at her, and she noticed beads of perspiration dotting his forehead. She recognized the strained look in his eyes.

"Kind of a bad choice of words right about now, Hope."

"Oh, yeah," she mumbled. "Sorry about that."

She shut her mouth then and busied herself, hooking the front wires together. "More Band-Aids, please," she requested clinically.

He handed them to her. She taped down the remaining wires and suction.

"Okay." She stood up and stepped back from him. "We're all done here. You're good to go."

Chandler let out a deep breath, wiped his brow with the back of his hand and swiftly grabbed his shirt from the bed. She didn't think she'd ever seen anyone button up that many buttons so quickly in her life. Or be so nimble with a pair of cufflinks and bow tie.

She watched in silent amazement as his hands moved deftly, swiftly. She was still staring when he unzipped his trousers even lower than before to tuck in his formal shirt. Embarrassingly for her—and probably for him, too, she guessed—he looked up and caught her gawking.

"Oh . . . I'm . . . sorry . . ." She turned away, sure that her face was as red as the roses in the Waterford vase on the nightstand.

Finally she heard the rustling of his shirt, and his pants zipper slide up.

Safe from temptation at last!

"All set?" he asked.

She turned to see him all decked out in his formal attire, looking dark, handsome and very male. Like every woman's dream.

Well . . . maybe not safe just yet.

"Um . . . your tie." She pointed to his neck. "It's crooked."

He tugged at it from the left, pulling it down.

"No, the other way." She pointed again, to his right side this time.

He pulled it up from the right side.

"Almost. It's still just a tad lower on the left though."

"Can you just fix it?" he asked, impatience creeping into his voice.

"Sure. I can do that."

Sure, she could . . . Until she took several small steps toward him . . . and stood up slightly on her tiptoes . . . reached out her arms to touch him . . . saw a muscle quiver in his jaw, and felt the hardness of his legs through the sheerness of her gown . . . That's when she realized why Chandler had been dressing so quickly, like he was going to a fire. They had to get out of the room—fast—before they started something they couldn't put out.

Righting the bow tie into position, she used his chest to push herself off, away from him. It was her turn to dab at her sweaty brow.

"*Now* are you ready for a drink?" he asked.

Yet another major understatement for the evening, she thought, nodding mutely in response.

"Me too," he confessed, throwing on his tux jacket. "Let's get out of here."

Chapter Eight

Sela stood on the terrace gazing at Giorgio. How sweet! He was not only attempting to sing, but he was trying to dance for her, too. The gondola swayed this way and that underneath his happy feet.

The only man who had ever danced for her before was that bloke from London. She'd met him when she was there on an assignment for the Queen. He worked in the Parliament, yet wasn't nearly as stuffy and pent-up as she had imagined he'd be. In fact, he had been thinking of starting a new career. He liked to practice an entertaining, choreographed number called a "monty" for her, as she remembered.

She had to admit, the monty was more vivacious than Giorgio's jig. But at least her Italian admirer was aiming to please, and that's what counted the most.

Only, wait a minute! She held onto the terrace railing and leaned over as far as she could. Giorgio wasn't dancing at all. Something—or someone—was beneath the water trying to topple him over. And they were succeeding, she realized, as his legs finally gave way, and the gondola overturned.

Sela had wished to start the day with a nice, hot bubble bath. But that was out of the question now, she realized. The canal would have to suffice, she thought, as she plunged into the cold Venetian water to save him.

"Mrs. Chandler, would you like to dance?" her pretend, but very handsome, husband leaned over and inquired.

"I'd love to, Mr. Chandler." She smiled up at him demurely.

Chandler excused them both from the other two assigned couples at their dinner table, and with a hand at her elbow guided her toward the dance floor.

For Hope, it was a relief to be out among people. The honeymoon suite, as opulent as it was, was getting much too crowded for the two of them, what with all the sexual tension that seemed to pour out from every nook and cranny there. Out in public, in the company of others, they were safe. Safe to act like themselves, safe to act out their roles.

"So the people who are sitting at our table," Hope questioned him as soon as they had settled into a comfortable groove on the dance floor, "who are they really?"

"Really? Aren't they *really* the Ginsbergs from the Upper East Side and the Brockmans from Connecticut? Isn't that what they said?"

"No, I mean, they're people from your agency, right?" she quizzed him.

"No." He laughed. "They're just people. Didn't the Brockmans say they represent some new artist? And the Ginsbergs . . . aren't they long-standing patrons of the museum?"

"So the Brockmans and Ginsbergs are just regular people?"

"Guess it happens to the best of us." He gave her a fond smile.

Hope frowned, feeling dashed at the thought. She had come along on this venture hoping to gather some fodder for upcoming novels. Yet all day they'd been holed up alone, no criminals or artsy people in sight. *Not that it would've been so easy to think shop anyway,* she thought. She'd had to struggle all day to act flip and indifferent, as though they were merely partners on the prowl. But it wasn't as simple as that.

Trying on the gowns, of course, had been her first mistake. It was hard to forget they were two people alone in a hotel room with him looking at her that way. Not that he was leering by any means. In fact, he was very gentlemanly, giving his honest views about each dress till they'd agreed on the shimmering blue one. But even with all he'd said, or left unsaid, she could detect a hint of appreciation in his eyes and had forced herself to act as if it wasn't there at all.

And then there was the bubble bath. She had only meant to find a way to extricate herself from his presence to let the vibrations between them—or hers for him anyway—simmer down for a while. But a walk in the park would've been a much better idea. Knowing he was just on the other side of the door as she lay soaking in the tub didn't exactly evoke the relaxing feeling she was going for. She'd tried humming every show tune she knew, but it hadn't really helped.

Evidently though, her bathing hadn't provoked the same sensual feelings in him at all. By the time she emerged from the bathroom, he'd been out cold, curled up, napping with an empty champagne flute resting by his side.

But slinky dresses and hot, bubbly baths aside, the donning of the wiring device was the worst yet. That had been excruciating with Chandler's tux pants only partially zipped, his rippled stomach up close—at eye-level, for goodness' sake—paving the way to other mystical body parts. And then, of course, the bow tie experience—that had her in knots, too.

Yes, all in all, they'd had quite a titillating day together.

She felt his arm tighten around her waist, and saw the amusement bright in his eyes. The feelings of desire that had pelted them from every direction all day didn't seem to threaten them at this moment. As Mr. and Mrs. Chandler out in front of the world, their moods were light and fun-loving. Here they could afford to be close, witty, intimate, charmed by one another. They were performing, after all. And, anyway, what could possibly transpire between them when they were surrounded by a roomful of people?

He tightened the circle of his arm around her and pulled her closer to him. "This is okay to do, since you're my wife, right?"

"I suppose so. Yes, it's okay," she agreed verbally, yet physically she was feeling apprehensive. This felt good . . . way too good.

"I can't believe you told our dinner companions that you were a spy hunting down art frauds." She had almost sputtered out a mouthful of Chardonnay when he'd announced that to their table.

Chandler chuckled boyishly. "And did they believe me?"

"No. Incredibly enough, they didn't." She shook her head, grinning along with him. "They all laughed."

"Exactly. You didn't believe me either." He tilted his head back, looking her full in the face.

"Well, if you would've had a British accent . . ." she teased.

He laughed easily, bringing out the sweet crinkly lines around his eyes. For some reason, the thought skipped across her mind that he'd remain a good-looking man at any age.

"I knew it," he told her, still smiling. "An English accent does it every time."

Without missing a beat of the song, he released one of

his hands from around her waist, tucked it under her chin and raised her face up to meet his eyes. "But would you believe me if I told you that you look beautiful tonight, Mrs. Chandler?"

Yes, you've told me a hundred times with your eyes. That's what she wanted to say. That's what Sela had said to the Prince of Anatolia in her second book. But Hope wasn't nearly as outspoken as her fictional counterpart. Though she wished she were, at times.

"Thank you," she said simply.

It was true. She did feel beautiful tonight. She had swept back her hair in a loose knot on the top of her head, letting wavy, sexy strands of auburn outline her face and fall capriciously down the back of her neck. She'd strived for a natural look with her make-up, yet tried to dramatize her thickly-lashed eyes and accentuate her full lips. And the sequined dress was exquisite. It seemed to be made for her in every respect, with its sensual yet classy style, its perfect fit and alluring color.

But mostly, it was true because of Chandler. It was the way he made her feel when he looked at her. The way she saw herself reflected in his eyes. It had been a long time since a man had made her feel so beautiful.

Comfortable with the ease of their faux relationship for the time being, she nestled her head on his shoulder. He must not have minded, because he laid his head lightly against hers. For the moment, his aftershave, the hardness of his body, the touch of his hand . . . none of these things seemed to be turn-ons. They were simply there to be enjoyed overtly—the delicious, increasingly familiar parts of him.

What would it be like to really be Mrs. Chandler or Mrs. Adams or whomever? her mind taunted her . . . though she tried to push the thought away.

"Adam Chandler?" A female voice interrupted Hope's thoughts and their newlyweds' embrace. It seemed to be an occupational hazard with Chandler, Adam or whomever. "I'm glad you made it tonight."

Chandler looked up. "Ms. Dreyer. How are you?" He extended his right hand to shake Ms. Dreyer's. His left arm remained curved around Hope's waist. "Hope, this is Melanie Dreyer. She's one of the curators at the museum."

A curator? Hope's mind skittered. Weren't they supposed to be old, hunchbacked and gray? Melanie Dreyer was anything but. By contrast, she had a biological clock that still had years to blow. Her attractiveness could've probably won her Ms. New York in a beauty pageant. And she appeared to be a paragon of the young, successful professional.

"Melanie, this is my wife, Hope." He turned to Hope. "Melanie heads up the department of ancient art and sculpture," he explained while Melanie preened under the spotlight of his explanation. "She's a genius when it comes to artifacts of ancient civilizations."

A genius? A gorgeous, glamorous genius? Was nothing fair in this life?

"Mrs. Chandler, it's nice to meet you. I'm sorry to be so brusque, but could I borrow your husband for a few minutes?" Evidently the woman was ingenious, too, at stealing husbands, pretend or otherwise. "We need to catch up on some things."

Some things?

Right off, Hope didn't like Melanie Dreyer. It had nothing to do with her great looks. Or the "V" of her black dress, which stood for "very, very voluptuously low." Or even the way she had put a possessive hand on Chandler's arm.

No. It was merely an intuitive feeling. An impression

135

that the curator was a capable woman all right—capable of anything. But before Hope could even answer, the competent Ms. Dreyer had whisked away her husband, albeit her pretend husband, to another part of the dance floor.

It took a moment for Hope to close her astounded mouth and move her frozen legs. Her mood dampened, she made her way back to the dinner table. Noting Adams' absence, Mr. Brockman and Mr. Ginsberg were kind enough to ask her to dance.

After a not-so-thrilling round on the dance floor with each of the kind gentlemen, their pair of wives filled another half-hour or so with small talk. When it seemed apparent to her and probably everyone else at the table that Chandler wasn't coming back, Hope stood up to excuse herself from the couples.

"Are you sure we can't trip the light fantastic one more time?" Mr. Brockman asked her.

He was just being polite, she was sure. But she didn't think she could handle him stepping on her toes any more in one evening.

"Adam had to make an important business call," she fibbed. "Then I promised to meet him back in the room." She forced a blush. "What can I say? Newlyweds, you know?" She feigned a girlish giggle.

The women sighed longingly. The men grinned roguishly. And Hope tried to hold her head high and act out her wifely role when, in truth, she was feeling an urge to divorce the creep from her mind—her life—her everything.

At the end of Melanie and Chandler's first dance, Hope had scanned the dance floor for the pair. And even though she didn't spot them, she still expected to see Chandler back at the table at any moment.

But no such luck. Trying to keep in mind that they *were* here on business, the thought still nagged at her . . . *could Chandler be here on personal business as well?*

Or was there an off-chance that her groom really could be in trouble? After all, Melanie did look the part, with a capital "T." Although, the curator also looked like the kind of trouble men couldn't get enough of. Just the same, Hope decided to take a peek around the hotel for her long-lost and possibly endangered hubby.

Leaving behind the music and people inside the first-floor ballroom, she wound down several hallways. After finding her way back to the hotel lobby, she stood for a moment surrounded by the inordinate grandeur there, feeling small and vexed.

Now if Sela were setting out to locate her partner in crime . . . hmm . . .

There appeared to be only one answer.

Hope would start looking for Chandler systematically, floor by floor. She'd stop and listen at each door until she heard sounds of—her stomach tightened at the thought of Chandler and Melanie making any sort of "together" sounds. *Okay, best not to think about that right now.*

Rounding the corner to the row of elevators, she was stopped short by a pair of familiar-looking black leather coats. It was the trunk thugs, looking like the trendy villains they were, the gangster boss in his versatile full-length coat and the gangster gopher in his hip blazer.

Instinctively, she turned away from them, in case they might recognize her. Bending down, she pretended to attend to a strap on her high heel. All the while, she glanced up surreptitiously, studying the lit-up numbers above the elevator they entered. No doubt about it, the mobsters' elevator had stopped on the third floor.

Luckily, the doors of an adjacent elevator popped open, void of people. She rushed into it, moving as swiftly as she could in her clingy evening gown. In a flash, the elevator deposited her on floor number three, right on the thugs' heels. Peeking out the elevator, she saw them duck into a suite down the hall.

She had to admit the gangster guys gave her a bad case of the creeps. Something about people who lock you into trunks of cars can do that to you, she supposed. Leave you virtually intimidated. Still, she made herself leave the shelter of the elevator and forced herself to tiptoe down the hallway, until she was standing right outside their room.

Her body trembled involuntarily as she leaned against the door. Glancing around, she realized that if the thugs decided to leave their room in a hurry, there was no place she could hide. There were no decorative plants nearby for cover, and no cubbies to duck into. She'd have to hoof it in her tight-fitting gown all the way to the end of the hallway and around the corner.

How suspicious would that be? An unwelcome tremor shook its way down her spine.

With her heart pounding in her ears, it wasn't so easy to make out just what the crude crooks were saying behind the closed door. But, finally, with her head pressed against the frame, she made out some of their plans. Having had enough espionage for the time being, she made a break for it back to the safe haven of the honeymoon suite. Mr. Adams, she figured, would just have to make it back safely on his own.

The honeymoon suite.
Ha! It's not much of a honeymoon when you're all alone.
For a while, it had been fun being the cherished Mrs.

138

Adams. But thank goodness she wasn't really married to this spy guy. If this were the normal course of events in his life, with him running off with some museum hussy right in the middle of their evening, who needed it?

Disgusted, she headed for the suite's mini bar first thing, pouring herself a much-needed drink. Kicking off her heels, she plopped down in an overstuffed chair in a corner of the room where she had full view of the door. She'd be ready for him whenever he decided to come back. She crossed her legs, and, with drink in hand, she settled back in the chair to wait.

For the next couple of hours or so, her emotions flip-flopped between fury and worry. Every minute seemed like forever, until finally, Chandler came in the door with his black tie undone, his shirt unbuttoned at the neck, wearing a sappy grin on his face.

Clearly, she could rule out the worry. It was obvious he hadn't been detained in a torture chamber. Or if he had, it was a method of torture he hadn't minded.

"And just where have *you* been?"

She had thought all along that she'd stay cool and reserved. But as soon as he entered the room, she sat up straight and lashed out, surprising even herself.

"Now that sounds just like a jealous wife. Good role-playing, Hope," he complimented her.

"A jealous wife?" She reared up. "How about a concerned partner? A worried friend?" No way she'd want him to think she was jealous.

"I was with Melanie."

"Tell me something I don't know."

"I was trying to get something out of her."

"More like trying to get something in her, I would have thought."

139

His head jerked to attention. "Did you say what I think you said?"

"Did you do what I think you did?" Oh! How she hated that he made her resort to such lowlife stuff as this.

"I was trying to get her to put out, Hope."

"Well, let's not sugar-coat it for my benefit."

"Put out information."

"Oh, that's right. You're a spy. A spy who's on a mission. I almost forgot." She rolled her eyes at him. "Or perhaps it's *you* who almost forgot."

"What does that mean?" He mimicked her rolling eyes.

"You tell me."

"Tell you what?" He screwed up his face and shook his head. "It's all just business, Hope. You know that. Besides, I didn't do anything major with Melanie. What kind of husband do you think I am?"

He appeared sincerely taken aback. But she wasn't falling for it.

"So it was all minor-league play, huh?" She arched an eyebrow at him. "How far did you get? Second base? Third? A grand slam?"

"Not *play*. Business," he reaffirmed.

"Of course, it was," she snipped. "And I don't want to tell you how to go about your business, but you might want to be more discreet. You could blow our cover, you know."

He nodded so readily it felt patronizing. "What can I say, Hope? You're absolutely right."

Tugging at his tie, he slid it from around his neck and then stuffed it into his pants pocket. Then he removed his tux jacket, and headed for the closet to hang it up. The happy tune he whistled irritated the heck out of her. Apparently he wasn't about to let their little tiff dampen his good mood . . .

"And, um, one other thing . . ." She tried to keep her voice strong and authoritative.

He paused in mid-step and looked at her questioningly. She continued, "I think it's time you tell me what's going on."

"Ah, Hope." His shoulders slumped, and the tux jacket skimmed the floor. "I really don't want to get you too deeply involved. It's for your own safety."

"Did you ever think it could be the best thing for my protection?"

He tilted his head, as if considering her question. But she knew from the look in his eyes that he wasn't going to budge. Not easily anyhow.

It was time to play her trump card. "I saw our creepy Cadillac buddies a little while ago."

"No kidding?" His eyebrows shot up. His eyes did a sobering double-blink. "I knew they'd show up here. I just wasn't sure what time they'd arrive. Hmph," he said almost to himself, "Guess I'll have to figure out which room they're in."

He started off again to hang up his tux jacket. She halted him in his tracks with her smug reply.

"Three-twenty-two."

Information disclosed, she sat back in the enveloping folds of the cushy chair. She crossed her legs again, making sure the slit in the dress fell open just right to reveal every inch of her thigh.

He was flabbergasted by her answer, and she could tell the sight of her leg took him aback, too.

"What?" he exclaimed, lifting his gaze from her exposed thigh to her eyes.

"They're in room three-twenty-two. From the elevator, it's the fifth door down. Right side of the hallway."

"How did you find out?" She watched his eyes drift to her nude leg again.

Men! So predictable . . . so—like men!

"Did you ask Griggs?"

"Are you kidding?" She flashed an indignant glare. "No, I did not ask Griggs. I followed them."

"You what?" Chandler's head popped, a look of alarm contorting his face. "Hope, you really shouldn't be snooping around on your own."

"Well, if you recall, dearest hubby," she replied sweetly, "you were a little tied up this evening."

"Well, I . . ." His worried expression quickly gave way to a devilish smirk, a look that told her more than she wanted to know.

She cringed. "Oh, my gosh! Don't even tell me." She held up her hands and uncrossed her legs, tugging at her dress to pull it together. "It's just lucky for you that I found out what their next move is going to be."

"So . . ." He inched a bit closer. "Are you going to tell me?" he asked, responding to her bait. But she was playing hard to get.

"Sure, I'll tell you," she said sweetly, tilting her head and folding her arms over her chest. "But you have to make me a promise."

He instantly raised his right hand. "I hereby promise that I will not spend any more time alone with Ms. Dreyer."

"Oh, I don't care about her," Hope shrugged indifferently. "Past, present or future."

"No?" He looked a mite disappointed. "You don't?"

"Uh-uh." She shook her head and hid her crossed fingers under her arm. "Not at all."

"Okay then." She watched him struggle to shrug off her rejection. "What's the promise?"

Chapter Nine

Like so many other situations in life, Sela had dived into the canal without much forethought. And like other times, too, she had come up empty-handed . . . well, except for a soggy ricotta cheese package that was wrapped around her wrist like a bracelet.

But no Giorgio.

Wet from head to toe and smelling like a dumpster, she sloshed her way back to her apartment. She was fretful about Giorgio's safety and was thankful when the phone rang. How she prayed it would be him!

"Giorgio!" She all but shouted into the phone.

"Ex . . . <gasp> . . . actly." Her superior's familiar wheeze caught her off guard. "When are you . . . going to . . . bring him in?" he panted.

Clearly the man needed more oxygen going to his brain. The lack of it was affecting his judgment. "Bring him in? He's done nothing wrong."

"We have . . . proof," he sputtered.

"So do I," she countered.

"Bring . . . him in, S. T. Or else—"

She knocked the phone receiver against the wall and blew into it, mimicking a mini tornado. "Sorry. I'm losing you, sir. Try you back later, okay?" She crashed the receiver back into its cradle.

Giorgio guilty? How ridiculous, she fumed. He was being framed. Duped by Cirella Carducci, the woman she had seen in his villa. Oh, he may not be a total innocent, she smiled dreamily, remembering the luscious way he kissed. But he certainly wasn't guilty of a crime, for goodness' sake!

"Promise me? Cross your heart?"

"Oh hell, Hope." He wished she'd stop looking at him like that with those gigantic, gorgeous eyes of hers. It made him feel so weak. He may have spent the last couple of hours with the curvaceous curator, but somehow just two minutes with Hope could impair his better judgment.

"You know I won't be any trouble. In fact, I might even be a lot of help," she persisted. "Let me be a full-fledged Mona with you on this."

"I don't know." He shook his head. "I mean, I know you found out about the Caddy crew in a matter of minutes, while I couldn't get much out of Melanie in two hours."

Hope arched a disbelieving eyebrow at him.

"Well, that is to say, not much in the way of information anyway." He came clean. "But I'm concerned, Hope." He could feel his own eyebrows pinching together in a serious frown, his shoulders tensing underneath his tux shirt. "You could get hurt."

"Now how on earth would that happen," she purred, batting her eyelashes his way, "when I have you to protect me?"

Some women were easy to ignore when they put on a flirty voice like that. It came off as trite or too pushy. But with Hope, somehow it seemed adorably captivating. Maybe because there was a certain shyness attached to it. Whatever. However she did it, it was working really well on him. And he could tell she knew it too, by the way she cunningly used those eyes of hers for an extra dose of persuasion. Not only were they tantalizing him and hard to turn down, they were lit up with excitement, too.

Why does she get to me like this? he wondered.

"So . . ." He sighed like a man defeated. "The goons are meeting someone downstairs in the Oak Room after it closes?"

She nodded. "That's what it sounded like. I think I heard them say someone had a bartender cousin who would let them in."

"Hmm . . . wonder if our Ms. Dreyer will be there, too?"

"Mel is in on this caper?" Hope's eyes widened. "Chandler, this is driving me crazy. Please tell me what's going on."

He hesitated, sauntering toward the mini bar instead. "Would you like another? What are you drinking? A screwdriver?" he asked.

"Orange Crush. Sure, I'll have another."

"Orange Crush?" He almost laughed aloud. She was such a knockout, and so sophisticated-looking, too. Appearances would dictate that she was sipping on a Courvoisier or Zambuca. But then there was that dichotomy about her again.

"I wanted to be able to think clearly." She seemed to read his mind.

"Ah-hah." He grabbed himself a brandy and sat down on the bed across from where she was seated in the chair.

"It's kind of a long story, so here's the abbreviated version." He took a sip of his drink, the miniature snifter feeling too small and delicate in his hands.

"As you may have guessed, there are many forgeries in the art world. Many times it occurs with artifacts and sculpted works from ancient civilizations. I suppose that's because it's a lot easier replicating those than, say, a famous painting, for instance."

"That makes sense." Hope nodded, looking thoughtful and distant all at the same time.

"Wow. That was fast."

"What was fast?"

"You're already thinking about book number five, aren't you?" He cocked an eyebrow at her. "I can see the wheels churning."

"Possibly," she replied, eyes gleaming.

"Anyway," he swirled the brandy around in its glass, "as with so many other luxury items, an international black market exists for these artifacts. In particular, we've zeroed in on a group that's dealing in Pre-Columbian art. It seems forgeries are fairly prevalent with the pieces from that era and area of the world."

"So you and Mona have pretended to be part of the bad guys, the forgers, right?"

"Correct. Except, obviously, we're really the entrappers." He took another sip from his glass and felt the smooth liquid leave a burning trail down his esophagus. His shoulders were beginning to relax. And his thoughts were too, his eyes slipping over her dress, his mind recalling how incredible it felt to have her pressed against him on the dance floor. "Mona and I were actually supposed to deliver a replica to the Cadillac guys yesterday, but we hadn't gotten it from the lab yet. So she had to go back out last night and make the drop."

"By herself? While we were at your mom's eating? That stinks."

He shrugged. "Some days are like that. Anyway, the authentic piece will be up for grabs in the silent auction tomorrow."

"What is it exactly?"

"Actually, I have an extra replica in my suitcase just as a backup."

He slid off the bed, making his way to the closet on the other side of the room. Rummaging through his suitcase, he came up with the fake artifact and presented it to Hope.

"That's it?" Hope held out her hand for the crafted wooden piece, a figure resembling some kind of tribesman. "Why, it's adorable. And kind of exquisite all at the same time."

It crossed his mind that the description aptly fit Hope too.

"Like a little soldier," she mused, turning the miniature six-inch statue on its side. "My gosh, look at all the gems on this. Turquoise, mother-of-pearl—"

"Lapis lazuli, greenstone, silver," he continued. "It actually dates back to around 600 to 1000 A.D. It's a rare Huari figure of a dignitary."

"How much is it worth?" she asked.

His gaze met hers. "Well, that depends. The one you're holding is only worth the value of the materials it's made from, because it's a forgery. But the real piece could bring a price as high as a quarter of a million dollars."

Hope whistled. "Wow!" Her luscious-looking mouth hung open. "So tomorrow at the auction, I mean, how will—?"

He shrugged. "Probably what will happen is that somehow the pieces will get switched after the gavel comes down and before the piece is turned over to the buyer."

"Melanie?"

"It's a good possibility," he nodded. "Although like I said, I couldn't get much out of her."

Hope muttered something he couldn't quite detect. Something like, "Maybe you're slipping?" *Naw!*

"Pardon me?" he asked, leaning closer.

"I said, why even switch them?" she asked. "Can people really tell the difference?"

"Believe it or not, the crooks dealing in the black market know their art better than the rich and famous. The rich have money to burn, while the crooks need money to earn. And if they have an unscrupulous curator helping to make the switch for a small fee, it's not too tough. Everybody makes money; everybody's happy."

He sat the glass down on the nightstand. "So that's the story. But we're merely talking about one piece right this minute. This kind of thing goes on all the time."

From the look on her face, Chandler knew she could barely contain herself. She glanced at the clock sitting on the armoire. "We'd better get down to the Oak Room and get situated before they get there, don't you think?"

"Hope, seriously." He shook his head at her. "I'm really not crazy about the idea of you coming along."

"Hey, remember? You wouldn't even know they were meeting, if it weren't for me. Plus, you promised material for my writing."

He sighed, knowing all along that his stalling was useless. Hope was already arching those shapely calves of hers, putting her heels back on.

"But how will we get into the bar, since it's closed?" She tugged at her shoe.

"Huh?" He found himself momentarily distracted, watching her. "Oh, never fear." He gave her a half-hearted grin. "I've watched a lot of 'McGyver' reruns over the years. Believe me, getting in is the least of our worries."

The potent, intermingled scents of cigar smoke and charbroiled steaks lingered in the Oak Room. The atmosphere was clubby, to say the least, with handsomely-carved oak adorning the décor and hunter-green leather furnishings placed all about.

Hope had helped Chandler redo his tie before they left the honeymoon suite, and she had spent a moment to touch up her hair. Still decked out in their evening attire, they would have been among the best dressed in the place, if it had still been open to patrons. But it wasn't, of course.

Luckily, Chandler easily picked their way into the secured pub, and then relocked the door behind them.

Once inside, they scoped out the lay of the room, deciding it best to head for the massive, wooden bar. It seemed the logical place to hide out and wait for the gangsters and whomever else to arrive. Hope's stomach churned. Hopefully, she had heard the thugs correctly. She'd be embarrassed if she'd botched up the information she'd given Chandler.

Not a minute after they had settled in behind the bar, they heard someone fiddling with keys in the lock of the main door. Hope's adrenaline instantly shot up. Chandler, meanwhile, slid open the door of a man-sized cabinet behind the bar, a storage area for bar napkins and other paper products. He hurriedly swished the supplies out of the way, climbing into the makeshift cubbyhole. Hope stood staring at him, till he yanked her inside right along with him.

Landing in the cradle of his lap, facing him, the silvery blue dress rose up her legs and she could feel the solidness of his thighs from under his tux pants. With quick hands, he pushed up the slippery material of her gown even farther, past her thighs, setting her legs free. Then taking a calf in his hand, one at a time, he positioned her legs so that she was straddling him.

A gasp escaped her, and she blinked at him in wide-eyed disbelief. Not that it wasn't the prime position for them, considering the space they had to deal with. And not that she didn't feel surprisingly at home conjoined with the international spy. But still . . . a guy could ask a girl before he went wrapping her legs around him like a boa, couldn't he?

However, her indignant stare didn't seem to register on him. Instead, he merely raised a finger to his lips, signaling for her to be quiet. Then he pulled her tightly against his chest. And, no, he didn't ask permission to do that either.

Both so quiet they were barely breathing, their bodies were bound together in a tense hug. Consequently, they jumped out of their skins when the blurry ringing of Hope's cell phone broke the silence.

"What the—?" she heard Chandler curse as she pulled the phone from its holding place, a bra insert sown into her dress.

"Uncle Cary?" she whispered. "What are you doing up so late? Poker, huh? Yes, I know . . . I had planned on being home. But it's getting so late, I'll probably just stay. Look, can I call you back later?"

She listened to his response. "You ran into who? Old Mrs. Gallina? A man in a Porsche kidnapping me?" Pause. "Good, I'm glad you set her straight. You're right. Chan's your man. Of course, I'm fine with him. But how exciting can a dinner for accountants be? Skimpy on dessert, yeah. We were just meeting some friends of his in the lounge now. Yes, if it gets too late, we'll stay in the city for the night . . . Yes, we have separate rooms," she fibbed.

Pause again. Chandler rolled his eyes and made circles with his hand, giving her a signal to wrap it up. Still, Uncle Cary kept talking.

"What?" she spoke faintly. "I don't know. I'll ask him."

She covered the phone, speaking to Chandler. "Norm Hobbs is over at Uncle Cary's. He wants to know if you'll do his tax returns, too," she whispered softly.

"Anything. Just get him off the phone," he hissed.

"Tell Norm 'yes.' Okay . . . love you too, Uncle Cary."

Hope flipped the phone shut and inserted it back into her cleavage.

"Great timing," Chandler grunted, pulling her against him again.

The bar's door creaked as it opened, and the sound of footsteps followed. The footsteps definitely sounded male, thumping loudly as they hit the hardwood floor. But there was only one set, which was puzzling. The person kept coming nearer to the bar, until it was obvious that Chandler and Hope had a visitor they weren't expecting.

With the wooden sliding door still open, they could see the man's legs move behind the bar, and heard him open a glass decanter and pour a drink. He sat the glass down on the bar right over their heads. Next, he moved to the end of the bar, where he opened and closed some kind of container. Then he moved back to where his drink was sitting. They could've reached out and knocked on his knees, he was so close.

The sound of crinkling cellophane was the next thing to be heard. Then the visitor struck a match and the distinctive smell of a cigar began to fill the air. That was when the muttering started.

"Always watching the home shopping channel . . . twenty-four hours a day . . . impossible spoiled cat in her lap . . ." He paused and puffs of smoke shot into the air. "Work, work, work so she can buy, buy, buy . . . good-bye is what I'd like to say."

Hope looked at Chandler. Chandler looked at Hope. They nodded in silent realization, both recognizing the man's voice. It was definitely Griggs.

Chandler moved into action, taking the most obvious precaution just in case Griggs caught them in their peculiar hiding place. First, he slipped the straps of her dress off her shoulders. Then he cradled her head, smothering her with his lips, kissing her as if the rest of the world was totally nonexistent. It all happened so fast that she wasn't certain it was really happening. Except there was one thing she was sure of—something was stirring between them, and it wasn't just her heart.

Chandler's timing was pretty good, too, because next they heard Griggs' glass tip over on the bar. He cursed aloud and reached underneath the bar into their cabinet for some napkins to wipe up the mess.

Knowing they were about to be exposed, Chandler hoisted a handful of napkins up to Griggs, while maintaining his lip lock on Hope.

"Aaahyee!" Griggs screamed slightly effeminately, when his hand met Chandler's alien one. Out of the corner of her eye, Hope could see from below as Griggs' legs did a visible, heart-jumping skip. Next, they both spied his startled face as he bent down to investigate.

"Mr. and Mrs. Chandler?" His eyes were wide and befuddled-looking, his usual aplomb gone. "My, you two really do like to 'romp' around most anywhere, don't you?"

But Chandler wouldn't be rushed through his exhibition. Still grasping Hope by her shoulders, he held her in a long, passionate, heedless kiss. Then for special effect, he gave her several more abbreviated, loving smooches. Slow and deliberate. Brushing, tickling her with his lips . . . as if he had to wean himself from kissing her . . . as if breaking apart from her was nearly impossible.

When his lips finally parted from hers, she was left completely dazzled. Although, after catching her breath, she still had enough wits about her to mentally give his performance a five-star rating.

Meanwhile, Chandler appeared in total command, finally acknowledging Griggs's greeting. "Good evening, Griggs. I'd give you a proper handshake, but as you can see my hands are full at the moment."

Hope gazed up at her husband dreamily as he spoke, acting her part superbly, which wasn't all that difficult. Modestly, she crossed her hands over her chest to cover the curves revealed as a result of her fallen dress straps.

Griggs cleared his throat. "Are you finding the honeymoon suite is uh . . . lacking, sir?"

"On the contrary," Chandler assured him. "It's fabulous, Griggs. It really is. But, you know, we don't want to fall into the same old tired habits."

"Er . . . yes . . . same old tired habits," Griggs grumbled under his breath.

"I'll bet you and your wife make a date to stay in the honeymoon suite quite regularly, don't you, Griggs? I know I would take advantage of that, if I were you. That room can really put some zip in your doo-da, if you know what I mean."

"Why, I . . . yes, the honeymoon suite," Griggs stammered. "Our, um—actually our anniversary is coming up in the next couple of weeks, and I . . ." He paused and a glimmer of hope shone in his eyes. "Yes, I think we may be booked for that. But you know, I should go and check on it again, now that you mention it." He swiped up the spilled drink hurriedly and put out his cigar. "Well, it was a pleasure running into both of you again." He started to go, and then looked back down at them. "By the way, how did you get in the Oak Room? The door was locked."

"Love knows no obstacles, Griggs," Chandler answered profoundly.

"How true," Griggs agreed with a nod.

153

Hope stifled a giggle until after Griggs was on his way; then she and Chandler climbed out of their cozy hiding place. But their reprieve was short-lived as they heard a new wave of approaching footsteps. They squatted down, out of sight, behind the bar.

The gangsters' Brooklyn accents were easy to identify, their voices as loud and full of bravado as if they owned the place. Surely, Chandler's wires would be sensitive enough to pick up their conversation from where they stood in the middle of the room.

"Yo, your cousin Mickey's a cool dude," the boss man was saying. "Tell him thanks for hooking us up, man." Chandler and Hope could hear the two cronies in crime slapping their hands together, probably giving each other a high-five.

"Think she'll show?" his underling asked.

"Are you kidding? She likes nice things, and she needs money to buy them. She'll be here," he reassured his subordinate.

Hope stood up slightly from her crouching position and peeked curiously over the bar at the twosome. She caught a quick glimpse of the paunchy, shorter thug holding the replica of the Huari figure. That was right before Chandler yanked her back down by his side.

"I was kinda getting used to this little dude," they heard the hired help say with a sad, wistful tone in his voice.

"Hey, for the kind of money we're going to make, you can get yourself all kinds of fakes like that one."

It wasn't long before Melanie showed up. In minutes, the transfer of the Pre-Columbian forgery and money was made, and the deal was sealed.

"I can take Melanie if you can take on the two thugs," Hope whispered to Chandler.

He looked at her like she was fourteen-karat crazy. "Are you out of your mind?"

"You're going to just let them walk out of here?"

"Since they haven't committed any crime yet . . . yes."

"But—"

He put a finger up to Hope's lips. "Good things come to those who wait."

For a moment Hope wondered if he was just rifling off another platitude for the evening, or if his words held any prophetic meaning.

Dressed in her new sleepwear, Hope peered into the gilded framed bathroom mirror, quizzing her reflection. How had so many things happened all in one, short day? Had it really only been this morning that Chandler had come to her door begging—okay, asking her ardently—to be his wife for the evening? It seemed nearly impossible, like another lifetime ago.

After she had said yes, she'd rushed out to Mitchell's department store as soon as it opened and did some quick shopping for the trip. Mostly she had scooped up some basics that had long been lacking from her wardrobe.

First on her list were undies, the ones she was supposed to have bought the other day. Hers were in dire shape, having been laundered at least ten thousand times. They were so stretched out and barren of elastic, it was hard to tell which hole was for what.

Then, too, she needed a new nightgown or a pair of pajamas. As comfy as her old ones were, they were extremely faded and threadbare. Even though she hadn't figured on a roommate at that point, she'd still be embarrassed to answer the door for room service. Or worse yet, what if there was a fire drill? Somehow it had seemed fitting to visit the

Plaza with these new basic essentials.

Now, as things turned out, she wished she had her sloppy old long-johns with her. Chandler had seen her in those plenty of times. What would he think now when she stepped out of the bathroom and into the bedroom wearing the pink, slinky robe she had bought the other day with the newly-purchased matching nightgown underneath? Would he think she was ready for action? Plotting to seduce him?

Well, I can't stay in the bathroom all night, she told herself, *even if it is as big as my bedroom back home. Maybe if I act totally nonchalant, he'll never notice what I am—or am not—wearing.*

Stalling a few minutes more before making her grand entrance into the bedroom, she went about her nightly business with deliberate slowness. First she took out her contacts, opting not to put on her glasses, preferring to go semi-blindly into the night. Then she brushed every last tooth, flossed twice, and re-pinned her hair into a loose knot. But having done all that, she knew she couldn't put it off any longer. She took a deep breath and gave her reflection a final, approving glance in the bathroom mirror. Turning out the light, she retreated to the bedroom of the honeymoon suite.

Chapter Ten

Mom,

Chelsea Reye—wear deodrent before boys do even though boys need it more than girls. Does that make sense? I don't think girls ever make sense. She said next year some boys will wear deodrent?????

1,234,579

"What are you reading?"

Her face felt fiery, at least five shades pinker than her lingerie. Still, she worked hard to make her voice sound casual—as casual as if they were two fully-clothed strangers, sharing a seat on a crowded bus or something.

However, nothing could be further from the truth. Chandler was stretched out on the right side of the king-sized sleigh bed farthest away from her. One hand rested behind his neck; the other held a paperback. His hair was loose and soft-looking now that the gel had lost its hold. He still had on his tux pants, black socks and white dress shirt with onyx cufflinks.

His shirt was unbuttoned from top to bottom, and Hope tried not to look. She felt naked in her mere two-piece ensemble with her new pair of lacy panties hidden underneath. That was three items of clothing compared to his six pieces. Luckily, they weren't vying each other in a game of strip poker. Though looking at him leisurely stretched out like that, she knew most women would think she was out of her mind for not suggesting to go a hand or two with him.

He held up the book cover for her to see, and she noticed his face was as carnation pink as her own probably was. Maybe he was doing his utmost to appear at ease, too.

"You're kidding." She laughed. "*Lovestruck in London Town?*"

"Your third novel, so it says here on the back cover. And you 'just keep getting better and sexier.' " He paused, and added with a glint in his eye, "What I want to know is . . . are they referring to you or your writing?"

"Very funny." She grabbed a pillow from the closest side of the bed and threw it at him.

"Hey, watch it. You'll make me lose my place." He fended the pillow off his chest. "I'm just getting to the part with Sela and Rupert."

"Oh, really?"

He had actually bought a book of hers! She was so delightfully flattered that she couldn't resist toppling onto the enormous bed. Ever mindful of her lack of clothing, she tried to sit a safe distance away in a guarded position. She sat with her back against the footboard and her feet resting by his upper body. Holding a pillow like a fluffy chastity belt protectively across her lap, she added, "The part where the Queen is kidnapped and Sela and Rupert find her?"

"Let's see, in this part Sela and Rupert are . . ." His eyes scanned the page. "Well, actually they're . . ." His eyes got wider as he continued scanning. "They're . . . um, well . . . it's the part that starts with, 'his hand lingered on the bodice of her . . .' " His mumble became less and less audible, until it came to a stop. "I'm not sure this is group reading material."

She crinkled up her nose, squinted her eyes and clenched her teeth in total embarrassment. If only she could disappear into the mattress, sink so deep never to be found again. Instinctively, she reached up and tried to pull the sides of her robe closer together across her breasts. However, the scant material didn't budge. It was already covering her to its fullest potential.

"Page sixty-two, right?" She finally found her voice.

"And sixty-three, and," he flipped through the pages, "wow, part of sixty-four, too." He could barely tear his eyes away from the text.

"It was their first time," Hope explained, trying to justify her writing.

"Is this the part my mom thought I should learn new tricks from?" he teased, looking up at her.

She gave him a tight, wry smile. "I think not."

He seemed to notice he might have gone too far and tried to backpedal with a compliment. "You must have a great imagination. Seriously. I mean, this stuff is from your imagination, right?"

"Well, of course, it is!" She felt it necessary to defend her virtuosity. However, at the same time, she didn't want him to think she was some kind of Rebecca of Sunnybrook Farm. "But I am of age, you know. I've been around some. Though I'm sure I couldn't hold a candle to your gadabouts."

"Gadabouts?" He laid the book aside and crossed his arms across his chest. His grin was so irresistible that she scooted back against the footboard as far as she could. "Oh, I get it. You're feeling embarrassed, so you're trying to turn the focus to me."

She tilted her head, arching an eyebrow at him. "No, but it's a given you get around a lot more than I do. What was your last assignment? Saving an heiress? Freeing a beautiful princess?"

"Actually, last month I was in Greece searching for a U.S. diplomat's daughter who'd been abducted."

"Ah, that's sweet. But I'm talking about a mission where the female is of age. Surely you've had plenty of those."

"Oh, she was of age, all right." He nodded in fond remembrance. "But it was nothing. Sometimes you have to play the part, act involved. In my line of work, saving lives comes with the territory. When you save someone's life, sometimes those people want to show their appreciation." He held up his hands in a hopeless gesture. "What's a guy to do?" He smiled impishly.

Hope looked down her nose at him. "My point exactly."

"Hey, if you knew me at all, you'd know that at heart I'm just a small-town guy with small-town, conservative values."

"Who just happens to know women on a world-wide scale, and I mean that in its biblical sense."

"I don't know why you're being so hard on me." He sat up and looked at her intently. He didn't seem to be laughing so much anymore. "You have an imagination; I have an image. It's not totally real or totally us. It's just part of the job, right?"

Now she felt bad. She should've never pushed the conversation so far in this direction. "I'm sorry. It's none of my business anyway." She shook her head and realized how tight her neck and shoulder muscles were. Tilting her head from side to side, she rolled her shoulders, trying to relieve the pressure.

"Stress from the day?" He looked concerned.

She half-grimaced, half-smiled. "It always seems to settle in my neck and shoulders."

"I learned some about massage therapy and reflexology when I was in the Orient—"

"Along with martial arts," she quipped.

He nodded. "See, I'm not always up to no-good. I actually learn some valuable things on my assignments, too." He popped up from the bed and came around behind her, lightly touching her shoulders. "Do you want me to give it a try?"

"You don't have to," she said with just a modicum of resistance.

"I know I don't have to." His hands had already started working their magic. He massaged her shoulders gently, kneading away the tension there. Intermittently, he'd reach up and rub the sides of her neck, easing the stiffness. In response, her body automatically relaxed, her shoulders falling limp under the caress of his soothing hands.

"Mmm," she moaned. "Thank you so much. This feels so good." She patted the back of his hand gratefully. "So martial arts and massage therapy? You really are a jack of all trades," she crooned.

"And did I mention? If you need help with one of the—" He cleared his throat. "You know, other parts of your book, I'm available too." His hands delicately stroked the area under her shoulder blades.

Kidding or not, just the way he said it made her giggle. "I think you already gave me a lot of material with that kiss in the elevator and the make-out session underneath the bar."

"Well, okay, then." He rubbed at her temples. "I just wanted you to know if you need any help . . ."

It seemed odd to her that she felt so comfortable being in this Manhattan hotel room with this man. Not scared. Not threatened. Not feeling guilty. Just enjoying their light banter and the therapeutic feel of his hands. In fact, his hands seemed such a natural fit to her, at home on her skin. It was becoming increasingly harder to deny that her body could so easily yield to his touch.

And would that be so bad? she wondered. It's not like she did this sort of thing all the time. And wouldn't it be better with Chandler? He wasn't really ingrained in her life or in Theo's. He couldn't hurt them the way they'd been hurt before.

She wouldn't have to put up with any entanglements . . . or disappointments . . . or heartaches later on, because there was no "later." There was only now. In a week, he'd be gone. Was it possible to just have this one night?

Lacking the nerve to turn around and face him with her thoughts, she looked straight ahead, her voice quivering as she spoke. "There is this one part . . ."

His hands shifted and he began massaging her upper arms. Admittedly, it felt delicious. "I'm listening."

"I was kind of thinking ahead to book five, like you mentioned earlier." Her mind went to work, quickly fabricating an impromptu scene. "And well, Sela and the hero are undercover as a married couple."

"Sounds oddly familiar." His hands kept working their magic.

"Anyway, they wind up snowbound in a log cabin together."

His hands stopped. "Is this pre-fab log cabin or an authentic one? In the foothills or on a mountaintop?"

"Does it matter?" She laughed.

"Just trying to get a mental image here." He continued rubbing at the cap of her shoulders.

"Okay. So they've kissed a few times that day when they were—"

He interrupted her. "Pretending to be married?"

"Right. But in the scene they're going to really kiss for the first time."

"Just as themselves, right?" His hands eased up. "Interesting."

"So, how do you think that would unravel? Step by step, I mean."

He was a smart man. He'd know this was her coy way of initiating something physical with him.

But what if he flat-out isn't interested? Her stomach felt hollow and sick.

"Hmm. I'll have to think about that a moment." He stopped massaging her then, and Hope's internal distress bordered on critical. What if he simply blew her off? Then again, what if he didn't?

He moved around to face her, and she wasn't sure what to expect next. Scooping her up in his arms, he turned her around in bed, resting her head on a pillow. He sat down on the comforter beside her, his voice deep yet soft as he spoke.

"First, I think the hero would look into her eyes." He sought her eyes and, syllable after syllable, his gaze never wavered from them. "That way, she'd know he was looking just at her. Not looking at her like she was someone else, you know. Really looking. Knowing. Seeing the very core of her being."

Hope's fixed look couldn't tear away from his, and she noticed that her inner turmoil had instantly subsided. A new sensation began to fill her. It was a trembling . . . it was a quivering . . . it was good.

"And then I think he would make every move deliberate and sure, like he was in slow-motion. He'd probably caress her face for starters." He reached up and let the same hand that had soothed her shoulders bring a surprising feel of electricity to her cheek. A shiver ran down the side of her face from her earlobe to her chin. "And then, he'd kiss her . . . a tentative, first kiss."

He cupped her face in his hands, and let his lips faintly brush hers. His lower lip teased at hers, taunting her . . . once . . . twice . . . three times. *How could something so simple, such a soft, wispy feel, ignite my entire body with such overwhelming, heated desire?* she wondered. Coming near, then pulling back, leaving her mouth wanton, longing for more.

"How would you describe that?"

"Wistful. Blissful. Wonderful." She smiled languidly.

"Is that something you could use? In your book, I mean?"

She nodded. "Definitely."

"Good. Because then he would search her eyes, wondering if she wanted more. And he would hope that what he saw there would tell him that she did."

She made sure to do an Academy Award–winning job of speaking to him with her eyes. He smiled. "Even better. Because then his next kiss could be more passionate."

Her lips were already parted in anticipation, ready for the thrust of his tongue, the full effect of his kiss. She wasn't disappointed, and even surprised herself the way her body countered with an unbridled urgency of its own.

He eased his lips from hers. "Are you getting all of this down, Ms. Starr?"

"All of it." She nodded again.

"Any way you plan to describe it?" he asked.

"I think I'm at a loss for words at the moment."

He chuckled. "God, Hope, I know there's been a lot of pretending today. But reality is I've wanted to do that since the first morning we met. Since the first time I saw Dani hold this robe up to you, I had visions of you wrapped in it." His hand slid over the silky material down her arm, squeezing her hand.

She didn't respond to his admission with words of her own. Instead, she sat up and slowly untied the sash of her robe. He parted the sides of the pink silk, his hands brushing across her breasts underneath. Pushing back the silk from her shoulders, his eyes washed over her appreciatively, seeming to savor the sight of her bare shoulders.

As she freed her arms from the robe, she noticed he had already started to remove his cufflinks. That done, she reached out and removed his shirt, marveling once again at the effect his body had on her. He came to her then and lay next to her.

His arms seemed to be the best place she'd been in a long, long time. Her pleasure was so intense just lying there; she felt she could stay that way forever.

That is, until her cell phone rang.

"Probably Cary," Chandler said matter-of-factly.

She looked at him and winced.

"You have to answer it," he declared, kissing her forehead sweetly. "Make sure everything is okay."

He rolled one way in the huge bed, and she rolled the other to answer the phone.

"Uncle Cary? Is everything all right? Is Theo okay?" Pause. "No, I'm doing fine. Really, I'm okay."

"More than okay . . ." Chandler whispered as he adjusted his pillow and reposed into a comfortable-looking position, his hands locked behind his head.

Hope smiled at his compliment, wanting nothing more than to roll back over by him, and take up where they'd left off. Still she tried to tune into Uncle Cary's main reason for calling.

"What about Fiona? Was it something she ate?" Pause. "Sure you can. No, it's too late for the drugstore. You have the key. You didn't need to call and ask." Pause. "Well, that's true, finding anything in my house isn't that easy. Let's see . . . Mylanta." Long pause. "First look in the upstairs linen closet, and if it's not there . . . could be under the sink in the hall bath . . . or try the cupboard in the kitchen where I keep the glasses. It's in one of those places, I'm sure."

Uncle Cary was so animated and talkative Hope wondered how many Mountain Dews he'd had while playing cards that evening. A few more minutes of polite chatter, and then she'd tell him her battery was running low. Though that was a bold-faced lie, she smirked to herself, glancing over at the hunk of a man next to her. Actually, she was all charged up and ready to go—just as soon as she got off the phone here.

However . . . too bad she couldn't say the same for Chandler.

When she had glanced over a moment ago, his eyes had been closed. Just resting them, she had figured. But now he was turned away from her, curled up in a fetal position, his chest moving evenly up and down.

It seemed impossible that only a few minutes before they had been locked in one another's arms, sparks flying and loins on fire.

How humiliating! She sulked, sinking into her pillows and to a new all-time low. She had been all set to shoot for the moon and reach for the stars. Meanwhile, he opted to snooze under them.

Chapter Eleven

Sela gasped. No sooner had she gotten off the phone with her superior when a woman in head-to-toe black scuba togs and a dazed, drugged man who resembled Giorgio entered her living room from the terrace.

Wait a minute . . . that was Giorgio! Although it was hard to tell, since he smelled like raw sewage and was covered in—oh, yuck! The Venetian canals sure weren't what they used to be.

The woman took off her mask and cap, and instantly Sela recognized her as the villainous Cirella Carducci. Sela wasn't frightened as much as envious. Here she was, a stinky mess from her impromptu swim in the canal. In contrast, Cirella not only looked great and curvy in the rubber suit, but her black-as-night hair was dry and styled in a chic, blunt cut.

"So you're not a true blonde after all?" Sela asked her.

"Ha! It was only a wig." The woman shook her head and sneered. "And I'm not really Italian either. Carducci is an alias."

"You're a liar? A fraud?" And a raven-haired beauty, Sela thought to herself.

Cirella scoffed. "Only a few of my many skills. I'm an executioner, too," she said, beaming proudly. "I had hoped to lure you into the canal once I tipped over this goofus." She pointed to Giorgio. "But you slipped through my hands like an eel. However, I have a new plan. One shot to each of your heads," she said, pulling a small revolver out of her cap, "and then it's off the balcony with both of you. I'll try not to get any blood on your carpet by the way," she added, swinging the gun in the air.

"You're a real sweetheart," Sela answered tartly.

No way I'm going back into that murky water, Sela thought. Plus, I'm desperate for a shower. Oh . . . and to save Giorgio, of course.

Come on, Billy Blanks, Jet Li. Sela conjured up inspiration. Let's rumble.

"You're leaving?"

Chandler sat up in bed, scratching at the minimal patch of hair on his bare chest. Hope was already completely dressed in a burgundy boat-neck sweater, gray mid-calf wool skirt and boots, and was folding a blouse into her suitcase.

Must be in one helluva hurry, he thought. She hadn't even taken time to pop in her disposable lenses. Without sparing so much as a look in his direction, she nodded wordlessly, pushed her glasses up on the bridge of her nose and continued packing.

Last night there had been the beginnings of bodily contact between them. This morning she'd barely make eye contact with him. *Things aren't looking too good,* he quickly surmised. Though he supposed he had no one to blame but himself.

He glanced at the clock on the nightstand and tried to get his bearings. It was around nine, late for him to still be in bed, but he hadn't gotten much sleep at all last night.

He rubbed at his eyes. "Hey, why don't I take you out to breakfast?" he offered, when she didn't answer his first question. "There's a great place about four blocks from here and—"

"Thanks," she cut him off, "but I remembered there are some things I want to take care of today. Theo's birthday is next weekend. I have no idea what I'm doing for his party. Or what I'm getting him. Or anything."

"Oh." *Conveniently remembered* is what she really meant, he knew.

Man, a guy can't win, can he? He shook his head to himself. *If you have sex with someone and leave in the morning, they're upset with you. And if you respect someone and abstain,* they *leave in the morning—and they're still ticked off at you.*

He watched helplessly as she put the last of her clothes in the suitcase and zipped it closed. *So I've really blown it with her, huh?* he thought as he watched her prepare for her departure. Even though blowing it with her was the last thing he wanted to do.

But, damn. He couldn't help it. Once they got started last night, the thought of making love to her didn't seem like such a great idea.

Scratch that.

It seemed like an incredible idea. Admittedly, one he'd been harboring in his mind for quite a while. But while she and Cary rambled on the phone, his thoughts had digressed too. Indeed, Cary's call brought a whole new meaning to the term "coitus interruptus."

Ultimately, after some consideration, he thought it best to forego the lovemaking and pretend to be asleep. Though it wasn't as easy as it had seemed. In fact, it was quite difficult.

And sleep? That was a joke. He'd watched the numbers on the clock glow red at him almost the entire night. It was nearly dawn when he'd finally gotten some shut-eye.

And think? That was a stretch, too. His mind was a muddled mess, a mass of confusion. After all, usually having sex wasn't a cerebral process for him. He didn't stop to probe the whys and wherefores of it. But all of a sudden he'd found himself thinking instead of acting.

Thinking . . .

About Hope. Focusing entirely on her. Not thinking about what he was going to get from her . . . but rather what he wanted to give to her. He realized he desired her in a much deeper way than he had ever imagined. Wanted to revel in the feel of her body till the moon faded away and the sun came up . . . wanted to explore every inch of her with his lips, and satisfy her in every way possible.

Why? It wasn't all entirely clear at the moment. He just knew he respected her as a person . . . as a single mom . . . what she was all about. Not that he didn't want to relish her as a very sexy female, too. But he'd backed off and feigned sleep, for his sake as well as hers—or so he thought.

Chandler felt helpless, watching Hope move purposefully around the room. Apparently as an afterthought, she remembered the icy blue sequined gown she'd worn last night and retrieved it from the closet, folding it gently, making a place for it in her suitcase.

He recalled the way she'd looked in the gown the night before, all lovely and luscious . . . the way she'd felt in his arms as he held her dancing, all curvy and sensuous. And then he'd found her, waiting for him back at the honeymoon suite, sitting patiently, sleek legs crossed, sipping on, of all things, her Orange Crush—

"Orange juice," he sputtered, bolting up in bed, snapping his fingers.

"Orange juice?" she repeated dully, zipping up her suitcase.

"I can call room service and order some orange juice for you." Maybe orange was the way to her heart? "Fresh-squeezed with pulp. Or—or no pulp?" he stammered. "Ice? No ice? Whatever you want," he offered magnanimously, dying for her to stay.

The mind did work in mysterious ways, didn't it? And his was working inanely. Her look told him she thought so, too.

"Hope, it's just that, well—" He shrugged his shoulders. "I'd really like for you to stay."

"For orange juice?" Again, her eyebrows pleated and she looked at him like he was crazy.

And he was, he realized in that very moment. Yes, crazy. Crazy about her.

"Well, not exactly. I want you to stay for—"

For what? For a minute? For five? Forever? For what, for God's sake?

He couldn't explain himself, even though she stood there waiting for an answer, her head tilted, her eyes mirroring her confusion. He already missed seeing the look of caring and trust—and well, sure, lust—that had been reflected in those eyes less than ten hours earlier.

Finally, when he didn't reply, she turned defiantly on her heels and headed for the bathroom. He jumped out of bed, clad only in his orange Hawaiian print boxers, forgetting he had shed his tux pants and the wire in the middle of the night. Before he could reach her, she slammed the bathroom door in his face.

Leaning against the frame, arms crossed over his chest, he listened to her gather up her toiletries, probably packing them into the navy pouch he'd seen lying on the counter. If he wasn't so stressed about her walking out of his life at the moment, he might have felt comfortable—at home even—standing there, listening to her doing even the most mundane of tasks.

171

In fact, it hit him that all through the night still-shots of Hope had flashed through his mind like an eight-millimeter projector gone rampant. Everyday images of Hope. Hope with Theo . . . Hope in her kitchen . . . Hope in Dani's salon window . . . Hope with the gangsters. A sensuous Hope. A curious Hope. A caring Hope.

As he lay there last night, he tried to visualize his neatly-typed five-year plan in his mind, but the brain cells wouldn't connect the dots for him. Was it because his heart was too busy visualizing other things?

Who knew? His mind was just as befuddled this morning as it had been last night. He had no idea what all these feelings meant, or what, if anything, he was going to do about them. But if Hope left now, would he ever know?

"Hope!" He knocked forcefully on the door. "Hope," he pleaded, desperation mounting in his voice. Would she really just leave? And what would he do? Follow her to Uncle Cary's? But he couldn't, not with the art auction . . . and Melanie . . . and the thugs, and . . .

"Hope," he yelled, resuming his rapping on the door, pounding like a madman. "I don't want to have to force you to stay," he threatened, his voice sounding oddly ominous.

At that, the door suddenly jerked open. Startled, he jumped back.

"Force me?" she snorted, waving her bulky blue make-up case at him. "Force me?" she repeated indignantly, coming at him, backing him into the heart of the suite. "What are you going to do? Tie me up with drapery cords? Zap me with a stun gun? What?"

Force her? She was right. He sounded like a jerk! What was he doing standing there in his boxers talking to her like that?

Grasping at straws is what I'm doing.

"Well, no, of course not."

He kept a pace behind her, making sure to dodge the flying kit she swung in the air at various intervals. Following her like a panicked pup as she moved deftly around the room, moving quickly out of his life. Depositing her make-up kit into her purse. Snapping it shut. Then picking up her suitcase and heading toward the door.

Leaving too fast, leaving him feeling fearful. Was she really walking out? It was a real role reversal for him. And it didn't feel good.

She set the suitcase down at the side of the door, and opened it a crack, ready to make her exit. She turned as if she were going to say something, but apparently changed her mind. And then without another word, she slipped out the door. Out into the hallway. Out of his life?

"Hope," he pleaded with her again, following her out into the corridor, watching as she pushed the button for the elevator that would take her away from him. "You know, leaving in the middle of an operation just isn't—well, it's not—" he grasped for a word, "professional."

"Professional?" she scoffed, swinging around and giving his brightly-colored Hawaiian boxers with their friendly *Aloha!* greetings printed all over them a derisive once-over. "Ha!" she laughed, seeming to look right through them.

She was right, of course. Standing there in the hallway in his gregarious underwear definitely wasn't one of his more stellar double-o-sevenish moments. James Bond would at least have been in black silk boxers or a gold robe flung open at the chest. Her eyes told him so, and so did the wary stares of an elderly couple making their way back to their room.

And he—James—wouldn't have been standing there begging, threatening, panicking. No, James would've hauled

173

this sweet, sassy, sexy woman back into the room and made mad, passionate love to her.

But then he—Chandler—never did claim to be the total Bond man.

"If you'll notice, Mr. Wise Spy," she huffed, "my suitcase is still in the suite. I'm not leaving for good," she quipped, her look at him pathetic. "I'll be back in time for the auction."

"You're not? You will?" He couldn't hold back the slight smile that was breaking across his lips.

"Yes, I'll be back," she told him curtly, as the elevator dinged and the door opened. "I, for one, don't start things I can't finish."

Did she mean—? Was she referring to—? Did she think—? How in the hell had things gotten to this point anyway? Here he was trying to do what was right, and somehow he'd made a giant mess of things.

Well, at least she was coming back. And he could still make it right. Maybe. *Yeah, I'll find a way to make it all up to her,* he decided as she got on the elevator, leaving him alone in the hallway in his tropical skivvies.

"Nine dollars and ninety-five cents? For a cinnamon raisin bagel with cream cheese?"

The burly man behind the deli counter looked down his pug nose at her. "You got an orange juice, too, didn't you?"

"Yeah, but . . ." Hope held up the container of juice. It was barely larger than the urine sample cup they gave you at the doctor's office.

"It's from Florida." The man shrugged as if that explained the outrageousness of it all.

"That doesn't exactly make it an import," she countered, feeling totally ripped off. Back home in Bearsville, she could feed bagels and juice to a half dozen of Theo's friends for the kind of money he was talking.

But obviously, the guy could've cared less. He shrugged indifferently again. "Hey, take it or leave it," he said, one hand hovering over the cash register. "Just make it fast. There's a line, ya know?"

Conscious of the impatient queue of bagel patrons glowering at her, Hope plopped down her money and grabbed the brown bag containing her pricey breakfast. Stomping out the door, back into the cold moist morning, she made her way across the street to the south side of Central Park.

In the midst of Manhattan's towering buildings and throngs of people, Central Park was the only thing that halfway resembled home to her. A quiet refuge of nature. A place where she could gather her thoughts . . . and maybe find some sort of solace. Or so she had hoped. Instead, all she found was that she was still fuming when she settled down on a slightly damp park bench with her breakfast.

Last night had really cost her big time! A hit to her wallet for this ridiculously-priced breakfast the morning after. And then the cost in damages for her bruised, possibly annihilated, ego—well, who could even put a price on that?

For just a second, she had almost said yes this morning to Chandler's offer of breakfast. She wanted so desperately to make *him* pay for something. But then she knew he wouldn't really be paying. His agency would. And she wasn't ready to look him in the face yet anyway.

After all, he had actually fallen asleep on her! Asleep! How was it possible? How was it possible that things were heating up between them one minute, and he was out cold the next?

Of course, now that she thought about it, she had found

him the same way after her bubble bath yesterday afternoon, hadn't she? Maybe the guy was narcoleptic or something?

The thought boosted her spirit momentarily. But much as she hoped that was true, in her heart she knew it wasn't. She just didn't have much luck with this boy–girl thing. And she should've never gotten started on it again.

Of course, it wasn't like she had been staking her future on the guy or anything. That was a far too complicated and scary concept for her to even consider at this point in her life. But it had felt really nice—surprisingly so—to be embraced by him, wrapped in his arms. And to stay that way for one night, would there have been any harm in that?

Though he'd kissed her several times throughout the day yesterday, those entanglements had all seemed like part of the roles they were playing. But last night, everything felt different. At least in her mind it had. With just the two of them in the luxurious suite, sans gangsters, curators or their friendly desk clerk, Chandler's kisses seemed amazingly passionate and sincere.

Had she really misjudged so badly?

And now in a few hours, after the auction, they'd be heading back to Bearsville. With his assignment complete, he'd be making a grand exit from her life sometime soon.

So why even think about it anymore? she scolded herself.

She pulled her wool coat more snuggly around her legs, and reached in the bag for her bagel. All the while, she worked to clear her head. She needed to stop thinking about the big guy waiting for her back at the Plaza. Instead, she needed to concentrate on more pleasant things—like the little man waiting for her back home. In fact, F.A.O. Schwarz was nearby, wasn't it? After she ate, she'd run over to see if they had anything affordable for Theo's birthday.

That would make her feel better, she decided.

Unwrapping her bagel, she got a whiff of its awful smell before she even laid eyes on the onion coating. It definitely wasn't cinnamon raisin! No way she could eat the disgusting thing. Repulsed and cursing the paunchy deli man who messed up her order, she wadded up the stinky mess and thrust it back into the paper bag.

What is it about the male species anyway? She seethed at the lot of them as she dumped her inedible ten-dollar breakfast into the trash can. They sure had a way of screwing up everything they laid their hands on, didn't they?

"Hope! Where are you going?"

Ever since she'd gotten back to the Plaza, she had been trying to keep her distance from Chandler. It just seemed easier that way. So she was at least a good three yards ahead of him when he called down the hallway to her. Swiveling around in her pointed black boots, she replied as politely as she could manage, "To the auction. Isn't it in the meeting room down the hall?"

He strode up to her side in the seconds it had taken her to answer him. His blue-striped shirt, black sport coat and jeans were a far cry from his formal attire from the night before. But he still looked incredibly attractive and self-possessed, a man most females would notice, for sure. She hated that she could still think nice things about him.

"Think we could walk together?" He smiled at her tentatively. "We *are* supposed to be husband and wife, aren't we?"

Husband and wife? They hadn't exactly performed their conjugal duties last night, had they?

Her face burned at the memory, a memory she was sure

177

would be etched in her mind for a long while. Like possibly for all eternity.

Before she could muster an answer, he grabbed her by the shoulders and pulled her to the side of the hallway. His grip was so solid, she couldn't wriggle her way out of it.

"What—?" She scowled at him. "What do you think you're doing?"

He mouthed a "shhh" at her and whispered, "It's the Cadillac duo. Don't turn your head."

So, of course, she did. She glanced around, and sure enough there were the pair of creeps, wandering up and down the lengthy hallway in their leather outerwear.

Do they ever take off those coats? her mind thought absently.

It was apparent the thugs were in search of the room reserved for the auction. A task that probably wouldn't have been too tough for a person of average intelligence, but for the two of them . . .

"This could take a while," Chandler said softly.

He clutched at her shoulders again and the unexpected tug pulled her totally off-balance. Before she knew what was happening, he had opened a door right next to them and hurled both of their bodies inside.

Of course, it was a door to a closet. A small, dark, confining space. A place with barely enough room for their bodies to stand—well, except for against each other.

Been there, done that, she inwardly seethed at him.

"Sorry I had to do that. But we need to let those guys get settled on the auction floor. Then we'll move in behind them," he explained in the darkness.

"I'm getting really tired of this," she sputtered, wanting and not wanting to be so close to him all at the same time.

178

It was crazy and frustrating. "All of these dark, little spaces. It's so—so trite."

She heard his hands feeling around the walls. "Is that better?" He managed to flick on an overhead light.

Not really. Now she could see every line on his good-looking face. Could see the way his inquisitive eyes and timid smile were asking to be forgiven. Could feel her resolve melting involuntarily . . . like an iceberg that had drifted into warmer waters.

Still, she tried to put up a fight. "If all we do is get holed up in places like this, what else am I going to have to write about? You promised me action on this trip."

Oh, did I really say that? She groaned to herself.

Chandler blinked at her, and clamped his mouth shut. Kindly—and wisely—he refrained from retorting with any sort of double-entendre.

"You're a smart woman. I'm sure you can think of something," he replied in a way that sounded sincerely complimentary. "Hope, look. I don't want you to think I'm trying to stifle your creative opportunities, but we have to be careful. Those two thieves are more dangerous than you think. They're sure to recognize you. I mean . . ." He paused, and his eyebrows drew together in an almost agonized expression. "You're not exactly the kind of girl a guy can get off his mind so easily . . ."

He had caught her completely off-guard. Normally a line like that would have sounded seductive or flirty. And he would have been looking at her with a totally inviting, desirous gaze. But instead, Chandler seemed befuddled by his declaration, perplexed by his feelings. His eyes searched hers, as if she'd have the answer for him there.

Her iceberg quickly dissolved to an ice cube. "Well, I . . ."

Was there anything to say really? Could she blame the

guy for being honest? For caring in a way he didn't comprehend? As a friend? As a whatever? Who knew? Did she?

He didn't look like he understood himself any better
than she did. And she decided in that instant it was okay.
As two human beings, they connected. In some capacity,
they cared. Right now, that was enough. It was all that she
needed to know.

"Did you see the look on Melanie's face when they
handcuffed her?" Hope asked quietly. She shifted her gaze
from the winter-barren trees flashing by outside the
Porsche's small window to look at him.

After the auction, at the beginning of their trek back to
Bearsville, her cheeks had been flushed with excitement
from rounding up the bad guys. But now concern suddenly
shadowed her face. "I can't imagine being so degraded like
that. Honestly, I felt kind of bad for her, although I don't
know why."

"Because you're a nice person is why," he replied,
touched by her expanse of goodwill toward the attractive
curator.

It felt like Hope had graced him with a dose of her goodwill, too. He felt lucky she would look him in the eye—even
talk to him—after what had happened last night. Clearly,
this morning she had been more than a little upset with
him. Why wouldn't she be? He wasn't stupid enough to
think a few hours had changed that completely. He'd created a horrible, demoralizing situation for her. But if she
only knew . . . And if he only knew so he could explain . . .

But he hadn't said anything. Actually, their return drive
to Bearsville had been fairly conversation-free for the most
part. Not that the silence around them had seemed excep-
tionally tense, really. But Hope had appeared lost in

thought throughout most of the ride. And since it looked like things had a chance of getting back on an even keel with them, he was apprehensive about saying too much. *It is probably best to follow Hope's lead,* he decided.

"Thank you for taking me along," she spoke up as familiar sights of the quiet town began dotting their view.

"Really?"

"Yes, really." She nodded. "I mean, for a while it didn't seem like I'd have much to write about," she said shyly. "But the auction clearly made up for that. It was great to see the shocked look on the gangsters' faces close up. Especially the creep who locked us up in the trunk. And then watching the FBI agents behind the scenes, that was a thrill. Now that I've witnessed some real action firsthand, it'll be a lot easier to write about."

"Well, I'm glad. Glad you could go. Glad it'll help."

He shrugged like none of it was a big deal. But he wasn't feeling that cavalier inside. Her departing words of thanks . . . Uncle Cary's bed and breakfast just in sight . . . made everything seem so final. Suddenly he wanted to say something. Explain himself. Although he wasn't so sure he could. "Hope," he struggled for the right words, "about . . . well, about last—" *night,* he had started to say.

Her groaning interrupted his jumbled thoughts. "Oh, no." She rolled her eyes.

Oh, no? She didn't want to hear his explanation?

He glanced over at her, only to realize that her mind was somewhere else. Sitting erect and leaning forward, she frowned out the smudged windshield. "What? What's wrong?"

"What time is it?" She turned to him.

He glanced at the dash. "Ten after five."

"Theo's already home."

He followed her line of vision and sure enough he could make out Theo and Cary in the side yard of the inn, hovering over a beat-up-looking black barbecue grill.

"Is that a bad thing?"

"Well, yeah, considering he wasn't supposed to be home until six o'clock. Any other Sunday Robert gets him home late, of course. But not this one." She sighed heavily. "I really didn't want him to see us together." She bit her lower lip anxiously, shifting uneasily in the seat. "I wonder what Uncle Cary told him." She said it aloud, though it seemed like she was speaking to herself.

"Don't worry. I'm great with kids," he boasted, trying to convince himself as much as her. "I'll handle this, no problem," he said as he pulled into the driveway and threw the car into park.

"No, really, Chandler, I think it'd be best if—" she began to protest.

But he was already bolting out of the car, wondering what the hell he *was* going to do. How was he going to make this situation comfortable for mother and son? How was he going to placate an almost eleven-year-old who was not fond of other males taking up his mom's time?

He had to think of something. And think of it fast. This could be the answer to completely salvaging things with Hope. It was critical. *Critical, but hopefully not a mission impossible,* he thought.

Hope had barely gotten to say hello to Theo before Fiona poked her head out the inn's front door and asked her to help with dinner preparations. Reluctantly, she made her way inside, while Theo glared back and forth between her and Chandler with huge question marks in his greenish-blue eyes.

Well, she promised herself as she dealt out silverware to each setting at the table, after dinner she'd talk to him. Tell him she was helping Chandler with some business. Which, as it turned out, was very much the truth. And which, as it turned out, was honestly for the better, wasn't it? After all, their one night would've only come to an end today. And the results may have made things awkward and embarrassing. All in all, things had probably worked out for the best, she told herself.

Except for . . .

They had been through so much together the past few days. Theo's rudeness and possessiveness. The fright of mobsters. Close encounters of the Cadillac kind. Life and death situations. Going home to Mom. More close encounters in the honeymoon suite.

Their getting to know each other had hardly started out in your typical dinner-and-a-movie fashion. And maybe that was why once they started touching . . . exploring . . . caressing with their eyes and arms, she thought she felt that extra special spark there. An excitedly familiar, coming-home kind of feeling. That is, until she'd clicked off her cell, rolled over and slipped her arms around him once more.

Her stomach roiled, recalling how humiliated she'd felt when he didn't respond to her . . . when he chose shut-eye over what she thought was going to be some pretty dreamy lovemaking. Then her stomach tightened even more as she heard the inn's front door open, and the trio of male footsteps clump over the hardwood floor in the entryway.

Most likely it would be an uncomfortable dinner, with Theo either pouting or being a smart aleck—she never knew which Theo she was going to get these days. *Maybe an after-dinner talk is too late,* she considered. *Maybe now would be better.*

But then she heard laughter coming from the hallway. Distinguishable laughter from all three of the guys.

What on earth? Well, she wasn't fool enough to mess with that. She'd just roll with things for now.

"What's so funny?" she asked, forcing a smile to light her face.

"Oh, nothing." Theo grinned, waving a hand at her.

"Guy stuff, huh?" she guessed, glancing at him as she set a glass of milk at his place at the table.

Theo looked up at the two men flanking his sides. "Kind of." He smiled.

"Okay," she acquiesced with a shrug, glad that he seemed happy. "Uncle Cary, those steaks look delicious. You're the master of the Weber."

"And it's perfect timing, too," Fiona's sweet accent broke in as she flew into the room, balancing several serving bowls in her arms. "Gentlemen. Lady. Dinner is served."

As they all settled down to the table, Uncle Cary turned to Chandler. "Norm dropped off the information for his tax returns today."

"Great," Chandler replied. He lifted his eyes to hers, and gave her a conspiratorial wink from across the table. She could feel her cheeks flush. "I should be able to get to it in the next day or so."

"He won ten grand in the state lottery last year," Uncle Cary added, passing the steak sauce to Chandler. "Care for some?"

"Sure, thanks." Chandler grabbed the bottle and poured a spoonful on his plate. "That's not such a big deal. I can work that out."

"Bought me a box of fine, imported cigars, too," Uncle Cary informed Chandler, pointing a fork at him with a chunk of steak speared on it. "We'll have to try a couple after dinner."

"Not inside, boys," Fiona warned, wagging her finger at her mate from the other end of the table.

Cary gave an exaggerated roll of his eyes and, holding up his hand, made it clear he'd heard the orders from head-quarters before. "I know, I know."

Hope noticed Theo giggle at the couple, clearly finding pleasure in Fiona admonishing Uncle Cary. She still couldn't imagine why he was in such a gleeful mood. *What could have possibly brought it on?* she wondered. Was Chandler really the miracle worker he claimed to be?

Curious, she glanced up at the spy man, but Uncle Cary was busy talking again. "So, Chan, how much longer do you think you'll be staying?" he asked.

It seemed like such a simple question. So why did Hope suddenly feel as if she could choke on her mouthful of sweet potatoes which were practically pureed, mushy as baby food?

"Probably for the week," Chandler answered him. "Then I'll have to get back to work."

Hope felt his gaze fall on her, but she tried not to look across the table at him. Was there something he was looking for? A reaction he wanted to see?

She tried to remain neutral, expressionless, and he went back to buttering his biscuit. Discreetly, she watched his hands and couldn't help but remember the feel of them. On her cheek. On her skin. Gently nudging her robe from her shoulders. Making her shiver, even now. *Yes, it probably had been a blessing after all that he had fallen asleep,* she decided.

"Awesome biscuits, Fiona," he was saying to the mistress of the house, who beamed in the glow of his compliments. No wonder she enjoyed cooking for the man. "And

the sweet potato casserole, too. Everything's delicious."
Then he turned and addressed Theo. "Well, what do you
think, Theo? Think this is a good time?"

"To tell my mom?" Theo squirmed in his seat excitedly.

"Uh," Chandler looked at him with raised eyebrows,
"knowing your mom, I think I'd be asking her instead of
telling her."

"Oh, yeah." Theo nodded. His smile was so broad and
contagious, Hope found herself smiling, too, never mind
that she had no clue as to why the guys at the table seemed
so darn smiley.

"Mom, can I please, please, please have a pool party for
my birthday?"

"A what?" she replied louder than she intended, her
smile quickly retreating.

"A pool party. In Uncle Cary's pool. Mr. Adams thought
of it, and Uncle Cary says it's okay with him," he added
quickly, presenting his show of support.

"A pool party? In the dead of winter?" Incredulous, she
looked around the table at the male collaborators who were
seated there. They were all nodding their heads and grinning
like it was the best idea they'd ever come up with.

*So this is how Chandler cajoled Theo out of an ill mood?
Smart man.* She had to give him credit. "And just who
would want to come to a pool party in this weather, Theo?"

"Everyone I know!" her son practically shouted. He was
so totally excited she wondered how he'd contained himself
this long. "Mr. Adams is going to make it so the pool water
is really hot. And he can hook it up so we can have hot
water running down the slide like a waterfall. He said it's
really fun, because when you're in the water you're all
warm. But your head is sticking out in the cold, so it gets
icicles all over it."

"And that's supposed to be really fun?" She grimaced.

"For my friends it would be." Meaning it was something she and her friends would never understand. Well, none of her friends except for Chandler, whom Theo glanced to for moral support. "Please, Mom." He looked back at his mom, his eyes taking on their most appealing look ever. "No one has ever had a pool party in the winter before."

"And there's a good reason for that," Hope replied, wincing at her own words. She sounded so much like a mother!

"Ah, geez, Hope," Uncle Cary chimed in. "It's not a big deal. Let the kid have some fun. It's not like some people don't have hot tubs. And Chan here says he'll do the work, setting it up." He flipped a hand at the handsome man to his right.

"And just what will I tell the other moms?" It wasn't a total concession, but she knew that they knew they were reeling her in.

"We knew you'd say that!" Theo squealed. He looked at the other two men again. Clearly, he felt a part of their club, and any reservations he'd had about seeing her and Chandler get out of the car together today were preempted by Chandler's crazy idea. "We can have big towels on the side of the pool for all my friends, and flip-flops, too. After we swim, everyone can come back to our house and get dressed and have pizza and stuff."

"So you guys really have this all planned out, huh?"

Chandler tilted his head at her. "I'll just need you to chauffeur me to a home improvement store. Cary said there are a few in some larger towns close to here."

"Kingston." She nodded.

She'd managed to elude his eyes most of the meal, but now he stared at her and smiled, making her feel so connected to him it was unsettling. For some reason, in her family's presence the two of them seemed more together than the couple they had pretended to be all weekend.

Maybe it was because he fit all too well into the setting. But why wouldn't he? It was obvious that Uncle Cary enjoyed talking to him, and that Fiona liked cooking for him because he was always so appreciative. And, of course, now that he'd become Theo's favorite party planner . . .

But didn't they also realize he wasn't really a part of them. He was leaving. Very soon. Maybe in less than a week. Which was probably for the best anyway. Yes, the sooner the better. So everyone's lives could get back to normal . . . mostly her own.

"So, Kingston, tomorrow?" he was asking her.

She certainly didn't relish the idea of spending more time alone with him again. Although a hardware warehouse sure didn't compare to a Plaza suite. How intimate a trip could it be?

Plus, get real, she told herself. She hadn't found anything in her price range at F.A.O. Schwarz. And it wasn't like she had any ideas for Theo's party. Certainly none that could compare to Chandler's. And time was drawing near. And everyone at the table seemed anxious to host such an event.

"All right, Theo, you can have your pool party," she conceded.

At that, Theo whistled out a victorious, "Yes!" And Fiona brought on the desserts.

Chapter Twelve

Finally! The shower beat down on Sela. She had never been so thankful for its cleansing ions before. Down the drain went the layer of canal sludge that had clogged her pores and coated her tresses, possibly damaging her most recent hair-color treatment. Washed away were any doubts anyone had ever had about Giorgio. And rinsed clean were the lingering remains of a case she was glad to be finished with.

As it turned out, capturing Cirella Carducci, or whatever her real name was, had been easier than she imagined. In fact, she never even had to lay a goopy, slime-covered hand on her. When Sela advanced on the Queen of Mean, Cirella had tried to back away. It was then that she tripped over her own flippers and fell, hitting her head on a classic Italian glass tabletop. She was still out cold when the authorities came to fetch her. The evidence Sela had uncovered would surely put her fraudulent, evil tush away for good.

There was someone else who was thankful the case was over too. Giorgio. Sela could see his olive-skinned, water-slick body wrapped in a fluffy white towel through the frosted glass of the shower.

Pulsating . . . steamy . . . and that wasn't just the shower, Sela melted just thinking what their future together might hold.

The cordless phone lay buried beneath magazine clips of male models Hope was using to help her characterize her

Italian hero. She located it just before the answering machine started to pick up the call.

"What's up, girl?" Dani greeted her.

"Not much. Just trying to get through this chapter."

"I'm not talking about Sela's life, silly," Dani said in her
sing-song voice. "I'm referring to yours. I know something's
up. Mrs. Gallina came in for her Saturday afternoon
backcomb and spray, and told me you'd been kidnapped by
a man in a black Porsche." She laughed. "Saw you leaving
town with him. She's such a nut," Dani mused. "But then
when you didn't show up yesterday at the Village Pantry for
our brunch with the twins, I started figuring gassy Gallina
might be right."

"Nan and Jan? That was yesterday?" Hope winced. "Oh,
Dani, I'm sorry. Have you been worried?"

"Worried? Ha!" her friend sniggered. "The only thing
I've been worried about is that I'm missing out on all the
juicy details. Now tell me what's been going on," Dani
urged her. "And don't leave out a thing."

"Well." Hope took in a deep breath and let out an
equally deep sigh. "It kind of all started in the trunk of a
gangster's Cadillac . . . and then ended with a weekend at
the Plaza."

Her delivery was so understated that Dani's whoops of
jubilation clanged even more loudly in her ear. Plus, she
could hear Dani dinging a comb or brush handle or something on a coffee mug, sounding out a victory bell.

"A weekend where?" she shrieked. "Tell me, tell me."

"Oh, Dani," Hope sighed again. "It's so long, and I'm so
far behind on my deadline."

"Okay, okay. I can get the details later, I guess. I was
just wondering, because Porsche Man stopped in here a
little while ago, sounding all excited about Theo's birthday

party. He's helping to plan it? I thought that seemed like a good thing. So what happened? Bottom line."

Bottom line? Was she referring to what Hope thought she might be referring to?

"Did you—or didn't you?" her friend boldly inquired.

You could never accuse Dani of beating around the bush. Hope had to smile. "Nope," she replied flatly.

"You're kidding!" Dani sounded confused. "Well, hmm. Porsche Man seemed like one happy guy all the same."

"Really?"

"Yeah. So it must have been somewhat of a good weekend, right?" Dani giggled, and Hope knew she was still digging for details.

"Actually, Dani, it doesn't matter. He's going to be leaving for who knows where any day now. Why even talk about it?" She tried to dismiss the subject . . . like that was possible with Dani.

"Maybe he doesn't have to, Hope."

"Of course he has to, Dani. He has a life. I have a life. Besides, it wouldn't work anyway."

"Why wouldn't it?" her friend countered.

"Well, why would it?"

"Gosh, Hope. You're the consummate romantic, aren't you?"

"Thanks. My editor would appreciate that comment." An awkward silence settled between them, but they were too good friends to let it hang there. Hope was the first to break it. "Dani, I know you want the best for me. Or what you think is best for me. But, I'm okay. Really."

"Okay. Last word." Dani made an attempt to be taciturn.

Right, Hope thought wryly on the other side of the phone.

191

"Stop writing it. Start living it," her friend scolded mildly.

"Thanks, Dani. I'll try," she promised, hanging up the phone and turning back to her computer.

"Hope!" Chandler's voice drifted upstairs from the front door of the house.

Hope's head shot up from the computer monitor, and she winced as reality set in. It wasn't that she'd forgotten their date with Home Depot, but she'd gotten so wrapped up in Sela's world that she'd lost track of time. Obviously Chandler had knocked, and when she hadn't heard him, he'd taken the liberty of peeking in the door.

"Hope!" he yelled out again.

"I'm up here!" she called back.

Her first inclination was to try and straighten the note cards, papers, Post-its, reference books and Twizzler wrappers strewn messily around her computer desk and on the floor. But then she realized doing so would take days—not seconds—which was all the virile Mr. Adams needed to sprint up the steps to her office.

Well, "office" was a stretch of the imagination. Her workspace was little more than a small alcove tucked away on the second floor at the rear of the house. The ceiling was pitched in alignment with the house's eaves, and the best part about it—besides its cozy feel—was the window. From the window she could look out on the day, or keep an eye on Theo while he was outside playing.

Or sometimes Theo would trudge upstairs when she was working. Sometimes it was to leave Post-it notes for her. Other times, he'd curl up in the dusty-blue over-stuffed chair that sat in the corner. Throwing an afghan over himself, he'd watch cartoons or ESPN on the small television that was perpetually powdered with dust.

This morning she had the TV on, turned down low for background noise, when Chandler came bounding into the room. Instantly the small space seemed entirely filled with his presence. Standing there in ordinary faded jeans and a worn caramel-colored suede jacket, she was struck by the realization that every time she saw him she was taken aback by his good looks.

"Ready to go?" he asked.

"Just a second," she turned from him, taking a moment to save her work, click off the computer and stabilize the rush of feelings that had begun wildly coursing through her at the sight of him.

"Damn!" He stood, rubbing his hands together, his breath making the slightest clouds in the air of the room. "I thought hot air is supposed to rise. Is it freezing up here, or is it my imagination?"

Hope grinned. "No, it's definitely not your imagination."

She was still in her ski hat from her morning's route, and if she could manage to type with gloves, she'd have those on, too. As it was, she'd sit on her hands from time to time to warm them up. Her customary fleece afghan was wrapped around her lap.

"But in the summer," she offered, smiling, "it's quite toasty. Blazing, actually."

"Aren't there any vents, or what?" He glanced around at the base of the walls in search of some, or one.

"I don't know," she replied offhandedly. "Uncle Cary tried to fix something once. I can't say I really listen much when it comes to pipes and duct work unless, of course—"

"—it's a lead pipe in the dining room with Colonel Mustard." He finished her thought.

"Exactly!" She burst out laughing. "Maybe someday I'll get some kind of climate control in here. But for now it feels like the place in the house most conducive to writing."

She paused and rolled her shoulders. They perpetually seemed tight and knotted from sitting at the computer for long stretches. She really needed to think more about her posture when she sat working.

Rubbing at her right shoulder with her left hand, she continued, "I can look out at the backyard from here, keep an eye on Theo when he's outside kicking around the soccer ball with his buddies." She motioned toward the TV, and felt a poignant smile tug at her lips. "Or sometimes he comes in and falls asleep in that chair watching a football game. The man of the house, you know?"

She didn't know what she had said. *Football? Theo playing outside the window with buddies?* Whatever it was, Chandler looked startled for a moment, like he'd remembered something or seen a ghost.

"Well, I'm ready for this, if you are."

She got up, and turned off the TV. Chandler swung out his arm, inviting her to descend the steps ahead of him.

Making her way down the stairs, she had to wonder. Why had he put so much thought into Theo's party? Did he really miss his own nieces and nephews that much? Or was he just the proverbial nice guy? Surely he wasn't doing all this to impress her. Why would he care? He wasn't long for Bearsville anyway.

"So you really don't mind rigging up this heated pool thing?" she asked once they'd reached the bottom of the staircase.

"Are you kidding? This is something Theo and his friends will never forget. They'll be talking about it till his thirtieth birthday."

She smiled and cocked an eye at him. "Pretty sure of yourself, aren't you?"

"In some cases, yes." His lips made a firm, thin line across his face. "But not always."

Half-expecting some kind of cocky, clever answer, his honest reply threw her off. Slightly ruffled, she grabbed her coat off the oak bench by the front door. "What made you think of it anyway? A winter pool party?"

"Actually I had an assignment near a ski resort in the Alps."

As if he'd done it a hundred times, he took her coat from her hands and held it up for her to slip into. She eased into it, trying to remind herself that it was no more than a gentlemanly gesture. Good manners that Alicia Adams had taught him well.

"After the mission was complete," he continued as she buttoned up, "I did some skiing there. But the hot tub at the resort was definitely the best part."

A reminiscent sort of smile lit his face. She couldn't help but notice. Arching an eyebrow at him, she said teasingly, "Maybe that's because of who was in the hot tub with you."

He scowled, pretending to be crushed. "You know, it's people like you who give spies like me a bad name."

"If the ski boot fits . . ." She shrugged with a chuckle.

Hope chatted blithely as she followed Chandler around Home Depot, not even paying attention to all the pipes and tubes and whatevers he was throwing into the cart. He did pretty much the same when they hit Wal-Mart, and she combed the aisles for party decorations, game prizes, snacks and a few extra-large towels.

Admittedly, it felt good having someone to help with Theo's party for a change. For so many years, she had done it by herself. Not that she minded. In fact, if you had asked her before today, she probably would've said it was no problem and she preferred doing it solo anyway.

But now that she was sharing this experience with Chandler, she had to admit it was truly double the fun. They fed off of each other's enthusiasm about the big day, both looking forward to delighting her son and his guests.

Before they knew it, the shopping was finished and Chandler suggested they drop into Woodstock for lunch on their way back to Bearsville. Surprisingly, he had never visited the town, and Hope hadn't been there for years.

Starting out with Jitters, they ate double-decker sandwiches. Afterwards they strolled up and down Tinker Street, browsing through the pottery and glassworks shops. At one point, a bundled-up woman on a motorized scooter accidentally almost knocked Hope down. Chandler grabbed Hope's hand to pull her out of harm's way. Once he did, he never let go. Finally, after hours of walking and talking, holding hands and enjoying each other's company, they made their last stop in Woodstock. They went to Heaven for dessert.

During the short ride back to Bearsville, Hope smiled to herself. She'd never had her emotions run parallel to restaurant names before. Jitters . . . Heaven. She felt like she was back in high school. That's how innocent and brand-new the day had seemed.

When they made it back to Bearsville, they sat talking in her driveway for a while—something she hadn't done for more years than she could remember. And right as the afternoon school bus pulled up to drop Theo off, Chandler leaned over and gave her a light kiss good-bye in the seclusion of his car. Another something she hadn't done for more years than she could remember. But that was okay. It didn't really mean anything, did it? It was just like back in high school. And merely a chaste ending to a sweet day.

Another day, another trip to the grocery store . . .

Hope's mind was lost in a swirl of daydreams featuring Sela, Giorgio and the spy next door, as she lugged plastic bags of groceries into the house. She startled when a man's figure stepped out in front of her.

"Aaaeeee!" she screamed out, reacting quickly, hurling the heaviest bag right smack into the man's abdomen . . . which was unfortunate for Chandler.

"Holy crap!" she shouted when she recognized him. "You scared me to death!"

Doubled over, hugging his stomach, he rocked on his heels, attempting to soothe the effect of the blow. "Damn. I knew you were dangerous, woman. Just didn't know you were armed," he winced.

"I am so sorry," she apologized, feeling helpless. All she could manage to do is stand there, grimacing as the poor guy crouched over in obvious discomfort. "I didn't know it was you."

"It's okay," he groaned. "Cary let me in. Should've told you. Looked at your duct work."

Her own personal handyman. And she'd almost killed him!

Slowly sucking up the pain, he managed to make his way to a normal, upright, *Homo sapiens* position. Then he automatically grabbed the loaded grocery bags from her—also known as her supermarket weaponry—and carried them into the kitchen.

Her own personal bag carrier, too. *A girl could get used to this kind of service,* she thought, watching him take over.

"I think I figured out how to solve the heating problem in your writing room," he told her.

"Really?" Now she felt even worse. She'd truly overreacted with the bag heaving. "Chandler, I really am sorry," she stressed. "I nearly bludgeoned you to death."

"Well, it's good to know you can protect yourself," he said, though his eyes looked askance. "I guess."

He set the bags down on the counter, and then reached for the one that had taken his breath away. "What's in this fifty-pounder anyway?" He peeked into the bag cautiously, eyeing it as if it was a loaded gun. "Let's see. Lots of canned goods. Always good for a belt to the stomach . . ."

Hope winced at the thought.

"And—ah-ha! Stouffer's frozen lasagna. I should've known. Well, at least it's my favorite." A weak smile managed to tweak his lips. A light started coming back into his eyes.

"I thought *my* lasagna was your favorite." She put a hand on her hip.

"Yours. Stouffer's. I'd say they're pretty much one and the same, wouldn't you?" His grin was lazy, but still flashed at her all-knowingly.

"You knew?" she squealed. She covered her eyes with her hands and talked through them. "You knew that night?"

"Don't be embarrassed." He pulled her hands away from her face. "I'm trained to know everyone's little secrets. Even your culinary ones."

He laughed and squeezed her hands. His touch felt so affectionate to her. So natural. "Anyway, it doesn't matter, does it?" he continued. "It's very tasty lasagna. In fact, if I were invited, I wouldn't mind trying it again."

"Think you'll be fully recovered by dinnertime?" she kidded, glancing down at his stomach area.

His stomach. Hard. Flat. Smooth. She remembered from her firsthand experience, wiring him with the recording device. Remembered from the honeymoon suite, tugging the tux shirt from his broad shoulders. Suddenly his touch felt too affectionate. Too natural. She pulled her hands away from his as nonchalantly as possible, hoping he wouldn't detect her sudden unease. Dutifully she began unpacking the groceries.

"Well," she yakked on, willing the image of his bare chest from her mind, "I suppose all your hard labor does deserve some kind of reward. How about dinner and a rented movie?"

A nice PG-movie void of any rippled stomachs . . . touchy-feely hands . . . lazy, sexy smiles.

She glanced over at him sheepishly, hoping he couldn't read her lascivious thoughts. But he was busy peeking into the other grocery bags, snooping.

"Anything else in here?"

"Hey, now. Stop prying. Is it necessary you know all of my secrets?"

Obviously just like the other male in her life, the eleven-year-old one, Chandler suffered from selective hearing. Undaunted, he continued rifling through the bags.

"I'm warning you. Get your nose out of there." She swatted playfully at him with a bag of frozen Country-Crisper French Fries.

His reflexes were uncanny. He grabbed at her wrist, laughing as he did so. She loved the way he laughed. It seemed to come from the depths of him, full and hearty, like he meant every vibration of it.

He pulled her toward him, reeling her in till her wrist was practically under his chin. The bag of Country-Crispers dangled between them as he gazed deeply into her eyes.

"I was looking around . . ." he said hoarsely, seductively, ". . . wondering if I got dessert, too."

Dessert! Her wrist went limp, and the Country-Crispers crashed to the floor.

Kicking the fries out of his way, he slowly edged near her. His legs pressed up close against hers, he leisurely pushed the hair back from her shoulders. Unhurriedly, he began tantalizing her earlobe with his lips. Kisses given tenderly, yet the heat of his tongue pricked her ear. Circling. Enticing. Melting away any common sense she still had in her head.

She could hear him breathing heavily. Hear the urgency of his desire.

Regrettably, that wasn't the only thing she heard—

"Moooom!" Theo burst into the house, letting the back door bang behind him. Instantly the two adults broke apart, their heat dissipating like fireworks falling from the sky on the Fourth of July.

"Theo. I thought you were playing at Taylor's until dinner. Did something happen?"

She patted self-consciously at her hair, still feeling so breathless she wondered that she had managed to pull a sentence together at all.

"Isn't it dinnertime?" Theo asked, surveying the kitchen as he always did, searching for any sign of food preparation. "I'm hungry," he announced, which translated meant it must be time to eat.

"Um, as soon as I microwave the lasagna," she stammered, grabbing the Stouffer's box and tearing at it mercilessly. Trying to ignore the sensations trembling through her. Attempting to still the thoughts that pervaded her mind.

"And, uh, Mr. Adams makes the salad," she added,

turning to slip the frozen entrée into the microwave.

"Make the salad?" repeated Chandler, who didn't seem to be flustered in the least. He'd certainly recovered from their entangled moments more easily than she had. *Was that from years of experience?* she wondered. "I thought I was in charge of dessert." He grinned easily.

Dessert. There was that word again. A sensation of warmth rushed from her cheeks to her toes, and unfortunately spread to all the spots in between. "Uh, no. I'll take care of dessert," she assured him. *Ice cream seemed like a good idea. Frozen juice bars. A bowlful of jagged icicles yanked off the eaves of the house.*

"Promise?" He winked at her, his eyes twinkling and teasing.

Her own personal resident devil, too.

You are so bad, she mouthed at him when Theo wasn't looking.

He just smiled at her victoriously, mischievously. "Okay then." He clapped his hands together. "Theo, help me out here. Will you, pal?" Chandler motioned to him. "Find the biggest bowl you can. We're going to make the best salad your momma has ever tasted."

"Aw, Mom." Theo rolled his eyes. "Why can't I stay up? Mr. Adams and I didn't even get to play my new video game."

It had been a nice evening at the Hathaway house. The three of them had shared a very easy-to-prepare lasagna dinner and salad, plus chocolate chunk ice cream for dessert. The accountant-turned-spy had even helped Theo with his math homework while Hope did dishes. But being the nag she was . . .

"Sorry. It's that time." She nodded toward the staircase

leading to the bedrooms. "Let's go, mister."

Reluctantly Theo got to his feet and followed her over to the steps, grumbling all the way. But Hope mentally commended him for remembering his manners.

" 'Night, Mr. Adams," Theo called out to their guest.

"Theo, you think you could call me something besides 'Mr. Adams?' " Chandler asked from his spot on the family room couch.

"Isn't that your name?" The boy looked confused and glanced over at Hope.

"Well, yeah, it is," Chandler chuckled. "But I wouldn't mind if you called me Chandler."

Theo looked at Hope again. This time she knew he was seeking her approval. She nodded and smiled her consent.

"Okay. Good-night, Chandler," Theo said boldly, then bounded up the stairs.

"I'll be right back," Hope told Chandler before padding up the steps behind her son.

After the usual ritual of prayers and kisses, Hope started to leave Theo's bedside, but he reached out and grabbed her hand to stop her.

"Mom, do you like Mr. Adams? I mean Chandler?"

She nodded. "He's nice," she said as objectively as she could manage. "Very nice."

"I like him a lot." A broad grin crossed Theo's face, and Hope felt her own face contort in concern.

"Theo, Mr. Adams is being very good to you, planning your birthday party and all. But you didn't seem to give him much of a shot until he was doing something for you. Giving you something you wanted. You know that doesn't sit well with me," she chastised him.

And am I doing the same? she wondered in that moment. The man had to keep doing things, proving himself to her, proving he could be trusted, chipping away at the icy wall around her heart.

"I know," Theo replied, looking up at her sheepishly. "But I like him for other reasons, too."

"Oh, yeah? Like what?" She was curious to hear what he'd have to say.

"I also like him because he didn't get mad when I took his spy decoder ring."

"You what?" she exclaimed so vehemently that Theo flinched.

"Oops." Theo made a sick face. "We weren't going to mention that." He sat up in bed instantly, pleading with her. "Mom, Mom, you don't need to be mad though, I only borrowed it. Chandler didn't care."

Now it is exclusively "Chandler," huh?

"Well, I do care, Theo, and I am mad. And you'll make it up to me by doing extra chores tomorrow and—and—" she stuttered, trying to think of a punishment to fit the crime. "And you're grounded from your James Bond video games for a week."

"Aw, Mom," he whined. "I thought you wanted me to like Chandler."

"Well, I—"

She was afraid of this. Afraid of Theo getting too attached to Chandler. It seemed to be happening so suddenly. But why wouldn't Theo get attached? The personable spy behaved extraordinarily with her son; his rapport with Theo seemed so genuine. Although she couldn't believe Chandler had hidden the ring incident from her. That was a little disturbing.

Her first instinct was to rush downstairs and confront Mr. Wise Spy about it. But then, again, why even bother? Why get him more involved in her and Theo's affairs? She could take care of it from her end, and with his spy mission complete, he was leaving soon anyway. She just hoped that when he did make his departure from their lives that Theo wouldn't be too crushed.

That she wouldn't be too crushed.

"Theo, I hope you realize that Chandler is only visiting Bearsville. He doesn't have a home here. It's kind of like when we went on vacation to North Carolina and you met that boy Matt Hemming, remember? You played for a while and then when vacation was over, we came back home. That was it, you know?"

"I remember." Theo sighed, pausing thoughtfully. "Well, if Chandler does want to make his home in Bearsville, tell him I'll share my room with him. I don't mind," he added, nestling down into his comforter.

Hope winced inwardly, and then tucked the downy blanket around her son, doubting sincerely that the subject would ever come up.

Chandler surveyed his surroundings, finding them quite palatable. The plaid family-room sofa was comfortable. The glow of the fire was mesmerizing. And upstairs, tucking her son into bed, there was a woman whom he found totally captivating.

It was strange, but he couldn't imagine anything feeling better. He couldn't imagine anywhere else he'd rather be.

He'd been all over the globe in the most exquisite abodes . . . at the most famous restaurants . . . on the most scenic beaches . . . and with the most gorgeous women. And none of it compared to this feeling.

How could that be? How had it happened?

Suddenly, he didn't care about the reasons anymore. He had spent his whole life analyzing and charting his future, and now he wasn't sure why he ever had. Unless maybe it was to get him to this moment, to this place in time? Who knew really? At this point, who cared?

After putting Theo to bed, Hope puttered back into the family room, and sat on the couch next to him. She tucked her slippered feet underneath her, and he noticed she tried to politely stifle a yawn. Days were long for her, starting at dawn.

"Hey, I know you're tired," he told her. "We can do this another time, Hope. Really."

"No way," she insisted as she sorted through the remotes, looking for the one that belonged to the DVD player. "I promised you dinner and a movie, and I'm a woman of my word."

They settled in to watch the movie, but it wasn't long before Hope's sleepy head dangled and found its way onto his shoulder. He wrapped his arm around her, and moments later her head lolled again and sunk into his lap.

He glanced down at her face and pushed back a lock of russet hair that had fallen across her cheek. A smile came to his lips, and he felt something endearing stir in his heart.

God, she's adorable, he thought. So unassuming . . . so beautiful. Someone intelligent he could easily talk to. Someone caring and funny and loving. Someone real and honest. And oh, yeah, there was that whole sexy thing too; he smiled, thinking of their playful encounter in the kitchen just hours ago.

She might not like it, if she knew what he was thinking at the moment. Especially after eleven years of being by herself, protecting her son . . . protecting her heart. She might not like it at all, if she knew he wanted a space in both of their hearts—in hers and Theo's—and hoped to take up residence there.

Because it was true. Accountant-turned-spy or not, he'd always been a man of numbers, yet he would've never calculated on this. But damn it, it didn't matter. Everything had changed for him now, and he'd just have to come up with a new equation for his future. That was all there was to it. Because there was no way he wanted to subtract Hope . . . Theo . . . or this feeling from his life.

Chapter Thirteen

"Danielle, you've got to help me."

"Sela, it's the middle of the night. Are you all right?" Her friend's concern traveled over the phone. "When did you get back?"

"I'm not back," she paused. "And, no, I'm not all right."

"Don't tell me you got shot, Sela. I'll kill you if anything happens to you."

Sela was momentarily puzzled by her friend's incongruous statement. "No, no, nothing like that."

"It's a man then? That Giorgio babe from the photo you showed me?"

Sela smiled at her friend's intuitiveness. Even an ocean apart, they were of one mind.

"What happened with him?" Danielle wanted to know.

"I don't know. It's just—well, we spent hours together last night kissing, making love . . . first in the kitchen making dinner, then on the furry rug in his office, then in front of his fireplace, until finally we fell asleep in each other's arms."

Danielle's laughter was sweet. "Doesn't sound too awful so far."

"Well the fact is, when I woke up this morning, he was gone."

"Probably just went out for milk." Danielle assured her.

"No, he's definitely lactose intolerant. And he's been gone all day."

"How many rooms does he have in his house?"

"What? The villa?" Sela counted in her head. "About nine."

"How many did you visit last night?"

"Uh, three."

"Well, then, just sit tight," Danielle advised her. "It sounds like you have more loving to do. I'm sure he'll be back soon."

Hope tried to keep the viewfinder of the video camera steady, but it wasn't too easy with the way her body was jiggling with laughter. The boys were in the pool having the time of their lives, thanks to Chandler's madcap idea, and it was hilarious to watch. Doing cannonballs off the side . . . swatting at the icicles in each other's hair . . . bobbing up and down to get the full effect of the cold air and the hot water. Their voices were unusually high-pitched, shrill as a bunch of banshees. Plus, snow had been accumulating since dawn, making the setting even more preposterously perfect. Rolling around in the white mounds like playful polar bear cubs, they'd shock their bodies further by plunging into the steamy water.

"Hey, Mom, tape me," Theo called over to her.

Hope focused in on him as he hustled over to the slide, hugging his underdeveloped chest to stay warm. He climbed the ladder as fast as he could, and once the river of hot water hit his bottom, he was in heaven again and plunged back into the hot-as-Hades pool.

Meanwhile, the other boys in the pool were concentrating on creating icicles in one another's hair. They were especially set on splashing Nick Hahn, Larry Lighter's nephew, who had a super-thick head of long, unkempt hair. The boys shrieked at the way the clumps of ice formed spike-like dreadlocks all over Nick's noggin.

While the boys enjoyed the warmth of the water, Fiona and Uncle Cary were huddled around the fire pit, sipping hot chocolate. Hope turned the camera in their direction, and also managed to get some footage of Larry and Dani standing nearby, too. Dani looked adorable as always in her cream ski jacket, with its fur-trimmed hood wreathing her orange-red hair, her new color for the month. And Larry appeared quite comfortable in the frigid weather with his tan barn jacket left unbuttoned over a bulky navy sweater. Both were laughing openly at the boys' antics.

And then—Hope moved the camera just a bit more— there was Chandler, standing alongside them. Chandler who was—

What? Taking off his jacket, and peeling off his shoes and socks. And—she zoomed the camera lens in closer—removing his black sweater and customary white T-shirt.

And there was that—zoom, zoom—totally fit, arousing chest of his!

Then he—zoom the lens all the way in—oh my, undid his blue jeans!

Oh my gosh! He was stripping at her son's birthday party right down to his—navy trunks!

Then, practically loping toward the water, the man-turned-boy took off down the slide and made the biggest splash in the pool yet. The boys went wild, whooping and screaming, thrilled to have him create such a stir. Bobbing in a circle around him, they took turns climbing on his back. One by one, he tossed them through the frigid air and back into the welcome heat of the water.

After about an hour or so of such horseplay, Hope knew she had to make a judgment call. She steeled herself for the boys' resistance.

"It's time to eat. Everybody out!" she yelled, making all of the boys, including the six-foot hunky one, get out of the water and head back to her house.

"Aw, just when we were having fun," both Theo and Chandler complained at her.

With much prodding, the boys reluctantly retreated from the fun and heat of the pool. But once out in the cold air, they practically knocked one another over grabbing for flip-flops and oversized towels. Then they raced and whooped all the way back to the house, to the warmth of the crackling fire that awaited them.

All except for Theo and Nick, that is. Shivering and snickering, the mischievous pair grabbed every last towel in sight and went running away as fast as their frigid legs would carry them, leaving Chandler towel-less. Laughing uncontrollably, they fell over the towels and themselves as they tried to make their quick getaway. No doubt Chandler could've caught up to the boys easily. But instead he played it up like they'd really done him in, leaving him stranded and freezing. It was definitely a scene that made Hope smile.

After changing into dry clothes, devouring a half dozen pizzas, and playing video games, the group of boys huddled together in the center of the family room. Watching the video of themselves in the pool, their howling started all over again. The adults standing around the periphery of the room couldn't help but join in, too.

Unable to contain himself, Theo peered over the heads of his friends, noticeably seeking out Chandler's attention. "This is my best birthday ever!" he exclaimed to him. "Thanks, Chandler. Thanks, Mom." He gave them both one of the widest grins Hope had ever seen on his face.

Seeing Theo so overjoyed, and surrounded by so much

love, released years' worth of overwhelming feelings in Hope. Unconscious feelings, that seemed to well up and come out of nowhere. Divorce or not, Theo was going to be all right, she realized, relief washing over her, bringing her an inner peace. Despite Robert's abrupt departure at their son's birth, Theo was going to make it, after all.

Standing next to her, Chandler beamed with satisfaction at Theo's words, and rightfully so. And though not a part of them touched, she felt totally at one with the spy from next door.

"Thank you for this," she uttered, her emotions too full to say more. But her expression must've said it all.

Reaching over for her hand, he squeezed it, his touch so knowing . . . so sweet . . . so warm . . . it nearly brought tears to her eyes, her heart feeling as though it could overflow again and again.

It was a slice-of-life scene, she knew. The kind she used to write television commercials about. Purely a Kodak moment. And, as hard as it was, she tried to remember that. It was only a brief second . . . a moment of life without its mars and blemishes. Her past history had taught her there was no guarantee for more. She'd be a fool to look beyond the special moment . . . or this extra-special day.

"We're taking off soon," Dani said as she and Hope finished cleaning up the mess from the birthday cake and ice cream. "We're spending the night in Merker's heated barn. They've got a sick racehorse Larry is trying to nurse back to health. We're taking Nick with us. He wanted to know if Theo could come along, too."

"Do you do that often?" Hope folded the dishtowels over the sink to let them air dry.

"You mean have overnights in barns? Yeah, usually

when Larry has to, I'll go with him. It can actually be pretty romantic sometimes." Her eyes glimmered. "That 'roll in the hay' expression didn't come out of nowhere, you know."

Hope laughed. "Well, won't the boys cramp your style?"

"We have Nick for the night anyway. Larry's sister and her husband are out of town. Besides," Dani confided, "we need the practice."

"Oh, yeah?" Hope grinned. "Is there something you're not telling me?"

"Me? Not tell you? Impossible, darling." Dani reached for her purse on the kitchen counter, extracting a lipstick and compact from it.

"Well, then?" Hope folded her arms across her chest, ready for details.

"We're getting there. We're getting there," her friend tittered. She held out the compact and filled in her lips with a dark, raisin-colored lipstick. "We both know we're going to end up together. It's just kind of an unspoken thing. But right now," she snapped the compact closed, her eyes glinting capriciously, "the chase is so much fun, why not enjoy it?"

Hope couldn't help but look concerned.

"No need for that worried look on your face, Mom," Dani assured her. "I won't blow it, I promise. This isn't like changing my hair color. Trust me, I know the difference. I'm committed to Larry. He's definitely the one." She fluttered her eyelashes. "But speaking of blowing it, what about you?"

"Me?" Hope raised her arms in surprise.

"I wouldn't let Mr. Tall, Dark, Handsome, Sweet and Wonderful get away, Hope." Dani paused thoughtfully. "Oh, and did I mention Sexy and Successful, too?"

"And who says I've got him?"

"Oh, come on." Dani waved a hand at her. "The chemistry between you two is undeniable. The way he looks at you like there's no one else in the room—or even on the planet. The way you look at him . . ."

"I don't look at him like—" Hope started to protest, but her best friend wouldn't hear of it.

"Hope, why are you fighting this?"

Fighting it? She wasn't fighting anything. She had almost succumbed to him in this very room just days before. And in a hotel room several days before that. But getting involved was quite another thing. Wasn't it best to keep her and Theo's world intact, free of any more possible hurt? That just made good sense, didn't it?

"I don't understand you." Her friend was shaking her head at her. "Do you really think this guy just happened to land right next door at your Uncle Cary's? That you both happen to have common interests? And both happen to be single? And nothing's supposed to come of it?"

"Dani, I don't need metaphysical right now."

"Okay, how about something real? Like the way you feel about him? Hope, I'm your best friend. Can't fool me, honey. I can see it."

Okay. So it was true. She did ache for him. She did want him. But wouldn't any woman in her right mind? And if it wasn't for Theo, maybe—just maybe—she'd let herself explore another man completely, without reservation, let her feelings be exposed to another man. *And he could so easily be that man,* she admitted to herself.

But Theo did exist, and what about him? Was it right for him to be tangled up in all of that? He was eleven now, sure. But that was still young enough to be really hurt when things between two adults didn't work out.

"Oh, Dani, he's a big-time spy. Think of all the stunning women he meets from all over the world."

"So that's what this is about? Other women?" Dani cocked her head as if she hadn't heard correctly. "That doesn't make sense, Hope. I mean, everyone is tempted. And with Robert, the scumbag, it only took one woman. One woman right here in Bearsville. One woman right under your nose. A ditzy office assistant who wasn't even that cute."

"Boy! Now that makes me feel much, much better," Hope grunted.

"I didn't mean it that way. I'm just saying tempting things are everywhere, all the time. But everyone is different. And Chandler may be a big-time spy, but he's a good-hearted small-town guy, too. Eventually they all come home to roost."

They stopped talking momentarily, caught up in the scene unfolding outside the kitchen window. Under the glow of the back porch light and the early evening moon, they watched Chandler and Larry and the two boys outside in the snow.

The men had gone out to get more firewood, and Theo and Nick had tagged along. But apparently the boys had other things on their minds besides the wood. While the men were involved in their own conversation, the boys were rolling up snowballs, preparing for a fun-loving skirmish.

"He's so good with Theo." Hope sighed, and then caught herself. She didn't realize she had said it—admitted it, actually—out loud.

"He's an all-around good guy, Hope. You can feel it about him. Don't let him go." Dani wagged a finger at her.

But he was going. And even if she did trust her innermost feelings, which she didn't at the moment, she wasn't going to stop that. The operation was complete, and he'd be getting his next assignment soon. In fact, maybe he'd already gotten it. He could end up in another country. Or another state. With another woman. She had no control over it.

"I haven't even known him for that long." She raised another argument that had evidently been lurking in the back of her mind.

"Does that mean anything?" Dani countered.

Hairdresser. Psychiatrist. Litigator. Hope smiled inwardly at her friend.

"You knew Robert, that idiot, since fourth grade. You guys went back and forth for decades. Did that help?" Dani stressed the point with her hands. "It's not the amount of time you know someone. It's the amount of time you both put into loving each other."

Hairdresser. Psychiatrist. Litigator. Philosopher, Hope mused fondly. "You really never liked Robert, did you?"

"Ha! That's being kind." Dani shook her head. "The point is, Hope, love doesn't exactly have a formula. That's the magic of it. And deep down in your, your—"

"Untrusting heart?"

"Yeah, in your untrusting heart, you know that's true."

"I don't know. It's all confusing. I think I need to spend my time concentrating on Theo."

"And, it wouldn't help if Theo had another person pouring love into him, too?"

Outside the boys had barricaded themselves behind a snow-covered patio bench. The tide had turned quickly and now they were yelping as the men were showering them with snowballs. Involuntarily, the scene made Hope ache longingly inside.

"It's more complicated than that, Dani."

"Only if you make it that way. Just think, if you and slimeball Robert—"

"Could you ever say my ex's name without attaching a nasty modifier to it?" Hope raised her voice more in amazement than anger.

Dani stood quietly, apparently considering the question seriously for a moment. "I don't think so," she admitted honestly. At that, they both broke down and laughed.

"Anyway, what I started to say was . . . if you and dirtbag Robert made something as beautiful as that," she pointed out the window toward Theo, "what other wonderful possibilities does life hold with the right person?"

"Well, Chandler hasn't exactly asked me yet, Dani. So I don't think we have much to worry about."

"Well, I know people, and—"

Hope raised her hand. "I know. You've got the chair. You've got the insight. You know it all."

"Exactly. He's hooked on you, Hope." Dani eyed her intensely. "Don't let him get away, fisherwoman."

Chapter Fourteen

The sky grew darker, and Sela's concern grew more grave. Giorgio had been gone the entire day. Where could he be?

She busied herself, flitting from room to room throughout the villa. Turning on lamps . . . burning candles . . . symbolically lighting the way for his return.

But as the hours passed, she began to pace the floors more vigorously. Calculations mounted in her head. Seventy-nine. One hundred and forty-eight. Her brisk strides had probably burned up a good two hundred and sixty calories or so, though not nearly enough to cover the half dozen cannoli she had devoured in her lover's absence.

Suddenly she heard a crash on the marble-tiled floor in the foyer.

Then another. Topped off by yet another!

Curious, courageous—and hopeful there wasn't some big mess to clean up—she rushed to the front of the villa to see what it was.

Hope and Chandler stood by the front door and waved as Larry's Grand Cherokee pulled out of the driveway into the star-speckled evening. Still all keyed up, Theo and Nick rolled down the Jeep's rear window and waved wildly back at them. Seconds later the foursome was gone, out of sight. Hope and Chandler still stood where they were, staring out into the night.

After a day of uproarious fun, punctuated by unflagging noise, the house seemed oddly quiet. Only a sliver of music from a slow-tempo CD filtered through the air from somewhere in the house. Hope wondered who had turned it on.

She finally broke the silence. "Thank you again."

"No problem." Chandler turned a generous smile to her. "I think it was my best birthday party ever, too."

There seemed like there was so much to say, but also as if nothing needed to be said. They turned their gazes back out into the night again, where a cluster of multicolored balloons danced around the top of the mailbox. They were put there mostly to mark the day's festivity, since everyone in town knew where she lived anyway.

"I got my next assignment."

The sound of his voice was so soft. So weak. Hope wondered how the force of it could possibly take her breath away. But then it wasn't his tone, she knew. It was his words.

This day had always been coming. It was always imminent, unavoidable. Now she couldn't believe how many times she had wished for it to speed up, to come right away, so he'd be swept out of her life.

Why hadn't she wished for more time with him instead? Did she think less time would equate to less disappointment? That it would all rush by her and skip over her feelings, never making so much as a nick in them?

"When do you leave?" She stared straight ahead, trying not to relay the surprise she was feeling within herself. She felt so foolish. Why hadn't she known this moment would leave her feeling so limp . . . shaken, like life's energy had flowed right out of her?

"I'm supposed to hook up with Mona tomorrow. I've already settled the bill with Cary." He put his hands in his jeans pockets. His shoulders sloped, and he didn't turn his head to look at her as he spoke.

"So soon?"

She felt him nod beside her.

"Do you know where you're going?"

"The United Kingdom," he answered vaguely.

"Something with the Queen?" Her mind flashed back to the night at the Plaza, when he was reading her London book out loud. The whole thing seemed sweet to her now, funny rather than embarrassing.

"Something with a female leader of an IRA group. You know I can't disclose much."

Another country. Another woman. Hadn't she said as much to Dani just minutes ago?

More somber silence stood between them. She thought about how glad she was that she had never gotten around to replacing summer's screen door for the storm door this winter. She needed the cold night air on her face right now.

"Hope, I—" He turned to her and took her hands into his. He looked so helpless, like he was sifting through his words, searching desperately for the right ones to say. But she wasn't sure she wanted to hear any words—even if he found the right ones—if there were such a thing at this moment.

No, she decided for sure, she didn't want to hear anything right now. Slipping her hand from one of his, she put two fingers up to his lips to silence him. She just wanted to feel him, be near him before he was gone. If she heard anything at all, it would be the anticipation in his breath, the beating of his heart. That's all she wanted to hear this minute.

"We never finished our dance," she said softly. "At the Plaza."

"You're right," he replied, his voice just as quiet.

As he gathered her in his arms, poignant piano tones and lonely saxophones drifted through the room, circling around them. Totally enfolded in his caress, she laid her weary head against his shoulder.

His arms . . . his shoulder . . . his hand as it stroked her face, all felt so strong. Sinewy. Safe. Yet it was the overwhelming tenderness she found enveloped in his embrace that brought tears plucking at her eyes.

This dance is so different, she thought. So unlike the one they had shared at the Plaza. Their slow dance in the grand ballroom had been far less intimate, not so telling. But then their time at the Plaza had been designated as pretend, hadn't it? *And what is this?* she wondered. *Real?*

She wasn't sure what to make of all the emotions surfacing within her. But as the CD paused, marking its end before it started all over again, she knew one thing for certain. She didn't want their time to be over. Not just yet.

Somehow Chandler seemed to sense her thoughts; somehow he seemed to share her feelings. Because wordlessly, holding hands, they left the music behind, and floated up the steps to her bedroom.

Moonlight poured in the window as, together, they lit the decorative candles placed about the room. A row of scented pillar candles on a white wooden wall shelf reflected into an antique mirror, casting an amber glow about them. The winter night and snow-covered world seemed especially far away in the hush of the second-story retreat. Silence embraced them; all was quiet except for the sound of their movements. And, of course, the beating of Hope's heart, which she imagined Chandler couldn't help but hear, too.

Apparently he realized what she was offering to him.

Something—a part of herself—that she hadn't shared with many others before. It was evident in the way he led her, almost reverently, over to the bed. He sat her down and searched her eyes, love and caring gleaming in his own.

"You need to be sure," he told her, sitting down next to her, clasping her hands.

She reached out and with timid, almost jerky movements, she slowly removed his sweater. Underneath, a white T-shirt clung to him. With a bolder touch, she grabbed at its edges, pulling it over his head, exposing the muscular torso which she had only seen but never felt. She ran her hands down the rippled hardness of his chest. She thought she heard him gasp slightly at her touch.

"I am sure," she whispered back.

He lifted her chin and looked into her eyes before he laid her back onto the bed. Seeking her mouth, he pushed ardently against her lips, his tongue probing . . . provocative . . . passionate, letting her know he wanted more . . . telling her he'd been waiting for so long.

She was surprised, thinking this first kiss, under this new moon, would be more tender and searching. But she realized, as his lips aroused the very depths of her, that she was glad it wasn't. His kiss was raw and real . . . totally undeniable. Its effect on her left her with no choice, no decision. She had to respond to it . . . and she did.

Her body arched toward him, yearning to be lost in him and whatever they could share this moment. She was ready and willing to abandon all thought. But then he pulled away from her lips, seemingly intent on orchestrating the waves of her desire.

He pushed the hair back from her shoulder, and dipped his head there, his sweet lips and tongue leaving a tempting trail of tingling sensations. All the way down the soft contour of her neck to the deliciously forbidden vee of her sweater . . . the sensations did make her think after all . . . sensual thoughts about how much she wanted him.

Her chest was rising and falling rapidly under the torturous wisps of his stimulating kisses. And just when she thought she couldn't stand it any longer . . . something new . . . his hands grasped at the hem of her sweater, inverted it and drew it over her head.

She readily helped him free her arms from the sweater, wanting him so desperately now that she surprised herself. It had been a long time since she had bared her skin or her soul to a man. It would've been natural and easy to feel shy or uncomfortable, or ashamed even.

But not so with Chandler.

Whatever the reason, she had always felt remarkably comfortable with him, unabashedly at ease. And, of course, he was driving her so crazy with his lips, his touch—few other things could come to mind.

With the lightest of touches, he circled his finger around the curve of her breast on the outside of her bra. Her nipples were peaked and hard against the cloth, longing for his touch, just as they had been since the first moment his lips met hers. She imagined those lips swarming over every part of her. However, he wasn't a man in a hurry.

Instead, he slid one bra strap from her shoulder, letting it fall limply on the top of her arm. Then he nestled his head in the crook of her shoulder, placing kisses that sent more shivers through her and more wishes for him to hurry and release her from the delicious agony he was putting her through.

She was growing impatient. Wanting more, wanting it faster, when he finally released her from the binding cloth that stood between her skin and the touch of his lips and hands. The look on his face when he gazed upon her bare flesh was one of pure adulation. "God, Hope, you're—"

Again, she put her fingers to his lips to stifle his words. But that didn't stop the searching of his curious hands, and she was glad. She didn't want to think right now . . . she only wanted to feel his touch. And that she did.

With a feathery fingertip, he traced over her skin like a sculptor admiring the feel of his cherished work of art. Following the swells of her breasts, making tantalizing swirls there, trickling down her ribcage, and then lingering over the very core of her desire.

Delirious, she arched upward to him. Yearning, she ached for him. Finally unable to contain herself, she reached out, dipping her hand below his waistband. Her passion a strong match for his own, he moaned at her touch. His hands on her body stilled completely. And for a few moments she knew he was lost in pleasurable sensations of his own. Sensations that she had created. The thought filled her, gratifying her in a totally different way.

But then he seemed to shake his sensual reverie, recalling the ultimate mission of his heart.

He leaned over her and whispered hoarsely in her ear, "Tell me what feels good, Hope. I want this for you . . . I want to make you feel *so* good."

The sweetness of his words caressed her just as he already had with his eyes, his lips and his touch. "You feel good." She stroked his chest, teasingly circling the tips there with her fingertip. "It all feels so good," she moaned as she strained once again to reach out to him.

He allowed her hand to fall on him fleetingly, letting her gauge for herself how very much he wanted her, before moving away from her grasp. She felt him unzip her jeans, and it seemed only an instant before she lay there naked before him. He never took his eyes off of her—nor she off him—as he stood up to remove the rest of his clothing.

Settling back down next to her, they took their time exploring every part of the other with their hands . . . their senses . . . their kisses. But when it seemed apparent neither could wait any longer, he sheathed himself in a condom from who knows where. She didn't care to question him; she was just glad he was prepared, because she was incredibly ready for him.

She had been resisting her attraction to him all along, she knew, but now she relinquished all of that. Let it all fall away . . . without a thought or a concern for anything outside the moment. She opened herself up to him and let his passion pour into her, filling her. And right before his pleasure overflowed, hers did, too, and she dug her fingers into his shoulders and cried out his name.

Both spent, he lay still on top of her momentarily, their bodies still quaking in the aftermath. The solid weight of him made her feel warm and enveloped in the special act they had shared.

Finally, he lifted up on his arms and searched her eyes, seeming to be unsure of what he would find there. Her unrestrained smile met his gaze. A smile of satisfaction and happiness . . . an expression void of guilt or remorse. His relief was evident in his eyes, and he beamed at her. He looked at her adoringly, as if he couldn't quite comprehend his good fortune. Then he bent his head down to kiss her lovingly before parting his body from hers.

Lying in the crescent of his arm, it took a moment before their breathing became even. And a few moments more before words intermingled with their snuggling.

"You know," he started, "I have a confession to make."

"Oh, yeah?" She smiled languidly, figuring it would be

something cute or spy-like. He was always saying something cute or spy-like.

"I kind of lied to you," he said abruptly.

What? She tensed up in his arm. *That was definitely neither cute nor spy-like. Oh, no,* her mind wailed, *it was starting already.*

"At the Plaza, you know the night we almost—" he started, and she nodded. "Well, I wasn't really asleep. I just pretended to be."

"What?" She shot up in bed, taking part of the sheet with her, covering herself, suddenly not wishing to be naked in front of him. "You did that to me? Do you know how terrible—how awful that made me feel? I didn't even tell Dani, I was so embarrassed."

"I swear it was for a good reason." He raised his hands in self-defense.

She eyed him suspiciously. "Really? I can't wait to hear it."

"Well, the thing is, I realized I felt differently about you," he explained in a rush. "I wasn't sure how. And it's taken me a while to sort it all out. But I knew I didn't want making love to you to be just some act of carnal pleasure. It was hard as hell though," he admitted to her, "having your luscious body lying next to me. I was awake almost the entire night, wishing we had been together. Hell, if you want to know the truth, I've been awake almost every night since."

Soothed by his admission, she gushed over his words. "Seriously?"

He nodded. The sheet went limp in her hand, exposing a part of her flesh and much of her feelings for him. She leaned over, eager to kiss the amazing lips of this most amazing man, her chest grazing his. Then she sat back up, taking the sheet with her again, ready to make a confession of her own.

"Well, as long as we're being honest here, you should know I lied to you, too."

"You're kidding?" He appeared taken aback.

She shook her head. "Remember when I said I didn't care if you were with Melanie that night or in the future?"

He shook his head, feigning total lack of recall. "Not really."

"Oh, yes, you do. Don't tease me," she said, laughing. "I saw the surprised and rather hurt look in your eyes that night."

He grinned. "So you *did* care?" He let his finger trickle an imaginary line over the sheet, down her tingling torso to her belly button.

"Well, sure. I'm not exactly the type to be making love— well, almost making love—to some man in a hotel room, if I didn't care."

"I know, that's why I didn't want to make love to you that night," he told her. "I'm glad we waited until now."

He held out his arms to her, and she lay back down in their safe-feeling haven once more.

"But I have to tell you, Hope . . ." He held her close. "I've done a lot of thinking this week, reevaluating my life. And I've come to a realization." He paused, and the silence around them framed his words. "I don't want to leave you, Hope."

He kissed the top of her head, softly, sweetly. Meanwhile she felt her body go somewhat rigid in his arms. *He didn't want to leave when? Tonight? Tomorrow? What was he saying?*

"Well, I—" She wasn't sure how to respond. "I mean— Dani has Theo for the night. Of course, I thought you'd stay."

"No." She felt his lips brush her hair as he shook his head. "I mean I don't want to leave you . . . or Theo. I don't know how it happened. It's hard to explain. But all along I've had this five-year plan, and now it doesn't seem like it's going to work out."

She chuckled as she rubbed her hand delicately over his bare chest. "Believe me, you don't have to explain to me about plans not working out," she replied, thinking back to that one particular evening when Robert scurried out of her and Theo's lives. Not at all what she'd had on her agenda.

He must not have felt like he was being heard, because he pushed himself up and balanced on one elbow. Looking into her eyes, he seemed intent on stressing the importance of his words. "Hope, what I'm trying to say is—I don't care about my five-year plan anymore. Since I've been here, things have changed. I've changed. It isn't just about me anymore. I want you and Theo to be a part of who I am." He paused and looked at her. She tried not to appear as dumbstruck as she really was.

"Hope, I love you," he said without hesitation. "I want the three of us to be together. Always. As a family." He rubbed soft circles on her belly with the warm palm of his loving hand. "Hopefully, someday, an even larger family," he dreamed aloud.

Having someone tell you after sex that they loved you should've been a good thing. And that they wanted to marry you, even better. Instead, for Hope, his declaration brought on a panic attack of the worst kind. She fought to breathe. Fought to slow the wild palpitations of her heart. Tried to shake the clamminess that had instantly covered her body like a wet blanket.

Had she always known these were the words he held true in his heart? Is that why she had silenced him? Because she didn't want to hear words of commitment? Promises made that might not be promises kept? Vows voiced, that might never stand the test of time?

He stared at her waiting for an answer. The one she gave him probably wasn't what he was looking for, she knew. "I, uh . . . gosh, Chandler . . . your job," she stuttered. "I don't know. It would be very stressful to know you were out there—somewhere. Never knowing . . . I mean, hmm . . . I don't know that I could handle it."

Am I really saying this inane stuff? she wondered. *For real? Or does this rate as an out-of-body experience?*

"Hey, I know I've thrown a lot at you all at once," he conceded. "And I realize I've been thinking about this for a while now, and it's all new to you. And that's okay. I understand . . ."

Reaching out, he took her in his arms once more, spooning her body with his own. "Just let me hold you tonight, Hope. I want to hold you all night long."

With every inch of his body caressing her, he seemed totally content and drifted off to sleep within minutes. Meanwhile, she lay awake tormented by the feel of him. The incredible feel of him. She didn't know of anything that felt more right . . . or any place on earth she'd rather be.

So, why had she lied to him? To herself? Why was it so hard to trust again? Did she want to lose this? Was she willing to turn her back on him and not even try?

She listened to his breathing next to her. Such a simple sound that brought her immense joy. His arms wrapped so sweetly around her, making her feel secure and loved.

Yes, loved.

He had said he loved her. And she knew in her heart that she loved him, too. She would've never made love to him otherwise, would she? Not only that, he had said he loved

Theo. And from what she'd observed, there was no doubt that was also true. Plus, could she even conjure up a hero with more admirable qualities? Chandler Adams was a man that Theo could respect. A man her son already liked, and someday might come to love in return.

So, no, she finally decided. No. She wasn't going to give that up. She would learn to believe in love again.

But she wouldn't disturb his dreams to tell him so. She'd tell him everything in the morning . . . in the light of their new tomorrow.

Morning came too late.

By the time she woke up, Chandler had already slipped from her arms and vanished from her life. It seemed so impossible after the night they had shared.

It seems impossible that he's only been gone for fourteen hours now, she thought, studying the clock on the mantel. Especially since each hour that passed by felt like an entire lifetime. An eternity.

As her first day without him neared an end and the skies outside darkened, she realized she would have many painfully slow, torturous days ahead of her. Days just like this one had been.

Theo had turned into bed earlier than his usual time, tuckered out from his sleepover the night before. Normally, she would've seized the opportunity to cozy up in bed and read after he fell asleep. But she dreaded the thought of retreating to her bedroom any earlier than necessary, now that it was filled with taunting memories of Chandler.

Instead she moved listlessly around the house, performing chores. Plodding through the rooms like a domestically-programmed robot until an unexpected knock sounded on the door.

Momentarily a breath of life . . . a flicker of hope . . . ignited within her. But it was put out all too soon.

"Sorry it's so late." Dani stormed into the house before Hope could utter the words to welcome her in. "I just had a late dinner with Larry at the Village Pantry. I came over as soon as I heard. Are you okay?"

Hope led her friend into the light of the kitchen, where Dani automatically sat down at the table. Normally, Hope thought sadly, her kitchen was a bright and cheery place to be. But now she only felt exposed in all that brightness, her pain illuminated. And she could feel the concerned eyes of her friend observing her, as she moved rigidly around the room, teeth steeled. Filling the kettle with water for tea. Placing two cups on two saucers . . .

"Oh, no. You're not okay, are you?" Dani answered her own question, and Hope knew she had zeroed in on the red-rimmed eyes beneath her glasses.

"How did you know?" Hope asked sullenly. Extracting two spoons from the silverware drawer. Removing two tea bags from the canister . . .

"Shirley waited on us at dinner."

"Shirley? How did she know?" Confused, she scrunched up her nose and closed the lid on the canister.

"Because when she switched shifts with Becca this afternoon, Becca told her."

"So the whole town knows I'm a loser? That I couldn't hang on to yet another man?" She banged a spoon on the counter. "That's great."

"No one thinks any such thing, Hope," Dani assured her. "They just know that Chandler left Bearsville at the crack of dawn this morning, after Becca served him three eggs over-easy, four sausage links, home fries, wheat toast, a large buttermilk pancake, a small orange juice and a coffee-to-go with cream and sugar."

"Glad to hear his departure didn't hurt his appetite," she scoffed. Meanwhile, she hadn't been able to eat a thing all day.

Dani tried to calm her friend. "He told her he was leaving town, and he left her a nice tip. That's all."

"Well, he told me that, too. I just didn't think it would happen quite the way it did."

Dani lowered her chin and raised her eyebrows quizzically. "So what did happen, Hope?"

"I'll tell you if you'll stop looking at me like I blew it," Hope all but shouted.

"I'm sorry. Am I looking at you that way? I don't mean to." Dani switched tacks. "I'm sure it was entirely his fault," she said earnestly enough, her eyes all sympathetic. "What a jerk!"

Hope didn't reply, but continued with her rote movements. Pouring the steaming water in their cups. Steeping the tea bags. Adding spoonfuls of honey to each cup. Placing the cups on the table . . .

With that done, however, her self-control seemed to have run its course. Her shoulders began to shake. Her mouth quivered. And before either of them knew it, she threw her glasses on the table and slunk down in the chair across from her best friend. Burying her face in her hands, she sobbed uncontrollably.

Dani reached over, placing a comforting hand on Hope's forearm. "Shh . . . it's going to be all right." Dani rubbed her arm. "I know it. We can fix this. Just tell me what happened. I still have a good feeling about this."

"Oh, Dani." Hope raised her head, rivulets of tears streaming down her face. "I don't know if this can be fixed," she half-choked on her words. "I think I really did blow it," she blubbered. "I wrote to him this afternoon and tried to tell him I messed up. That I was lying to myself about the feelings I have for him. But I don't even know where," she stammered, caught on a sob, "—wh-where he is." She sniffed. "So I mailed the letter to his mom in Nyack, hoping she'll forward it to him. Where—wherever. But maybe he doesn't want to be found. Who knows? It hurts so bad, Dani," she wailed.

"I know, honey, I know." Dani patted Hope's hand consolingly. She pushed back her chair and retrieved a box of Kleenex from the kitchen counter. She held one up to Hope's nose. "Blow hard," she commanded.

Hope blew and felt herself settle down a bit. "Okay, now back up," Dani said, "and tell me exactly what happened after we left last night."

"Well." Hope tugged a Kleenex from the box and twisted it self-consciously in her hands. "We held each other . . ." Her voice cracked at the sweet memory, and she had to fight from breaking down into sobs again. ". . . and we, you know . . . and it was wonderful. I mean I'm not that experienced, as you know. But it was so perfect. It felt so right."

"That doesn't sound like a problem." Dani smiled encouragingly. "Did he seem to feel the same?" Hope knew even though Dani tried to ask the question nonchalantly, she was holding her breath waiting for an answer.

"I thought so." Looking down, Hope realized she had twisted the Kleenex into a skinny-looking earthworm shape. Discarding it, she plucked another one from the box and started mutilating it, too. "He told me that he didn't want to leave," she explained to Dani. "And I thought he meant last night. But he said, 'No, I don't mean that.' "

She paused, reflecting on the highlights of the conversation. Meanwhile, she could sense Dani was on the edge of her seat, waiting as patiently as she could for more information. "He said he didn't want to leave me or Theo. He wanted the three of us to always be together."

"Oh, Hope, that's so sweet." Dani appeared to be nearly on the verge of tears herself.

"And then . . ." Hope had a faraway look in her eyes. "He rubbed my stomach, and," she squelched a cry rising from the back of her throat, "he said something about a family."

"So what did you do?" Dani inquired tentatively.

"Why, I freaked, of course!" she blurted, flailing her arms in the air. "I stiffened up. I saw another fatherless child I'd have to raise. I saw flashes of Robert lying to me and—"

"Argh. Damn that Robert! The sleaze!" Dani shuddered at the mention of his name. "So you never answered him?"

"Oh, sure, I gave him some lame excuse." Hope tilted her head, ashamed to admit how she had lied to him. "I told him his occupation was too dangerous. That I couldn't handle the worry. But it was all a lie," she said flatly. "I lied to myself about my feelings for him. I lied to him . . . all because I didn't know if I could trust someone again."

Dani waved a hand at her, dismissing what they both already knew and trying to get back to the nitty-gritty. "Then what? Was he upset? Did he leave? What?"

"No, he asked me if I would stay in his arms all night long." Hope sighed.

Both women were quiet for a moment. A single tear escaped down Hope's cheek.

"He fell asleep," she said softly, "and I lay there thinking how right it felt to be next to him, to have his body wrapped around me. It never really felt like that—even with Robert, you know?"

"I know." Dani acknowledged the comment with a nod and a sigh.

"I thought I'd tell him everything this morning. Everything. But, when I w-w-woke up," she started to sniffle again, "he was gone." She pulled a folded-up piece of paper from her overall pocket. "All that was left of him was this note."

She swiped her runny nose with the back of her hand while Dani read the note aloud. " 'Hope, I'll always love you. Chandler.' "

Dani sat staring at the paper, mute for a change.

"You're not saying any of your usual positive things, Dani. It doesn't look good, does it?"

"Oh, now. I'm sure—I'm sure it's fine." Dani said, trying to sound resolute, though Hope noticed her stammering. She folded the note and handed it back to Hope. "So you wrote a letter right away and told him how you felt? And sent it to his mom?"

Hope nodded. "Hopefully, his mom will forward it to him."

"I'm sure he'll be calling you any day then," her friend said confidently, as she sipped at her lukewarm tea. "Any day," she repeated.

It was a nice thing for Dani to say. But Hope wondered if she was trying to convince her as much as herself.

Thankfully Dani stayed for hours, keeping her company till well after midnight. But finally it came to a point where they both knew she had to go. She had clients to clip early in the morning. And Hope had a bus full of kids to look forward to.

Mechanically, Hope locked the front door behind her best friend and turned off the lights. But then she couldn't put it off any longer. Reluctance weighing heavy on her heart, she plodded over to the steps leading upstairs to her bedroom.

They were the same steps as the night before, but tonight there was no gliding upward . . . no slice of heaven awaiting her there. Tonight, she groped onto the banister, nearly having to pull her weary body over each step. All the while, a vision of her bed loomed gloomily in her head.

Hours earlier she had changed her bed linens, mostly feeling her way around the mattress blindly. Her eyes had been too blurred by tears to see. But clean sheets on her bed couldn't erase the events that had taken place there . . . or dim the memory of Chandler that seemed to linger everywhere.

Staring at the bed, she knew there was no way she could bear to be tucked in it. Not a chance she could lie under the same warm coziness of her comforter the way she had with Chandler the night before. Instead she grabbed an afghan from her bedroom closet and wrapped it around her numb body. She lay down on top of her made-up bed, not really expecting to sleep.

Something shimmered at her from the open closet in the dim light of her room. Oh, yes. The silvery-blue sequined dress she had worn the night she had pretended to be his wife. She had wondered that night, as the music played and their bodies simmered at each other's touch, what it would be like to be his. But at the time, she had managed to push the thought far, far away.

But this night was different. Tonight every thought she had was of him. Tonight . . . she wished she could dance in his arms once more . . . feel the possessiveness in his touch . . . see the unspoken yearning in his eyes. Tonight . . . being with him again for a moment . . . an hour . . . a lifetime . . . was all she could think about.

Chapter Fifteen

"Giorgio!" Sela exclaimed, overcome with relief and joy.

"Sela." He appeared happy to see her and probably would've hugged her hello. However, his arms were laden with a pile of books and tapes.

She noted the titles of the books that had already dropped noisily to the floor. Favorite English Phrases. English Made Easy. Welcome to English.

"Tings were note wrecking," he said.

She gave him a puzzled look, straining her brain to understand.

"Wrecking?" she asked.

He let all the books drop to the floor except for an Italian-English Dictionary. *He skimmed through the pages. "Working!" he declared, apparently delighted at the discovery of the word. "Working!"*

"And so you went out and did all of this? All day? That's where you've been?" she asked.

His fingers flipped frantically through the dictionary trying to keep up with her. It was no use. He tried something else.

"Sela, you are—ah—" He paused to look up another word. "Bountiful."

Bountiful? How adorable! She almost laughed aloud. "I'm so glad you noticed," she purred provocatively.

She took a deep breath, making her already plentiful breasts swell. She felt the heat of his appreciative gaze.

Taking the dictionary from his hands, she chucked it carelessly over her shoulder.

"Giorgio, I could swear your eyes are saying you want me," she cooed flirtatiously, figuring he wouldn't understand a word she said.

But he did. Nodding eagerly, he took her in his arms, gently guiding her to the floor.

Men! Sela mused as Giorgio placed delicious, titillating kisses all down her neck. There were some things they understood naturally . . . in any language.

Freshly-made raspberry crepes. Hope had to smile, in spite of the fact that eating was the very last thing she felt like doing. Fiona was up to her kind-hearted nurturing again, trying to cheer her up.

The crepes had been waiting there for her when she got on the school bus that morning, a half-dozen of them nestled in a tin with a lovely, flowered lid. Lid cast aside, their scent filled the bus with a sweet aroma, one that conjured up warm-hearted memories. Like cozy, woman-to-woman chats in the bed-and-breakfast's kitchen . . . sharing desserts on summer evenings in wicker rockers strewn about the inn's porch . . . impromptu, backyard picnics with Theo, complete with pink lemonade, raspberry crepes and ants.

Comfort memories . . . that's what they were. Comforts dear to her heart. And that was just what she needed now.

The raspberry aroma must have cast a spell on her cargo of school kids that morning, too. They seemed more subdued and quiet, quite content to talk softly or look outside the window at the gleaming premature spring-like morning where the dew glistened, and the birds couldn't help but sing.

Hope wished she felt like chirping about the new day, too. But the sweet-tasting raspberry crepes would help, she reasoned, as she dropped her parcel of kids off at school. They always did. She'd eat them all day long, without a care about the calories, hoping the magical pocket of berries would fill up the empty void she felt inside.

She took her first bite, a very satisfying one, as she headed the bus back toward home. She knew she'd be fine . . . eventually. She was a survivor after all. Certainly she'd make it. Though she was tired of hanging tough and making it through all of the time. Was that her fate after all? How she prayed it wasn't! She didn't want to merely survive. She wanted to live. She wanted to love. She wanted to trust.

Why hadn't she figured that out sooner?

Dani had been right all along. It was a losing proposition to put all men into one category. One wrong man didn't mean there wasn't a Mr. Right. She'd come to the same conclusion too late . . . after Chandler had fallen asleep, as she lay there thinking how right it felt to have his body snuggled against hers.

Why hadn't she woken him up, instead of waiting to talk to him in the morning? By morning, it was too late. He had already vanished from her life.

Hope had hoped his mom would forward the letter she had written to him. She had hoped he'd reconsider. Dani had said he'd be calling any day. But now, after days and days without hearing from him, she was all out of hope. And it served her right, didn't it?

Letting out a deep, long, weary sigh, Hope turned the corner of Liberty Street, heading toward her house.

It seemed so odd that the quaint life indicative of Bearsville could still be going on around her. How could it when her life—at least her chance at a love life—felt like it was over for good?

And yet there was the postman still delivering the mail. Mrs. Gallina was shuffling north, walking her pug. A young mother was jogging behind her baby's stroller. Retired Doc Merchant was on his porch, perusing the morning paper. And who was that standing on the curb up there?

Hope squinted through the windshield. It looked like—

"Some guy out of an Eddie Bauer ad," Hope whispered, the words catching on her inhaled breath.

And he was waving, waving her down. Hope's face tingled, and instantly tears blurred her eyes. She pulled the bus to a stop, and opened the door.

"Going somewhere?" she asked, attempting to make her voice light, though it sounded a bit shaky even to her own ears.

"I hope not." Chandler stared at her intently.

She didn't know how to respond to his words, wasn't sure of what he was saying. So she kept silent, focusing her energies on trying to take one breath after another.

"May I?" He gestured toward the steps of the bus.

Hope nodded, and he walked up the steps and sat down in the first seat catty-corner to hers. She turned around to look at him, barely able to comprehend he was really there. In real live flesh . . . the scent of him teasing her . . . the unreadable look in his eyes taunting her . . . his haven't-shaved-for-a-day look reminding her of the first day they met.

She wanted nothing more than to fling herself into his arms. Yet she was pinned to the spot, anxiety and hopefulness wrestling around inside of her as she waited for him to speak.

"I hope not," he repeated, his gaze catching hers. "I'd like to stay right here in Bearsville."

Her hopefulness was winning out.

"But I don't know yet," he added.

"You don't?" Her anxiety returned.

Chandler shook his head. "Guess it depends on you."

"But you said . . ." Hope started. She was so confused. "Your note . . . it sounded . . . it seemed like . . . good-bye."

"Really?" He placed a finger on his chin, poised thoughtfully. "I thought the note I left said I'd always love you," he challenged her.

"Yes, but where did you—why did you—?" She wasn't even sure which question to ask him first.

"I made arrangements for an early flight and didn't want to wake you," he explained. "I could tell things weren't going to work out the way they were. So I changed them." He shrugged his shoulders easily, as if he performed a major turnaround in his life every week. "I didn't go out on my mission. I went back to headquarters instead, and have been there for quite a while. I got debriefed, Hope." He paused to let the news sink in. "I'm officially out of the spy business."

He shifted on the vinyl bus seat before sharing the rest of his thoughts with her. "Besides, I think our family can only handle one spy mission at a time, don't you?" He glanced at her, looking unsure. She knew he was trying to gauge her reaction. "So I'm leaving the espionage up to you. You and Sela, that is."

Family? Had he really said family? Yes, he truly had. And this time it didn't sound scary. Or negative. Or impossible. Instead, it sounded and felt just right.

"But what will you do?"

"Well," he rubbed his hands together as he spoke, "I've been doing a lot of thinking about that. And I figure I already have two clients in town requesting my accounting expertise . . ." He paused long enough to smile about that. "And don't forget, my hometown of Nyack isn't so far away. And neither is Manhattan. I think I can scare up enough clients around the area to make it work." He nodded with certainty, before his smile turned impish. "Plus, I could always act as your writing consultant."

"True," she nodded back, a smile forming on her own lips. "I could use the benefit of your spy experience."

His mouth turned down in a frown, but his eyes glimmered roguishly as he said, "Hmm. I was thinking more like the romantic parts."

She could feel her eyes twinkling back in answer to his playfulness. But her mind was still working, trying to put all the pieces together.

"So when *did* you get my letter?"

Completely puzzled, his eyebrows furrowed. "Your letter?" His hesitant tone disclosed that he wasn't sure if the letter was a good thing or a bad one.

She nodded. "I sent it to your mom's house, so she could forward it to you."

"Oh. Well, my mom's been out in Colorado for a while, visiting her grandkids." His face lit up at the mention of his family. "I don't know exactly when she'll be back."

He shrugged before adding tentatively, "You wrote a letter to me, huh? Anything important?"

So he had never gotten her letter? He had come back all on his own? A tingle rose up her cheeks. A feeling of happiness surged through her heart.

"Uh, no." She waved a hand, her entire body feeling suddenly light and buoyant. "It was just . . . just a letter."

He looked partially relieved, though still anxious, as he inched forward on the bus seat. "Well . . . are you going to leave me hanging here?" He raised his eyebrows and a nervous half-laugh escaped his lips. "Spies, or I should say ex-spies, have feelings, too, you know. What do you think, Hope? About us?"

"Well, I—" Hope bowed her head and looked into her lap, pretending to be studying her hands. But in reality all she really wanted to do is yell out her love for him all the way to Woodstock. Then she wanted to grab him and show him how badly, and madly, she wanted him. From the sounds of it, thank God, he still wanted her, too.

She lifted her head. "I don't know how to say this . . ." She was slow and deliberate. This was important. She wanted to do this right. "But about that de-briefing stuff . . ." Her eyes sparkled more coquettishly with every word.

Chandler laughed that rich, deep laugh she loved. "Now, now. There'll be no more talk like that, young lady, until I have a decision from you."

"Definitely."

"Yes, definitely." He nodded, reaching out and taking both of her hands in his. "Hope, I love you. And I want us to be a forever thing." His eyes were intent on hers, and Hope knew he was asking her then and there to seal their future together.

"I already said definitely, silly."

"You mean—?"

"Yes, Chandler." She beamed at him. "I definitely love you, too."

"With vows, rings and wedding reception napkins with our names printed on them?"

She grinned, crinkling her nose at him. "You really want napkins with our names printed on them?"

He shook his head. "It's whatever you want, Hope. The main thing is . . ." He paused, looking down at her hands in his, appearing suddenly mesmerized by them. Studying them as if he were seeing them for the very first time. Gazing at them as if his fate, their future, lay right in the palm of her hands.

With tender movements, he lightly stroked the length of her fingers from their base to their tips. For a moment she felt shy under his scrutiny, wishing winter wasn't so harsh on her skin. But that feeling quickly dissipated, as he made circles in her palm, the soft touch of his fingertip creating an almost electrical sensation that traveled from the cradle of her hand up to her cheekbone.

Then he clasped her hands in his, interlocking each and every one of their fingers together. Squeezing lovingly. Grasping tightly. Affirming their oneness . . . their solidarity . . . and a love that would be built on years to come.

She squeezed back, answering him breathily, "Yes? The main thing is . . . ?" Their laced fingers seemed such a simple gesture on his part, yet she felt a blending of hearts like she'd never known before. No wonder that she could barely breathe. Surely her heart had swelled enormously, leaving no room for her lungs.

"The main thing is, I just want you, Hope," he answered. He gazed at her longingly, before lowering his head to kiss her. It was a gentle kiss, so light, so tender and so unhurried. A kiss that said there was no need to rush. They had all the time in the world . . . and all of that time would be together.

As their lips parted, he pulled his head back from hers. Wordlessly, for who knows how long, they gazed at each other. She thought he looked as astounded as she felt. How had they ever found something so much larger than life, so astonishing, in such a small, isolated place as Bearsville?

Reaching out, he stroked her cheek gently. Then he

stopped abruptly, as if he'd had a revelation.

"Raspberry!" he blurted out. "I kept wondering what that was. I smell raspberry!"

His eyes were so wide and baffled-looking, Hope threw back her head and laughed. It felt like an eternity since she had done so.

"You never did get to try Fiona's raspberry crepes, did you?"

Chandler shook his head, and Hope had an idea.

"Have I got a treat for you," she promised. Closing the doors of the bus, she grabbed the tin of crepes with one hand and tugged on Chandler with the other. "Back of the bus, please, sir."

At the rear of the bus, there was a woolen emergency blanket. Chandler helped Hope throw it down over the rubber mat that made a black strip down the center aisle of the bus. They lay down then, with the tin of raspberry crepes between them.

Dipping her finger into the crimson jelly, Hope placed it to his lips. "Have a taste," she offered.

"I'd love to," Chandler leaned forward, sampling Fiona's specialty with his tongue. "Mmm, delicious," he moaned.

His lips moved from her finger to her mouth, a sweet hint of raspberry crossing her lips. His kiss was sensuous . . . seductive, making her yearn for him as intensely as ever. But she wanted to take things slow with him. To savor every second. After all, now they had a lifetime to do that, didn't they?

"Do you like it?" she pulled back from him, attempting to catch her breath.

"Like it?" He barely glanced up at her, his hand intent on parting the top of her blouse, exposing, exploring.

Nuzzling his mouth hungrily to the spot, she could feel the slightest bristle of his whiskers against her delicate skin, making her burn for him even more.

"I love it," he finally looked up, answering her hoarsely in a way that let her know he was in agony, too.

"You know," she made an effort to speak, a challenging thing since he was now placing a series of tingle-producing kisses up and down her neck. "I've been with a guy in the back seat of a car, and even in the trunk of one."

"Oh, yeah. A trunk, huh?" Taking a moment's break from his exquisite work, he smiled with her in remembrance.

"But I've never been with a guy in the back of a bus before. In the middle of town. In broad daylight. This is a first for me."

"And how do you like it so far?"

He had grasped her reddish-stained finger now and held it to his lips. Then with his tongue and his lips taking turns, first one and then the other, he began to kiss it clean in a way that was undeniably erotic.

It was the smallest act, but Hope could feel the sensation of it in every part of her . . . from the tips of her breasts to the essence of her being, which ached for him to the point of madness. "So far, I love it," she answered when she'd caught her breath.

"Well, good. Because we're going to have lots of firsts, Hope. A whole lifetime of them." He looked into her eyes and the truth she saw there made her gasp. "Trust me, Hope."

"I do," she said with all her heart. "Really. I do."

Chandler pressed more salacious kisses onto the palm of her hand. "Now about this debriefing business . . ." He looked up at her and smiled, his love for her burning bright in his eyes.

Hope laughed. "Don't worry. We'll get there all in good time," she answered, as she began ever so slowly unbuttoning his shirt with a lustful smile. "Trust me," she reiterated his words. "Trust me."

Mom,

It's your computer sticky note son again. I think Sela should get married so she can have an awesome son just like me who could help with all her spy stuff but he wouldn't have to help with dishes. ??????

1,234,589

About the Author

Cathy Liggett's mom worried about her as a young girl. Cathy was often indoors reading and trying to write when other kids were outside playing. As a teenager, her mom worried about her even more. Besides the reading and writing, there was another obsession in her daughter's life: boys.

Finally, Cathy has combined her two favorite things from way back when—writing and the opposite sex—by penning romantic fiction. Admittedly it's more fun than all her years of advertising copywriting put together.

She lives with her husband in Loveland, Ohio, where their son and daughter, ages sixteen and eighteen, manage to keep life quite lively. For that reason, she has a standing hair-coloring appointment every five weeks.